I0553736

THE XANDRA
Book One

Daughter of the Dark
By
Herbert Grosshans

Published by
Melange Books, LLC
White Bear Lake, MN 55110
www.melange-books.com

The Xandra: Book One - Daughter of the Dark by Herbert Grosshans
Copyright © 2006, 2011

ISBN 978-1-61235-205-3

Credits
Cover Artist: A. Bratt
Editor: Taylor Evans
Copy: Mae Powers
Format: Mae Powers

The Xandra: Book One
Daughter Of The Dark
By Herbert Grosshans

In the 30th century humans are reaching out toward the far stars. Earth is sending huge ships carrying thousands of colonists in search of suitable planets. Nu-Eden, 325 light-years from Homeworld, looked like an ideal planet--until the colonists discover it is already occupied by a sentient entity who calls herself 'The Xandra', and she is not willing to share her planet with the humans. The colonists are beginning to behave strangely. At night they have sex-orgies, which they don't remember by day. Tom McClary loves his wife, Anina, but the lure of the Xandra may be stronger than his love for her. Even the space-station may not be safe from the influence of the Xandra.

You can visit Herbert at his blog
http://www.hegro.blogspot.com

The Xandra Trilogy
Seeds of Chaos Book 1 Eden's Gate
Seeds Of Chaos Book 2 Hell's Gate
Stardogs, Book One, Return to Redsky
Stardogs, Book Two, Redemption

Dual Visions:
Orion—The Hunt
Cliffs of Time

The Xandra: Book One
Daughter Of The Dark
By Herbert Grosshans

Chapter One
Alpha Colony

Tom McClary opened his eyes, sat up in the dark and listened. Something awakened him. The night sounds were almost familiar now. The eerie calls of the swamp dwellers didn't seem so frightening anymore.

He lay silent, staring at the dark ceiling of the shelter and let his eyes adjust to the darkness. Noticing the seam of light framing the entrance to the shelter, he realized that the door stood slightly ajar.

Strange, he remembered closing it before they went to sleep.

Quietly, so he wouldn't disturb his wife, he slipped from the mattress and walked to the door. About to close it, he heard a soft moaning sound from outside.

Stepping into the night, he looked at the two moons shining brightly above, they were close together, almost touching. Soon they would part again, each going in a different direction.

Again, he heard a soft moaning. It came from the small clearing on the other side of the thick brush that separated the sleeping quarters from the recreational area. They called it that because of the pond and the small stream of fresh water that flowed into it.

Out of curiosity he walked around the cluster of shrubs, after a moment of hesitation he stepped back into the shadows. The bright light of the moons illuminated the slim naked female figure writhing on top of someone in the tall grass. Her face was upturned, and he recognized Orona, there was no mistaking her delicate oriental features. For a small woman she carried surprisingly large breasts, firm, conical shaped, with long nipples. Rotating her round buttocks with ever-increasing speed, she turned her face toward the moon, cried out softly. Then she stopped moving and sat quivering for a long time. Sighing, she lifted up.

Tom saw the stiff large penis of the man she made love to.

"That was beautiful," a man's familiar voice said. "But I can still go on for a long time."

4

Tom chuckled to himself. Even hot little Orona couldn't satisfy Stephan Tilus. Stephan was one of the young unattached men and well liked with some of the women.

"Maybe I can help you out," said a female voice from the shadows of a tall Corander tree. He froze when he saw the naked woman stepping into the open. The light of the moons made the soft curls of her pubis gleam with golden fire. "I thought you two would never stop. I was afraid there'd be nothing left for me."

"There is plenty left," Stephan said with a hoarse voice. "Come and take it."

Straddling the man below her, she reached down to grab his stiff penis, then she sank into his lap and with a loud moan, she took the solid pole deep into her.

Tom could see her face clearly in the pale light. His gaze moved down to her jiggling breasts, as she rode the man beneath her. They were beginning to sag, betraying her age. Tom looked down at his hands, that cupped those breasts untold times, looked at his fingers that dug into her wide hips at the moment of ecstatic release, and watched as his hands curled into fists.

Her cries of pleasure forced him to look again, forced him to watch her climax on top of another man.

Anina, his wife!

He couldn't move. He seemed riveted to the spot he was standing on, hidden inside the thick shrubbery.

Anina got off Stephan, stood up and stretched. She looked up toward the two bright disks and laughed. "I haven't felt this good since we've landed on this forsaken planet. In fact, I haven't felt like this for a long time. You're quite a man, Stephan Tilus."

Stephan chuckled, came to his feet and stood behind her. Reaching around, he cupped her full breasts. He whispered something into her ear. She laughed again and slowly sank to the ground, kneeling in front of Stephan. Her round buttocks gleamed pale in the moonlight. Stephan knelt behind her.

Tom could see the other man's stiff pole and watched as he guided it between Anina's spread thighs. It disappeared between her white fleshy cheeks. Arching her back, she pushed backward. Stephan grabbed her quivering hips, shoved his penis into her. Anina cried out, her arms flew apart and her face disappeared in the tall grass. Behind her, Stephan moved his hips with forceful thrusts.

Tom stood paralyzed, watched with a mixture of anger, frustration, and amazement as another man fucked his wife. Like an animal in heat, on all fours!

Anina, the woman who was never far away from her prayer book. She never did this with him. He felt betrayed. Anger made his blood boil.

What should he do? What could he do?

They pledged to do everything possible to ensure the success and survival of the colony. Did that mean sharing his wife with another man? A man like Stephan Tilus who was half his age and as virile as a bull in his prime.

Tom looked up at the dark cloud that suddenly covered the two moons. His fists reached into the sky. *Lord, what should I do?* He prayed silently. *Tell me what to do.*

The distant roar of a swamp creature couldn't block out the sobbing cries of pleasure from his wife's throat.

When the clouds were gone, and the clearing was flooded again with pale light, Stephan and Anina changed positions. Anina lay on her back, her legs spread wide, her knees up. Stephan moved between them, his hand fumbled for a moment, and then with a satisfied grunt he pushed deep into her.

Anina cried out softly and lifted her hips off the ground to meet Stephan's thrusts. Tom couldn't keep his eyes off the lean buttocks of the man who copulated with the woman who suddenly became a stranger to him. It seemed like a bad dream.

"I'm coming!" Stephan panted, grabbed Anina's hips and held her still while he came inside her with a suppressed cry. Anina whimpered and moaned loudly as she accepted his discharge. It was quite obvious that she was experiencing her own intense orgasm. Stephan collapsed into her arms; their ragged breathing a nauseating sound in Tom's ears, he felt sick to his stomach.

What if she became pregnant? She'd be carrying another man's child. At age 45, she was still able to bear children.

He thought of his own daughters, one of them eighteen, the other one twenty years old. He'd never see them again. They decided not to come to the colonies with them. The oldest, Cindy, had good reason not to leave Earth. She found a young man, who was willing to marry her, and he was not the adventurous type. Mandy, the younger one, his favorite daughter, even though he would never admit it to anyone, she was a special young woman. She was very bright and the Science Corps took an interest in her. She was better off back on the home planet.

He sighed, and taking a deep breath, he became aware of a peculiar, heady fragrance in the air. He didn't notice it before. And he was sprouting a huge, almost painful erection.

A loud splash made him look toward the pond, where he saw a naked figure coming out of the water. Orona. Laughing, she came running toward the couple in the grass. Wide-legged and panting, she stood beside them. Tom stared, fascinated by her conical, up-tilted breasts. His erection became even more painful.

"You two made quite a racket," Orona said. "I watched you from the water. It made me horny all over again."

Stephan laughed, reached for her and pulled her down; rolling between her parting legs, he gave one mighty thrust, and then they were locked together, thrashing around in the grass like two wild animals. Beside them Anina knelt; laughing and panting she straddled Stephan, pressed her naked body against his back and moved with him. Slipping off, she rolled onto her back. Stephan pulled out of Orona, moved on top of Anina. Her thighs flew open, and Stephan fell between them.

Watching them, Orona got onto her knees, pushed her buttocks up and began to imitate Stephan's thrusts.

Tom found himself stumbling toward the three beneath the tree. His erection grew so painful, and he reacted without conscious thought. Dropping to his knees behind Orona, he grabbed her moving hips and put his swollen member between her cheeks. She pushed backward, and without effort, he slid into her creamy, hot sheath.

As the soft tightness closed around his throbbing shaft, Tom sobbed uncontrollably and began to thrust into Orona's sucking sex-canal. His taut belly slammed into her soft buttocks. It wasn't long before he climaxed inside her with mind shattering force, but his erection did not go down.

There came a moment of clarity, and he realized suddenly what he was doing. He looked at the naked slim form of the female kneeling in front of him.

This was not his wife Anina!

When he stopped moving, the woman turned her head to look back at him. Staring into her almond shaped eyes, he whispered, "Orona! Oh my God!"

Orona smiled. "Hello Tom. I had no idea it was you. You surprise me. Just don't stop what you were doing."

"I'm sorry," he stammered. "Forgive me."

"Forgive what?"

"I didn't know what I was doing."

Orona laughed and rotated her hips. Her soft warm love channel tightened around his hard shaft. "You're doing all right, Preacher-man."

"Please, don't call me that. I'm an engineer, not a preacher."

She chuckled. "I've heard you preach at Sister Angela's church."

"I just help out sometimes." He kept staring at her curved back, the form of her slim hips, her soft buttocks that pressed against his thighs.

What was happening here? This was so wrong! He was having sex with a girl not much older than his daughter, and he liked it.

Orona moved forward, he slipped out of her. She turned onto her back, lay there smiling, her legs spread wide. Her pubic area smooth and her mound puffed up. Between her open legs her pink slit beckoned.

"Come on, Tom," she cooed, "put it back in. I see you're still ready."

He lifted his face up to the night sky, searched for the bright discs of the moons. They had separated, were almost halfway on their journey to the horizon. Then he remembered his wife and Stephan. When he looked, he found nobody beside him. He was alone with Orona.

Looking at her naked breasts and her taunting smile, he moaned, moved between her slim thighs and with a hoarse cry he slid his rigid pole back into heavenly bliss. Orona pulled him into her arms and kissed him feverishly. "I didn't think you had in you, Preacher-man," she breathed into his ear. "Always so proper and moral."

He didn't care what she said. All that mattered was her soft, tight sheath that enveloped his aching member, and the almost unbearable pleasure she gave him.

He felt her smooth belly muscles ripple, as she bucked underneath him, milking him with great expertise. Her rigid nipples pressed into his chest, her breasts were soft and warm against his skin. He lost all sense of time, just moved in and out of her. Orona pulled up her knees, it changed the angle of his penis inside her vagina, spurned him on to greater speed.

He could feel the pressure building up, waited as long as he could, then with a loud shout he let himself erupt inside her. He held her tight until he was empty. Her own discharge felt warm and liquid, and he knew that she did not fake her cries of pleasure.

Anina never came like this. He knew she faked her orgasm many times, just to please him.

With regret, he pulled out of the young woman's warm sex-canal and rolled onto his back. He felt satisfied the way he never felt before. Turning his head, he studied Orona's features. She looked beautiful, young, with smooth olive skin, her slim body firm and well muscled. He had to admit that he found women of her type exotic and attractive.

8

She sensed his look and turned over onto her side. Touching her finger to his nose, she smiled, rose to her feet and ran off toward the pond. He watched her solid round buttocks move enticingly under her smooth skin. A moment later, she dove into the water with a loud splash.

His gaze went up to the heavens. The bright disks of the two moons were gone. A third moon hung halfway up in the sky, swirling, dark clouds partially covered the red disk, promising rain.

He sat up, picked up his nightshirt, which he didn't remember taking off, then he stood up and walked slowly back to the sleeping quarters. Finding Anina fast asleep on their bed, he joined her under the covers. He reached out to touch her gently, pulled back his hand when he touched naked skin. He didn't remember falling asleep.

Chapter Two
Captain's Log
July 18, 2985

The Exploration ship has left. The abandoned alien space station has been adapted to support human life. We are in orbit around the fourth planet of the star system ACG 671-397-D. We've named the planet Nu-Eden. It seems to be the most suited for human settlement.

It has been six months now since the first shuttle with 25 colonists on board left for the planet below. Only 1,000 of the 2,000 colonists are living on the planet. The other 1,000 are still in cryogenic suspension.

I'll give the colony five years. If the colony prospers, the rest of the settlers will be revived and sent down to join the others.

I believe they have a good chance, though. The climate is good, the air is breathable, and the water quality excellent. It is an ideal planet. We'll see.

Unfortunately, the station cannot be moved, but we have one small exploration ship, a number of shuttles, and one small, but powerful battle cruiser. We have begun exploring the rest of the planets in this system.

There are seventeen of them. The one closest to the primary is too hot for anything living to exist. The side that faces the Primary gets surface temperatures in excess of 500 degrees Celsius. The second one is not much better, too hot on the sunlit side, too cold on the dark side.

The third planet is a giant, with a diameter of 51,000 km. There is some sort of life on it, but no human being could live there. Too hot and too humid. The oxygen content in the air is too low, and we've detected high concentrations of methane gas and traces of other poisonous substances.

Luckily, the fourth planet was more than we could have hoped for. This is the best planet the human race has discovered so far. With a diameter of 13,200 km, and gravity slightly higher than 1 G, it is so close to Earth standard, it is almost eerie.

There are three moons circling it, two large ones and one small one. How they affect the tides of the oceans that separate the three huge continents is still unknown. The sites of the two settlements are in the middle of the largest continent; we will worry about the tides when we have to.

The first survey of the fifth planet (we haven't given it an official name, yet) didn't create too much excitement. It is similar in size to Nu-Eden, a little larger, but not large enough to increase the gravity. About three-quarters of the planet's surface is land. There is only one ocean, and it is rough. A huge ridge of high mountains runs from north to south, effectively dividing the landmass into two separate continents.

High, rugged mountains cover much of the land surface, but there are also large flat, tundra-like areas with tall grasses and wild forests. Myriads of long and wide rivers snake through the flat lands and mountains, emptying themselves into huge and deep inland lakes.

It is a rough and savage world, with great temperature fluctuations between the seasons, plagued in the summer by vicious thunderstorms, hurricanes and torrential rains, and by snowstorms in the winter. The mountains and the poles are forever covered under a deep blanket of snow or thick ice; still, humans could live on this planet. The air is pure and clean. We found traces of, as yet, undefined elements in the air, but they seem harmless. Of course, these are only preliminary findings.

About two months ago, we set up a research station in the Western Hemisphere, which seems to have a bit more temperate climate. We have a team of five men and five women scientists doing closer studies, they will stay down there a year, longer, if they want to.

Maybe some day, even if things do work out on Nu-Eden, we will begin to colonize the fifth planet.

So far, we haven't found any intelligent life or any evidence that these planets have been host to visitors from other star systems. There are no ruins, no signs that anybody ever landed on the surface, which is quite puzzling because of the abandoned space station.

The space station is huge and old, maybe a thousand years or so. Who built it? We don't know. It certainly is not of human design, even though we are quite certain that a humanoid race built it.

Professor Romanof believes that it wasn't built in this system, but was transported by a method we have not been able to establish. Whoever built it possessed a technology superior to ours.

There is a space anomaly about three light years away, which gives cause to all kinds of speculations.

As I've said, the space station is huge; it could easily support 5,000 people. Of simple design, it is a giant sphere about 1.5 km in diameter, studded with twelve spikes 150 meters high and 60 meters wide. Each spike, or tower, as we call it, is divided into 25 floors that are connected through an elevator. At the end of the tower is an observation deck, with transparent walls and ceiling.

The station was not completely dead when we found it. Even though nothing was working, there seems to be some kind of power source in the sphere's center, because there is still gravity.

Each tower is completely sealed off from the main body, accessible only through a pressurized chamber. It is one of these towers that we have adapted to acceptable living conditions.

There was a team of excellent engineers on the Mother-ship, and they installed an independent power plant on one of the floors. The elevators are working and we have lights, heat and air.

We even have a hydroponics garden where we grow vegetables, enough to supply us with fresh greens at least three times a week.

Water we brought up from the planet below. We store it in huge tanks located on the first floor. From there it is pumped into pipes that run up to the top of the tower. Almost every third floor has a toilet and a washbasin. The main facilities are on the ninth floor, where we have showers and tubs for those who like to soak for a while. My old bones need that sometimes. The sleeping quarters are on the eighth, tenth and eleventh floor.

Most of the upper floors are used for storage, research labs, hospital rooms, and entertainment. The cryogenic chambers are on the 21st and 22nd floor. Both floors had higher ceilings, and only a few partitions. It was not difficult to convert them to our purpose. Computers monitor each chamber around the clock. Only technical personnel are allowed on those floors.

Did I mention that 217 men and women make up the crew? Actually, there are 137 men and 80 women living in the tower. Some of them may eventually decide to stay and join the colonists on Nu-Eden, but most of them will go back home with the relief ship.

The military personnel have taken over the fourth and fifth floor. There are only 27 Marines, but all of them are well trained, and they do provide us with a certain sense of security. Besides, their commander, Les Beringer, has become a good friend of mine, and he assures me that we are 'in good hands'. He keeps his men at constant alert, putting them through a rigorous training regiment every day.

They are training on the fourth floor, and it is a good thing that the floors are sound proof. My quarters are on the seventh floor.

A large porthole in what serves as my living room gives me a good view of the planet below us, and sometimes I sit for hours just staring at that huge globe. When the surface is not obscured by clouds I can see the continents and the oceans and I wonder what it would be like to brave the giant waves in an old-fashioned steam powered ship. What an adventure that would be!

Would I have the guts? I don't know. I envy the future younger generations who may do exactly that. There are many questions I ask myself. What if something happens to this station? What if the Mother-ship gets lost in the vastness of space and never comes back? This planet may be cut off for centuries, maybe millennia, from the rest of humanity.

Ah, but I'm transgressing, daydreaming, like some old fool. At 90, I'm still young enough to maybe set foot on Nu-Eden someday and sail those oceans. Mind you, not in a steam-driven boat. I'm not that crazy.

* * * *

August 18, 2985

It is autumn in the Northern Hemisphere of Nu-Eden. We'll have to adapt the calendar to the local conditions and seasons. However, there is still time for that and it is only of concern to the people living on the planet. There are no seasons on the station.

So far, the reports we've been getting are excellent. Alpha Colony, which is in the southern part of the northern continent, is probably the better location. The weather is a little warmer, and there are many fruit bearing trees and shrubs. Most of the fruit and berries are edible and can be eaten by humans.

Beta Colony is about 1500 km further to the north. The region is quite mountainous, and the trees don't grow as tall. Yet, it is still a very hospitable place to live in. All the settlers are healthy and seem to be quite happy.

Here on the station not much has happened. I've sent a team deeper into the bowels of the sphere. We've discovered a staircase that leads from one level to the next. There are many levels. Of course, there is no air, but we are proceeding with caution. We don't want to cause any damage to vital components.

Actually, we were quite fortunate to gain access to the sphere without great difficulties. Maybe the access doors were purposely left open. They are large enough to let our ships get inside. It was obviously a docking port, because we did find a number of small shuttles parked in what looked like parking spots, (at least we assume they are shuttles).

The outermost level has a ceiling one hundred meters high. Huge elevators go up to each tower. Unfortunately, we could not get them to work. We needed to build our own.

I have great respect for the builders of this station. They did have marvelous engineering skills.

* * * *

My contract is for five years. I'll be 95 then, and I hope they'll let me retire. Of course, I am assuming that Earth sends a relief team. I have no ties with Earth or any other planet. My wife and three children, two girls

13

and one boy, were killed in the revolution on Eldorado. That was forty years ago. I joined the Space Exploration Corps after that.

In those days, I used to be a hotshot pilot with the Terran Customs and Revenue Corporation. Nothing could touch me. I was a big hero. I've always blamed myself for my family's death. I should have been there, with them, but I wasn't! I was somewhere in the Alpha Centauri System, chasing after smugglers. I loved the thrill of the hunt, it was more important to me than my family. Oh well, that is all in the past. Now I'm just an old man waiting to be put out to pasture.

I know 90 isn't so old. Barring any accidents I could live to be 150 and beyond, but I'm just so tired of spending my time in the vastness of space. Maybe it's true what the opponents of space travel say: Man's destiny lies on Earth, not in Outer Space. A man needs solid ground under his feet.

Maybe I'll get married again, settle on Nu-Eden.

Who knows.

Chapter Three
Space Station

Captain Cunningham looked up from his desk when Lieutenant Striker walked into his office.

"You asked for me, Captain?"

Striker appeared young, with his square chin and steely gray eyes he would look good on a recruiting poster. "I understand you'll be leading Exploration Team Delta down to the fifth planet?"

"Yes, sir, that is correct." Striker gave him a salute. A little sloppy, but the Captain let it go. He saw a lot of himself in the young lieutenant, which was not necessarily a compliment. Suppressing a smile, he said, "You do understand the risk, Lieutenant?"

"Yes, sir, I do. Commander Beringer explained it to me, sir."

"At ease, Striker." He said it, but it wasn't really necessary. Discipline was not this man's strongest trait. "Have a seat." He waited until Striker was seated. "And stop calling me 'sir'. This is an informal meeting."

"Yes, sir. I mean, yes, I know." The lieutenant smiled tightly. "May I speak freely?"

Cunningham nodded. "Go ahead."

"I've studied the list of people who are on this mission. I'm not comfortable having Jeffro Remmington on the team. He's just a security guard, not military, won't follow orders. There is no reason for him to be on the team. He's a troublemaker."

"You know him?"

"Not well, but we've exchanged words."

"I see." The Captain looked thoughtful. "Unfortunately, Commander Beringer won't give me any more of his marines, except for you and Raymond Chu, the pilot. Chu is needed to fly the shuttle back to the station. Which leaves only you with the team. I'd like to have at least one more man, who is not a scientist, someone who can handle a weapon without endangering himself and others. Remington is the only one available, I mean, willing to go. Besides, we have more than enough guards. There is not much for them to do here on the station. I'm afraid you're stuck with him."

The lieutenant sighed, smiled. "By the way, are you expecting us to come across any inhabitants?"

The Captain leaned forward. "We haven't found evidence of any civilization. That doesn't rule out dangerous primitive indigenous life forms. Have you studied the maps of the planet?"

"I have." Striker shrugged. "They are very sketchy. Not much detail."

"Best we can do." Cunningham drummed his fingers on the tabletop. "We're only just beginning our surveys. If it were up to me, I'd wait a bit before we send people down. However, Professor Tennenboum is insistent. He can be quite persuasive. He says he needs more people. Actually, everyone on your team is quite eager to go. Some wouldn't mind staying the whole year."

"Not me." Striker grinned. "A couple of months, maybe. I don't think the Commander would be too happy to have me gone longer than that."

"Probably not. I'm surprised you don't want to stay longer. Don't you get bored here on the station?"

Striker shrugged. "Space is where I belong. Even though I grew up on Earth, I've spent too much time inside the confines of a ship. I don't feel comfortable on the surface of a planet with nothing above me but empty sky."

"I know the feeling." Captain Cunningham nodded. "I'm curious, why did you volunteer for this mission?"

"I didn't." Striker smiled. "Commander Beringer can also be quite persuasive."

Cunningham rose, held out a hand. "Good Luck, Lieutenant. If you run into trouble, you're on your own. I don't have another shuttle that is equipped for search-and-rescue missions, nor do I have a trained team ready. There are a lot of good men and women on this team. Take care of them. I want to see everyone back on the station, including you."

Striker shook the Captain's hand, stepped back, saluted and walked out of the door. Cunningham watched him go, sighed and murmured, "Good luck and be careful." In a way, he felt a little envious. There is nothing more exiting than taking that first step on a strange planet, inhaling that first breath of natural air, feeling the warmth of an alien sun. He'd never be able to experience that. As the Captain, he was stuck here on the station.

He got up and walked over to the porthole, stared at the large globe of Nu-Eden hanging in space like a huge balloon. Most of the land surface was obscured by clouds, only the ocean was visible. He had never been on Nu-Eden, and there was a good chance he may never touch its soil, or sail that large ocean. He turned when he heard the footsteps of someone approaching.

"Dreaming again, Jeremy?"

Cunningham smiled at the big man in uniform. "Les, what brings you here?"

Commander Beringer chuckled. "I hope you didn't put too many ideas into Lieutenant Striker's head. He is an idealist, like you. A bit of a hothead, too. Doesn't always follow rules. But he is a competent leader. That's why I chose him, and I want him back."

"He'll be back, don't worry." Cunningham walked over to a cabinet, pulled out a couple of glasses and a bottle. "Care for a drink?"

Beringer grinned, flopped into a chair. "How can I say 'no' to 50 year old scotch?"

"49, actually." Cunningham smiled, filled the glasses, handed one to the Commander. "Cheers, my friend."

"Cheers." Beringer held the liquid in his mouth before he swallowed it. "If you keep sharing your stock with me, it won't last," he said. "We're a long way from home."

A quick smile flickered across the Captain's lips. "I'm hoping the people on Nu-Eden will come up with some brew of their own. There are enough chemists among the settlers. Of course, we can always drink the synthetic concoction our chemists on the station are producing. By the way, have you received any reports from Sergeant Vicks? The only stuff I get coming across my desk are the usual reports, most of it is boring."

Beringer cleared his throat. "Actually, I did get a report from the Sergeant. It is confidential, but as the captain of this station, and as my friend, I think you should know about it. Apparently, some of the colonists are behaving strangely."

"Strangely? How?"

"They are having, as Vicks called it, 'bizarre sexual encounters'." Beringer grinned when the Captain's eyebrows went up. "I guess we should be so lucky."

Cunningham didn't smile. "At any other time I would dismiss it, but I've had a similar report from Beta Colony. Father Champaine left a message on the monitor this morning. It sounded somewhat garbled, there is a lot of electromagnetic interference in the planet's atmosphere. It seems that the colonists are practicing some kind of demon-worship. They meet at night and have sex-orgies. At least that's what we are getting out of the message. The Father was rambling on, talked about visions of a beautiful demon-goddess who wants to have sex with him and steal his soul."

"I've never had much use for these religious fanatics, and Father Francoise Champaine certainly fits that category. I guess that's why he was encouraged to go to the colonies." Cunnningham allowed himself the shadow of a grin. "Just kidding, of course."

"Demon-goddess?" Beringer commented. "Have they discovered intelligent life?"

Cunningham shrugged. "Nothing in the reports, so far, unless you want to call those *tree-elves* intelligent."

"They're some kind of monkey, aren't they?"

"No contact was ever made with them, but they live in trees, don't wear any clothing. I'd say they're about as smart as monkeys, and as ugly."

"You wouldn't say that if you were a monkey," Beringer joked.

"I guess not." The Captain chuckled, filled the two glasses to the halfway mark.

It was Beringer's turn to raise an eyebrow, but he accepted the glass. "Good stuff," he said after draining it. "I shall miss it." He looked at the Captain. "I know we are keeping contact with the settlers to a bare minimum. After all, we're here only to observe. But don't you think you should have these reports investigated?"

Cunningham nodded. "Maybe I'll send a couple of our Psych-teams down. Then again, what does it really matter if they go wild sexually? Aren't they supposed to populate this planet? Earth laws don't really apply here. A new planet, new morals."

"Even so." Beringer hesitated. "It's not my job to advise you, Jeremy. You're the captain, but I don't feel right about this. Why would both colonies experience the same thing? I took the liberty to study the types of people who make up the colonists. One thing struck me as a little odd, there are a large number of religious people who make up Beta Colony."

"I'm aware of that fact." The Captain touched his computer screen. It expanded, changed position to give the Commander a better view. Beringer looked at a list of names. "As you can see," Cunningham said, "most of them come from the Southern Americas. We've tried to keep them together. Alpha Colony is made up of people who have a more diverse background."

"Don't you find it peculiar that all those religious people would engage in sexual depravities? In my experience, religious people usually have many taboos and hang-ups when it comes to sex. They don't have orgies."

"Usually," Cunningham agreed. "I guess, you're right. I should have it investigated."

18

Chapter Four
Space Station

When Commander Beringer left the Captain's quarters, he walked out with mixed feelings. *He's getting old,* Beringer thought. *I would not treat those incidents so lightly.* Being a military man made him naturally more aware of hidden dangers, made him more suspicious of things that might look harmless to the ordinary private citizen.

He took the elevator down to the fourth floor where his men were training under the sharp eyes of Sergeant Stasnowski. When he entered the gym, most of the marines were engaged in physical combat. He didn't see Lieutenant Striker and Raymond Chu, but he knew they were busy getting ready for their mission.

Sergeant Stasnowski let go of the man he held pinned to the mat. The Sergeant was a big man. Many had been fooled by his great bulk, expecting him to be slow, but he was as agile as any one of them, and stronger. He saluted when Beringer walked up to him.

"At ease, Sergeant." Beringer kept a tight ship, but he preferred a relaxed atmosphere when talking to his men. He knew he kept their respect, mainly because of that attitude. He handpicked each one, and he knew their strengths and weaknesses. They were the best that the Academy produced. "I see you're still beating your opponents," Beringer commented, smiling.

Stasnowski grinned. "They're keeping me on my toes, especially Lieutenant Wang. He's the best."

"But not as good as you?"

The Sergeant lowered his voice, still grinning. "Actually, he's better, but don't tell him that I know. I think he lets me beat him, because he doesn't want to hurt my feelings."

"I didn't know you had any." Beringer laughed. "Tell the men to take the rest of the day off, and I'll meet you in an hour on the observation deck. I'll buy you a drink."

There were a couple of people in the elevator when Beringer entered it. A man and a woman. He nodded politely, but didn't say anything. They were strangers to him. He and his men didn't fraternize with the civilians, he felt it was better that way.

He did see the woman on occasion. She was not the type a man could easily forget, with her red hair and green eyes, but he never spoke to her.

"So, when are you leaving," the man asked the woman.

"Day after tomorrow," she answered.

"For how long?"

"I might stay the full year." She laughed softly. "Unless I like it so much. I just may decide to settle there."

The man shook himself. "I hear it's a rugged world. Nothing but snow and ice. And the weather is unpredictable, lots of thunderstorms in the summer and severe snowstorms in the winter."

The woman brushed a strand of hair out of her face and chuckled. "It's not as bad as all that. It'll be nice to breathe some natural air again. The air on the station is becoming stale."

"But it's clean and sterilized, free of germs and bacteria. You don't know what kind of stuff you'll breathe down there."

"Professor Tennenboum has been planet side now for a couple of months. All the members on his team are fine." She touched the man's cheek. "Are you trying to talk me out of it, Bret?"

"I worry about you, Breanna. I wish you wouldn't go. I'll miss you. Besides, who's going to look after you?"

"I'm not a little girl anymore. I can take care of myself." Breanna smiled at Beringer, who studied her with interest, but tried not to be too obvious about it. "He's my big brother," she said. "It's time I get away from him for awhile."

Beringer smiled politely. "Older siblings tend to be overprotective of their younger ones, sometimes." He thought of his own brother, almost twice his age now, who tried to talk him out of joining the military. A long time ago. They hadn't spoken since.

"I'm not overprotective," Bret defended himself. "It's just, Breanna can be so impulsive."

"This is not an impulsive decision, Bret. I joined this mission to discover alien life forms, intelligent life forms. I won't find them here on the station."

"This station itself is alien."

"An artifact, interesting to an archeologist. Maybe. I'm looking for the people who built it." Breanna sighed. "You wouldn't understand." She looked at Beringer. "All he's interested in are the *caskets.*"

"Caskets?" Beringer asked.

"I'm a technician," Bret explained. "I'm looking after the cryogenic chambers."

The doors to the elevator opened before Beringer could comment.

"Would you mind joining us at our table?" Breanna asked him. "Unless you're meeting someone?"

"Not for an hour."

"Good." Breanna flashed him a smile. "Come on, then."

Beringer followed the couple. The transparent ceiling above them gave the illusion that he could just launch himself into the air and float into the emptiness of space. Even for one who had spent most of his life in outer space, it took some time to get used to it.

There were not many people in the observatory, since it was daytime on the station. Most of the crewmembers were performing their assigned duties and the scientists were busy working on their research projects.

"Isn't it beautiful?" Breanna lifted her arms, reached toward the stars. The bright globe of Nu-Eden hung motionless to one side. She looked at it. "Did you know that I've only spent a couple of weeks on Nu-Eden?" she asked Beringer.

He smiled. "That's two weeks longer than I have."

"Oh. Aren't you wondering what's it's like down there?"

"Sometimes." He shrugged. "My job is here on the station."

"So what do you do all day?" she asked.

"He's a military man, Bren, can't you see that." Bret sank into a chair. "Come, sit down."

Breanna's green eyes flashed when she glared at him. "I'm not stupid. I can see he's a military man." Sitting down, she clenched her fists and looked at Beringer. "This is why I have to get away. I feel I'm being smothered."

Bret snorted, but didn't comment.

Feeling somewhat uncomfortable, Beringer took the seat across from her. She must have sensed his discomfort and reached across the table to touch his hand. "Forgive me. It's not your problem." She smiled. "You never told me who you actually are."

"Sorry." Beringer cleared his throat. "Les Beringer. Commander Les Beringer."

"Oh, you're the famous commander. I finally meet you."

"Famous?" Beringer chuckled. "Why would you say that?"

"Your Lieutenant Striker told me about you. He respects you a lot."

"You know the lieutenant?"

She shook her head. "Not intimately. But we've bumped into each other a couple of times. I just saw him yesterday. He's part of our exploration team. But you know that, of course."

"Of course." Beringer nodded, looked at Brent. "I've wondered. Why did they put the cryogenic chambers on the 21st and 22nd floor? Wouldn't it have been easier to keep them on the lower floors?"

21

Bret smiled. He seemed relieved and happy to talk about something else than the problem he had with his sister. "Accessibility," he explained. There is an exit on the 21st floor, probably originally designed as an emergency exit. The engineers attached a large pressure chamber on the outside of the tower, large enough for a shuttle to dock."

"Interesting."

"Both of the floors have an independent power plant. It is located on the 23rd floor." Bret was eager to explain it to Beringer. There probably wasn't anyone else around who would be interested in his work. "There are always four security guards on duty. We don't take any chances. After all, we're responsible for 1,000 human lives."

Breanna touched her brother's arm. "I don't think the Commander is interested in all the details, Bret. You don't want to bore him."

Bret shook away her hand. "He asked," he said, angrily. "Nobody seems to appreciate my work. I know, I'm just a technician, but I have a responsible job." He looked at the timepiece on his wrist and rose. "If you'll excuse me, I have to get back to my shift. A pleasure to meet you, Commander." He stalked away, his shoulders stiff and straight.

"Your brother is an angry man," Beringer said, after Bret disappeared into the elevator.

"That he is." Breanna let out a deep sigh. "Our parents were killed when I was quite young. He's been my guardian and protector ever since. Now I'm grown up, and he can't get used to it. As far as he's concerned, I'm still his little kid-sister. He never married, doesn't have any friends. I'm the only person he feels close to. And now I'm abandoning him."

"Maybe it's good if he's alone for awhile. Have you ever thought that it may be you who's smothering him?"

Her eyebrows arched delicately when she looked at him. "Are you also a psychiatrist?" she asked, almost sharply, but then she smiled. "You may be right. I've been leaning on him for much too long. I don't make friends easily, either."

"I can't believe that. A beautiful woman like you?" He looked into her eyes. *She sure is a beauty, and damn attractive,* he thought, a gentle flutter suddenly took life in his loins.

A bright smile smoothed out the frown on her forehead, made her look even more beautiful. The pounding in his loins became almost unbearable.

"You really think I'm beautiful?" she asked, her eyes partially covered by lowered lashes.

She's playing me, he thought. *Damn it, I'm getting an erection.* "You

22

want something to drink?" he asked, trying to cover his embarrassment. He had been much too long without a woman.

"Sure." She smiled again. He became aware of the way her breasts moved under her thin sweater. "It's warm in here, makes a person thirsty," she said softly.

He grinned foolishly, nodded, and got up to walk over to the bar to order a couple of drinks. He'd never asked her what she wanted, so he ordered double scotch on the rocks for both of them.

After she downed her second one, she waggled a finger at him. "You're a sly one, Commander," she said, her speech a little slurred. "I think you're trying to get me drunk. I can get quite naughty after a few drinks."

After her fourth, she asked him to take her back to her room. "I think I need someone to tuck me into bed," she slurred.

Beringer looked at his watch. Sergeant Stasnowski should make his appearance any time now. Then he thought, *What the hell, he can wait.*

Breanna's room was on the tenth floor. She shared it with two other women. Both were at work now. Breanna assured him that they wouldn't be home for at least a couple of hours.

The alcohol hit her fully, and she was quite drunk by the time they arrived in her room. Beringer started feeling the effects of the alcohol also, and he didn't object when Breanna tugged on his pants to free his erection. When her mouth closed over his hard member he was almost ready to explode inside her hot mouth, but he still had enough self-control. He reached down to pull off her sweater. Her breasts tumbled out, large and round, with nipples as thick as her small finger.

With feverish haste, he took off his own clothes, and then he lay between her spread thighs. When he entered her moist sheath she cried out sharply, thrust up against him with the ferocity of a wild beast. The alcohol slowed his reflexes, kept him from coming too soon. When it finally happened, he exploded like an erupting volcano inside her hot interior.

"Don't pull out yet," she sobbed, still in the throes of an orgasm. He waited until she calmed down. Her legs fell open and released him. He rolled onto his back. "I guess I better leave," he said after catching his breath. "Wouldn't want your roommates to find me here, in your bed."

She laughed softly. "They would just be jealous." She climbed on top of him, wiggled her bottom. "Don't worry," she said and chuckled. "I'm as exhausted as you are." She slipped off the bed, padded over to a small cabinet and took out a bottle. "I'm thirsty. Want some water?"

"No, thank you. Did anybody ever tell you that you have a perfect body?"

She struck a pose, smiled. "Hundreds. I sleep with a lot of men."

"Really?"

Pouting, she said, "You don't actually believe that, do you? I don't make it a habit to fuck every guy I meet."

"Why me, then?" Beringer kept staring at her, smitten by her beauty.

She shrugged. "I found you attractive. Maybe it was the alcohol. Maybe I just wanted to be loved by someone. Or maybe I was just horny. Does it matter?"

"No, it doesn't. I don't jump into bed with every woman I talk to, either. I'm not sorry it happened." He swung his feet off the bed, began dressing. "I better go before I drag you back to bed."

She came closer. Her naked, soft breasts pressed against his chest as she leaned against him. Lifting up, she kissed him on the lips. "Thank you, Les Beringer. I hope to see you again when I come back."

Chapter Five
Alpha Colony

He was awakened by a gentle kiss. Opening his eyes, he looked into Anina's smiling face.

"Good morning," she said brightly. "Time to get up." She was already dressed in her usual colorless robe. Most women in the colony wore similar robes, they were practical, easy to maintain, warm on chilly nights and cool on hot days. Unfortunately, they were not very attractive.

"You sound chipper," he said and sat up.

"I feel great this morning." She laughed and stretched. Even the coarse material of her robe couldn't hide the swell of her breasts. "Did you ever have a dream that seemed so real you didn't know if you were awake or just dreaming?" she asked.

He studied her face; it seemed a little flushed. He shrugged. "I guess I have." Images of her kneeling in front of Stephan Tilus flashed into his mind. Her cries of ecstasy echoed in his head, the memory of her writhing on top of the other man made his blood boil. Then he saw himself kneeling behind Orona. He could still feel the pounding in his loins and the ecstatic feeling when he slid his penis into the young woman's sex-organ. Had it been just a dream?

"Why do you ask?"

"No reason," she said, color creeping into her cheeks. "It was just a silly dream."

"Maybe it's the air," he said.

"Or maybe the moons. Did you see those moons last night?" She pulled her hair out of her face, bunched it together behind her head. "I think I'll wear my hair a little looser from now on. That bun makes me look older, don't you think so?"

He smiled. "You look fine to me either way."

She pulled her mouth into a pout. "Just fine? I want to look beautiful for you. It's been quite some time since you told me I was beautiful."

He got off the bed and walked up to her. Taking her into his arms he said, "You are beautiful, and I love you."

"Do you, Thomas?" She looked into his eyes. "So why do we hardly make love anymore." It was not a question, but a statement.

He let go of her, turned away. "Not that again, Anina. You know how hard I've worked ever since we landed. I'm just tired."

"Everybody works hard," she said in a low voice. She kissed him on the shoulder and put her arms around him from the back. He could feel her soft breasts pressing against him, felt her warm breath in his neck. Between his legs, his penis stirred. When he turned, his hard penis touched her hips.

She smiled and put her hand on his hardness. "Thomas," she breathed, "it's early in the morning, but if you insist." She stepped back, pulled the robe over her head. She was naked underneath. He stared at her coppery triangle, at the slit visible underneath the sparse pubic hair.

She put her hand on his stiff penis, pulled him gently toward her. Groaning, he put his arms around her, kissed her hungrily. She fell backward onto the bed, her legs parted and then he found himself sliding into her creamy moistness. She cried out, wrapped her legs around his torso and lifted off the bed to meet his thrusts. She writhed beneath him, whimpering and clawing at his back.

He moved between her soft clutching thighs with ever-increasing speed. When he erupted inside her, he felt the all-consuming fire rage in his veins. His whole body seemed to burn with a passion he never felt before. He pulled out of her, still stiff.

"Turn around," he said, images of Orona's pale buttocks flashing through his mind.

Anina turned onto her belly. He straddled her, put his hands on her hips and pulled her up. Her buttocks were fleshy, but round and full; he pulled them apart, pushed his finger into the slit beneath, felt her inner muscle contract around his finger. He mounted her then, sank his erect member deep into her.

"Oh, Thomas," she moaned, "what is happening? We've never done it like this before."

He didn't say anything, just stared at her arching back, held her smooth hips in his strong hands. She began to rotate her hips, milking him fiercely. He slammed into her soft buttocks until he felt the wave of pleasure rise inside him. When it became impossible to hold back any longer he let go, and roaring, he emptied his discharge into his wife's hot interior, dimly aware of her cries of pleasure and her own gushing eruption.

Sighing deeply, she stretched out. He fell on top of her, where he lay panting, her smooth buttocks warm and soft against his loins. After awhile she turned and looked into his eyes, searching. "What's got into us?" she whispered.

"I don't know," he answered and kissed her gently. "But I like it. I feel like a sex-starved teenager." He lay on his side and studied her face. He'd never seen her this radiant, never before did she completely

26

abandoned herself to her desires, the way she did just now. Sex to her had been something a wife did with her husband in the dark of the night, not necessarily something to be enjoyed. She had never been frigid, and he knew she enjoyed it most of the time, but she never had an orgasm like the one she just experienced.

"Did you like it, too?" he asked.

She put her finger on his nose, let it trail over his lips, his chin. Smiling dreamily, she said, "I didn't know it could be like this. Did you?"

"No," he said, thinking again of Orona and felt guilty. Had it been a dream or had he really been with her? He wasn't sure. The image of Anina kneeling in front of Stephan Tilus popped into his mind. Had that been a dream?

"We better get dressed," he said. "I have to check out the power generator at the lab. It's been acting up lately."

Before he could get out of bed, there was a knock on the door. "Thomas," someone called. "Are you in there?" Tom recognized Ted Cameron, the botanist.

"A minute," Tom answered. "I've slept in." He slipped into his pants, didn't bother with a shirt. There was another knock, and then the door opened. Ted Cameron stepped through, glanced first at Tom, and then at Anina, who was sitting up in the bed.

He stared at her exposed breasts. "I'm sorry," he stammered, "I didn't know," but he kept staring at her.

Anina smiled, pulled the covers up to her neck. "It's all right, Teddy," she said. "I'm sure you've seen me naked before, down by the lake, where the women are bathing. The bushes aren't that thick."

Ted blushed. "I only got a glimpse, honest."

"Adam and Eve walked around naked. It says so in the *Good Book.*" Anina stretched, she didn't seem to notice the cover slipping off again.

"What's on your mind?" Tom asked, stirring Ted out of the door. "And I don't mean right at this very moment," he added, grinning.

The other man walked out backward, his eyes glued to Anina's naked body, when she slipped out of bed. She stood for a moment, inhaled deeply, thrusting out her ample breasts, a mischievous smile on her face, her green eyes large. They locked with his.

Tom closed the door behind him. "What's up?"

Ted was still staring at the closed door. "She's a beautiful woman," he said.

"Who?"

"Anina."

27

"You didn't come to tell me that." Tom eyed the other man. Ted Cameron was a big guy, beefy, with a round, friendly face. It appeared obvious by the dark shadow covering his chin and cheeks that he didn't shave this morning. That was not like him, he was usually clean-shaven.

Ted closed his eyes, shook his head. Then he fixed the gaze of his blue eyes on Tom. "Something weird is going on," he said with a haunted look on his face.

"What do you mean by *weird*?"

"I had sex with Nurse Mabel last night."

Tom smiled and then he laughed. "You are talking about *Mabel, the Ice cube*?"

"That's right, and she is no ice cube, let me tell you."

"It may be surprising news, but not weird." Tom chuckled. "Count yourself lucky, Teddy. I guess we can put the rumors to rest that she doesn't like men."

Ted came closer and whispered, "This morning, when I saw her, I gave her a wink. She just ignored me, acted as if nothing happened."

"Maybe nothing did happen." Tom said, flashes of young Orona coming unbidden. He remembered the feeling of her creamy vagina squeezing his rigid pole, remembered her soft breasts warm against his chest, her solid round buttocks in his groin. These memories seemed real, but were they?

"You think I'm making it up?" Ted stared at Tom. "I admit I've had fantasies about making out with her, but this was no fantasy. It happened!"

"Did you talk to her about it?"

"No, she ignores me."

"Why not ask her." Tom shrugged. "You know, Teddy, I can't give you an answer." He hesitated, wasn't quite sure if he should confide in the other man, after all, they weren't really close friends. "I've had a strange dream last night, and so did Anina."

"Really?" Ted seemed hopeful. "Tell me about it."

"Nah, it was just a stupid dream. It's already fading," he lied. The memory of Orona's pumping soft buttocks in his hands stayed quite strong. "By the way, did you notice a strange smell in the air last night?" he asked.

"Come to think of it, I did. But don't ask me where it came from."

"It was stronger by the pond," Tom said. "Maybe you should check it out. You're the botanist."

"Maybe I will." Ted turned to leave.

Tom watched him walk away and then went back into the shelter.

Anina was up, dressed. He remembered how she just behaved with Ted. "You shouldn't display yourself like that to other men," he chided her.

She just smiled, looked at him, and then she lowered her long lashes over her green eyes in a demure gesture. "I believe you're jealous, Thomas McClary." She laughed. "That makes me feel good."

"I guess I am jealous," he said. "That's just because I love you."

"I love you, too," she said in a low throaty voice and gave him a sidelong glance, it made her look incredibly sexy and Tom felt a sudden, strong urge.

"You're still so beautiful and attractive." He stared at her, at the swell of her breasts. He reached for the belt around her waist.

Gently, she pushed his hands away. "We're already late for our chores. I hope they left us something to eat. Those berry-pancakes are usually the first to go."

Together they walked toward the blue-striped building that served as the mess hall. Ho Ling, the cook, proved a real artist in the kitchen; creating palate-pleasing dishes from the local plants and fruit as soon as the biologists deemed them safe to eat.

The pancakes were gone, but there were plenty of small cakes made from the seeds of the local pine trees and many different kinds of fresh fruit. The herbal tea tasted somewhat bitter, but Ho Ling assured them it was safe and quite healthy.

"You'll feel like a young tiger tonight," he said, winking at Tom.

"I heard that." Anina laughed and shook a finger at the little man. "You are nasty."

Ho Ling smiled. "It'll turn you into a blooming flower that will attract every bee in the neighborhood."

"I've seen the local bees." Anina shook herself. "How about a female tiger?" There was a mischievous light in her green eyes.

"Too dangerous," the little cook said. "Besides, it is more fun to be a flower. Everyone will want to taste your sweet nectar." He walked away, chuckling to himself.

"He seems awfully good spirited this morning." Tom commented.

"Maybe he had a beautiful dream last night," Anina mused. "I feel very good today."

They got up. "I'll go have a look at that generator," he said. He touched his wife's hand. "See you later."

Before he reached the small shed that housed the generator, someone calling his name stopped him. Turning, he watched a figure dressed in a black and white robe rush toward him. *Sister Angela.*

29

She was a little out of breath when she reached him. Tom looked at her and fleetingly wondered why a beautiful woman like Sister Angela would choose a way of life dedicated to spiritual experiences instead of enjoying more earthly pleasures.

Like Sex!

He stopped himself before his mind could tread on dangerous grounds. *What is the matter with me,* he thought, *I've never looked at her this way before.*

"Brother Thomas." Sister Angela looked into his eyes, her face seemed flushed. Tom didn't think it came from running. "There is a matter I'd like to discuss with you."

"What is it, Sister?" Tom asked, noticing her uneasiness.

"It is of a somewhat delicate matter. I don't know how to say it. I feel deeply disturbed." Lowering her eyelashes, she blurted out, "I've entertained thoughts of a carnal nature lately."

Tom smiled, touched her arm. She pulled away, as if experiencing an electric shock. She looked at him, again. He noticed that her eyes were a beautiful deep blue color. "Why tell *me*, Sister?" he asked gently.

"Because you're the oldest down here." She smiled a little. "And I don't mean that in a derogatory way. In addition, you're a man who believes in the scriptures. Besides, you are married, happily, I believe, and the chance of you taking advantage of a certain situation is quite small. I have to show you something, but it has to be done at night, you will understand when you see it. I'll meet you after dark down by the women's bathing place."

Before he could answer her, she turned and walked away. Shaking his head, Tom looked after her retreating slim figure.

30

Chapter Six
Beta Colony

A brisk breeze blew from the Mountain Lake, leaving small ripples on the clear water. Rosanha slipped out of her plain cotton dress and stood naked at the edge of the lake. Closing her eyes, she took a deep breath and inhaled the heady scent that clung to the breeze.

It was a beautiful place. Life proved harsh now, but it would be better some day. Sometimes she felt homesick for her home planet, Earth, but when she remembered the over-crowded conditions she once lived in, the pangs of pain evaporated quickly.

She ran into the water, dove in and swam toward one of the large floating plants. Something touched her thigh, something cool and slippery. There was a tickling sensation on her belly, then her pubic area. She felt suddenly aroused. A splashing sound behind her made her turn around. "You startled me," she said in a breathless voice, her face flushed.

"I'm sorry, didn't mean to." He was young, handsome, his voice pleasant.

She studied him. "I've never seen you before," she said, backing away from him. In the clear water she could see that he was naked, like her. The tingling between her legs became almost overwhelming.

"I'm from Alpha-Colony," he said, smiling.

"But that's far away from here." She held on to one of the giant leafs of the plant, covering her breasts with one arm.

He laughed. "Are you shy? I've seen naked girls before."

She blushed. "I don't know you. You are a stranger." Her thighs tingled, her loins throbbed softly, and she found herself drawn to this young man.

"You don't have to be afraid of me," he said. "Come, let's go ashore and out of the sun. There is shade and soft grass underneath that tree over there."

"I like the sun, and it's almost gone anyway," she said, "besides, I am naked."

"So am I," he laughed. "Are you ashamed of your body? Are you ugly?"

She smiled. "No."

"No to what? Ashamed or ugly?"

"No to both." She let go of the plant, swam toward shore. "Catch me, if you can," she called over her shoulder, suddenly feeling reckless and playful.

He caught up with her easily, swam beside her, and then he disappeared under the surface. She saw a distorted image of him, and then he was gone. He surfaced close to shore, way ahead of her, waiting for her.

"You are fast," she said, trying to catch her breath.

"I love the water." He laughed. "I was born in it." He reached for her hand, pulled her up from her crouching position. When her naked breasts grazed his muscular chest, it sent a tingling sensation through her nipples. He picked her up, carried her onto dry land and put her down gently underneath the big tree.

He stood above her, muscles rippling on his youthful body. His penis was large and half-erect. She'd never seen a man's penis from this close, and it looked almost intimidating.

"You are very handsome," she said, blushing again.

He laughed, showing white teeth, and shook his shoulder-length hair. Then he dropped down beside her and kissed her gently. She didn't struggle; her vagina burned with an unfamiliar desire, her insides felt hot. When he moved on top of her, her thighs parted willingly. Something hard and hot touched her belly, slid between her thighs. His fingers massaged her pubic area. She reached down between them, found his hardness.

"This is my first time," she whispered, "please, be gentle."

She lifted up, felt him enter her partially. There was a sudden sharp pain, but only for a moment, then he was inside her. He moved slowly in and out of her. Soon she began to experience pleasure beyond anything she ever experienced before. When he kissed her, his saliva mingled with hers, it tasted sweet and pleasant. Boys kissed her before, but they never tasted like this.

She swallowed eagerly, sucked on his tongue. She experienced her first orgasm. Trying to stifle her cries of pleasure, she failed.

He pulled out of her, told her to turn around and kneel. She could hardly wait for him to enter her again and cried out when she felt his hard penis slide back into her dripping young vagina. She arched her back, pushed up her buttocks, bucked beneath him. His hands cupped her small breasts, his fingers played with her stiff nipples.

Then she felt his penis growing inside her, hot liquid gushed forcefully into her young womb. She whimpered and clawed the ground with her fingers as another powerful climax sent a series of spasms through her body.

"You are killing me," she cried out, "I can't take much more."

He kissed her neck. "You'd be amazed how much you can take," he whispered into her ear. "This is just the beginning."

Rosanha had never been with a man before, not sexually, but she watched other couples. There were not many secrets in the small settlement. "Let me be on top," she said, when he pulled out to turn her around again. He nodded, smiled and stretched out on his back. His penis stood like a stiff mast. She straddled him, lowered herself down. When she felt the swollen head touch her labia, she closed her eyes, rubbed her clitoris gently across his slippery glans.

As the pleasure built her movements became more furious. Crying out, she doused him with her discharge, and then she sank into his lap, took the hard organ deep inside her. Opening her eyes, she saw him watching her.

The sun disappeared, but the two moons were bright in the sky. Their silvery light bathed his face. A strange glow appeared in his dark eyes, as if they were illuminated from within.

He lifted his upper torso, put his arms around her slim body, then, without uncoupling, he put her onto her back. Her young sex-canal was stretched to its limits by his hard, throbbing organ. He moved with forceful strokes on top of her. She pulled up her knees until they touched her shoulders to give him deeper access.

"Accept my gift," he whispered into her ear and then his mouth closed over hers. His penis pumped inside her, filling her young vessel, his mouth fed her his sweet nectar. She milked his penis, sucked on his tongue, her body shook in the throes of a tremendous orgasm.

It proved too much for her system. Blackness engulfed her as she lost consciousness. When she awoke, he was gone.

She stared into the star-speckled sky above, the two moons met and were parting again. If it hadn't been for the dull throbbing in her womb, she would have thought this to be a dream. She had daydreamed before. She touched her belly, then her thighs. Closing her eyes, she tried to recall the sensation of a man's penis sliding into her. What an ecstatic experience that had been! She needed to tell someone, maybe Mandy, her girl friend. Mandy was half a year older, and she was also still a virgin.

Rosanha giggled suddenly. "I am not a virgin anymore," she whispered. "Mandy will be so envious." She became aware of someone approaching. When she looked up, she saw two people running toward the tree she lay under. A man and woman, both naked. They were giggling and laughing, the man grabbed the woman from the back, cupped her breasts. They never made it to the tree. The woman fell to her knees, pushed up her rump. The man knelt behind her, fumbled between his legs.

Rosanha got a quick glimpse of his rigid penis before it disappeared between the woman's buttocks. Arching her back, the woman cried out softly when the man's pelvis snapped forward.

"Am I too big for you?" the man asked, moving slowly behind the woman.

"No," gasped the woman, "you fill me up just right."

"I hope your husband didn't see us."

The woman laughed, began rotating her hips in his lap. "Don't worry about Franco. He's too busy dipping his nose into those two young honey-cups. He thinks I don't know what's going on."

The man grabbed her hips, increased his tempo. "You mean young Mandy and Lillith?" His breath started coming a little faster now. The woman's fleshy buttocks clenched and unclenched as she milked him furiously.

"Mandy and Lillith," breathed the woman. "Those two little *stream-nymphets*. They could be his daughters. He's been fogging both of them for the last couple of nights."

Rosanha gasped silently. So much for surprising Mandy with the big news. Sounds like she's been busy. And Lillith! Who would have thought? Lillith, who wouldn't look twice at any of the eligible young bachelors. So, she liked older men!

Rosanha rolled onto her belly, propped herself up on her elbows. Who were these two people? The voices sounded familiar, but she didn't recognize them, their faces lay in the shadows. The woman had big breasts, they swung like a pair of pendulums beneath her every time the man thrust into her.

"I don't know what it is," the woman was saying, "but whenever I go into the water I get so turned on."

"Maybe it's those moons," the man said behind her, "or maybe the air. It smells different at night, and it seems to make me awfully horny." His breath caught in his throat. "I think I'm coming!" he said hoarsely.

"I'm ready," the woman gasped.

"Here I come!" the man shouted, grabbed her hips and slammed his belly hard into her fleshy cheeks. His buttocks clenched as he emptied his load into the woman's shaking body. Her clawed fingers dug into the grass, and her cries of pleasure rang in Rosanha's ears.

"That was some climax," the woman moaned, her buttocks still quivering in the man's groin.

He bent over her and took her breasts into his hands. "You ever come with Franco like that?" he asked, his voice breathless and hoarse.

"Never." She was still trying to catch her breath. "How about Eilleene? Does she?"

"Eilleene? Not like you." He kissed her neck. "Mind you, she's not frigid, she's quite hot, but you, you're something else." He began thrusting again.

She laughed. "You're still hard. It feels good. But give me a moment, I have to wash myself first."

"Now?"

"Yeah, now. I don't know why, I just have to. I'm kinda itchy down there."

He shrugged, pulled out. The woman got up and ran toward the lake. The man watched her; when she dove into the water, he turned. His eyes fell on Rosanha. "Hey," he said, "have you been there all the time?"

Rosanha rose, stood uncertain, nodded. She realized she was not in the shadows anymore. The light from the two moons shone fully on her nude body.

"You're Rosanha," the man said. "I recognize you. You're Mandy's friend." He came closer; Rosanha stared at his erection. "Have you been watching us?" he asked. His voice sounded strange, tight. "Did you like what you saw? Are you turned on?"

She didn't know what to say. She recognized him now, Roger Ransum, the geologist. He was married to Eilleene, the biologist. A good friend of Rosanha's mother. He stood in front of her now. She could smell his masculinity and it turned her on immensely.

"You're Theresa's little girl," he said. "Not so little from close up. Nice tits." He cupped one of her nubile breasts. When he kissed her, she didn't resist, and when his hand reached down to touch her vagina, she only moaned. She felt his finger enter her, let him stroke her clitoris.

He broke away, laughed. "You're all wet, you little vixen. I believe you want me to make love to you."

She sank to the floor, opened her thighs to him. All rational thought left her, all she wanted was his big, stiff pole inside her aching belly.

He knelt between her open thighs, stroked her small breasts, her taut, flat belly, and rubbed his finger over her puffed-up pubis. Her eyes were glued to his penis. He noticed her look, chuckled, then he stretched out on top of her, guided his stiff mast between her inviting slim thighs.

She watched it disappear in her dark, fluffy triangle, felt the thick organ enter, cried out when he slid into her. She felt charged up from the encounter with the young man from Alpha-Colony, and whimpering she squirmed underneath the older man.

He crushed his lips to hers, kissed her hungrily. His thick pole moved in and out of her young vagina. "You are extremely tight," he groaned. "I don't think I can hold it long...ahh...NOW!" he shouted. He stopped moving, pushed deeper into her. She felt his warm discharge as he erupted inside her.

"Great Nova," he moaned. "I think from now on it will be only young, tight honey-pots, like yours. Next time bring your two friends."

Rosanha didn't answer. She closed her eyes, her whole body shook in the throes of a huge orgasm. Whimpering, she raked her fingers across the older man's back.

When it was over, she just lay there, eyes shut. He remained inside her, still stiff. After awhile she began milking his pole, letting her inner muscles ripple the length of the thick penis.

"You surprise me," he moaned, "here I thought you were an innocent little virgin. Looks like you've had quite some experience. Who's been sampling your little flower?"

"Nobody you know," she said, "and I am not as experienced as you may think."

"You're sure fooling me," he said hoarsely, "that thing you're doing with your love-tunnel. You are a pro."

"I'm a fast learner."

He gasped. "Just keep doing it. Don't stop. Here we go again!" He put his hands under her small round buttocks, held her in a tight grip and filled her up again. A delicious shudder went through Rosanha's body as she experienced another orgasm.

He collapsed on top of her, breathing hard. "I don't know where this stuff comes from. I can usually manage a couple of good ones. The third time I can hold it for quite a long time and then it's nothing big. But with you, wah!" He rolled over onto his back, keeping her on top.

Rosanha sat up straight. She felt his penis inside her. It lost some of its hardness, but was far from being soft.

"How is your mother?" he asked. "I haven't seen her for a couple of days."

Rosanha shrugged. "She's fine. I don't see her much. She's been busy, people have been coming down with some kind of rash."

"She's a fine doctor, your mother." He looked at her; his fingers stroked her small breasts. She studied him and realized that he was quite a handsome man. A little too old, though, he must be at least thirty-five.

"Too bad about your father," he said. "Do you miss him much?"

She shrugged again. "A little. I didn't really know him too well, he was gone most of the time."

"He was a scientist, wasn't he?"

"Yeah," she nodded. "I don't know what he did, exactly. He worked mostly in space, checking out asteroids. That's where he got killed." She wiggled her bottom, giggled when he gasped. "Let's not talk about him, let's fogg."

"Fogg...hmm." he grinned. "I like that when little girls talk dirty."

Rosanha began rotating her hips, snapped her pelvis back and forth. A female voice made her stop. "I see you've found a little playmate."

Rosanha looked up at the woman. She recognized her now, Francesca Geomez, one of the botanists. "Hello, Mrs. Geomez," Rosanha said, smiling innocently, "I've kept Mr. Ransum company. You want him back?"

Francesca glared for a moment, then she laughed softly. "This is too much. My husband screws your friends and my lover screws you. Are you even old enough to realize what you are doing, child?"

"I'm sixteen," Rosanna said, "I'm not a child anymore, I'm a woman now." She lifted up, feeling suddenly empty as the man's thick organ slipped out of her.

Francesca looked at the stiff penis. "Well, at least you didn't use him all up." She straddled Roger, grabbed the stiff pole and fed it into her thick black thatch of hair. Then she sank down slowly. "Go, take a bath," she said to Rosanha, "it'll do you good."

Rosanha stepped back, watched for a while as the older woman bounced up and down, watched her large breasts jiggle. *Some day I'll have breasts like that,* she thought and turned toward the lake.

When she stepped into the water, she noticed something slippery slide down her thigh. She reached down, peeled it off. At first, it looked like a transparent piece of cloth, but then it began to contract itself into an oval egg-shaped ball with tiny tendrils protruding from its bottom. It moved, slipped out of her cupped hands and disappeared in the water.

She didn't know what it was, but somehow it didn't matter. There was something right about it. She swam for a while, and then went back to shore. The third moon began rising above the mountains. It was time to go home.

Chapter Seven
Exploration Team Delta

"Any luck?" Lieutenant Striker peered anxiously over the pilot's shoulder, hoping to hear at least some good news.

Space-marine Raymond Chu shook his head. "Sorry, Lieutenant, but I think this thing is fried. The lightning strike that hit the shuttle burnt a bunch of relays and the primary memory chips of the computer. We don't have enough spare parts."

"What about the transmitter?"

"Negative, sir."

"What are you telling me, Chu?"

The pilot turned away from the controls. His almond eyes were even smaller than usual when he looked at the lieutenant. "We are stuck here, sir. For good!"

Striker suppressed a curse. He wasn't quite ready to tell the rest of the team. "It's been a week. Maybe the Old Man will send another shuttle to rescue us." But he knew better, and so did Chu. There would be no rescue. Captain Cunningham would never risk another team, even if there were one.

The only other qualified pilot was Space-marine John Lambert, and Commander Beringer would not risk the life of another pilot on a futile search for a lost shuttle on an unknown, unexplored planet.

"We'll have to tell the others," Chu said.

Striker looked around the shuttle one more time, before he stepped outside. The morning air was crisp, cold, but fresh. There were some clouds forming in the sky, it looked like rain. If they were stuck on this planet, they would have to move, look for shelter in a more moderate climate, find a better, and safer location.

It was late summer, the nights were already getting cold. They would never survive a winter. The shuttle might serve as a temporary shelter, but they'd soon run out of food rations. They didn't pack for a long stay, since the shuttle was supposed to bring new supplies for the research station with regular trips. In addition, without the computer the heating and air conditioning didn't work.

That storm cloud they passed through on the way down, punished them with a series of lightning strikes. When one of those strikes knocked out the navigation system, Chu piloted the shuttle manually and sat it down on a huge, rocky shelf.

Striker looked to the peak of the snow-covered mountains in the north. Winter would bring heavy snowfalls, accompanied by strong gales of wind. One snow-slide could sweep the shuttle off the shelf, tumble it into the valley below. *"No,"* he thought, *"we can't stay here. Our destination lies south, away from these mountains. It will be a tough journey, but not impossible."*

He could hear the other team members laughing by the small pond that lay hidden behind a group of large boulders, in a glade sheltered from the wind by a row of stunted trees. Hating himself for being the bearer of bad news, he headed toward the sound of their merry laughter.

Breanna McGuinness spotted him first. She was the expert on alien life forms. She and a couple of other women were frolicking in the surprisingly warm water of the pond. He recognized Nurse Monaca Vargas and Dr. Liss. All three women were naked.

"Come, join us, Lieutenant," Breanna called. "The water is beautiful."

Striker smiled at her. Of the eight women, she was the most attractive. Not only beautiful, she was also smart and blessed with a pleasing personality. Some day she'd be the reason for much rivalry between the men in the team. Eventually couples would pair off. Since there were twelve men and only eight women, some compromises would have to be reached.

It would be best not to encourage couples pairing off, but to form some kind of commune, where a woman could choose any man she wanted, any time she felt like having sex. Or maybe they should form groups of three partners, two men, and one woman. That would leave two women without partners.

Oh, to hell with it, Striker thought. No sense to break his head over that now!

Three of the other women were sitting with a group of men, playing cards. He didn't see Sara Golman, the biochemist, and Concitta Sanchez, the geophysicist. Neither did he see Professor Josef Banca, the geologist and head of the research team.

"What's up, Striker?" Jeffro Remington looked up from the card game. "How are the repairs coming?"

Remington was one of the Security guards. Not military, he didn't adhere to any protocol, and never called him lieutenant.

"I'd like to call a meeting. There is a matter which needs discussing." Striker looked around the group, seeing suddenly anxious faces. He cleared his throat, never good at making speeches. "I'm afraid the repairs are not going well. Actually..." he coughed again, "...they're not going at all. It looks like we're stranded."

"What the hell does that mean?" bellowed Ewor Gregorchuck. His field marine-biology and something else, Striker didn't remember what else the big, beefy man did. His full head of thick hair and the wild beard lent him a menacing look. Striker didn't know him well enough to make a judgment about his temper.

"It means exactly what it sounds like," Striker said mildly. "We are stranded on this planet. There is no way the shuttle will fly again."

"Surely they'll come looking for us," Remington said. "Have you contacted the research-station?"

"The communicator is also down. Damaged beyond repair."

"This is not happening!" Rhea Rosetti threw down her cards and stared accusingly at Striker as if it were his fault. Rhea was one of the biologists. A small, but wiry, tough looking woman, hard to tell her age. She possessed one of those smooth, forever young looking faces. Quite pretty, too.

"Captain Cunningham would never leave us down here," Gregorchuck almost growled. "This team is far too valuable."

"There is no other shuttle of this class on the station. All the others are cargo-shuttles, meant only for transportation of people and materials. They were never intended for search and rescue missions. Besides, we don't even have the personnel trained for that kind of work." Striker surprised himself over how calm he felt.

Breanna, Monaca, and Dr. Liss climbed out of the pond and were standing behind the seated group, still naked, dripping water.

"So, what's going to happen?" Breanna asked.

Striker stared at her heaving breasts. *She sure is beautiful,* he thought, momentarily distracted. He noticed her back on the station, but there had never been an opportunity to really get to know her. He felt attracted to her, and he got the impression the attraction was mutual. She kept looking at him with her green eyes and a challenging expression on her face.

"We have to move," he said.

"Well, then let's move," Remington rumbled. "It's too damn cold up here in the mountains anyway. Professor Tennenboum is probably wondering what happened to us and his supplies."

"I'll second that," Rhea chimed in. "We can take the shuttle, fly it to the research station and try to fix it then. At least we'll be more comfortable there. I hear there is a nice big lake near the station."

"As long as that lake is as warm as this little pothole," Dr. Liss said, and laughed. Her full name was actually Andrea Liss, but everybody

40

called her Dr. Liss. She was a biologist, but also a very good GP.

Striker studied her for moment. Slim, tall, she kept her hair short. He noticed her full, sensuous lips, a trifle too large, but her dark, smoldering eyes made her look extremely attractive. It didn't seem to bother her to prance around in the nude, thrusting out her small breasts on an otherwise trim, well-built body, and have all the men study her.

"I'm sure it will be warm enough." Striker smiled, then became serious. "But it may be awhile until you'll swim in that lake."

"Why?" she asked.

"Because we can't take the shuttle."

"Why the hell not?" demanded Gregorchuck.

"As I said before, the shuttle has been damaged, we don't have the necessary parts to make repairs. It won't fly, ever again!" There, he said it!

"What do you mean by it won't fly? It looks fine to me." One of the other men, Acram Mian, broke into the conversation.

Striker shrugged. "There is nothing physically wrong with the shuttle. It may look fine, but it won't fly. The computer has been damaged. We might get the shuttle into the air, but we can't control it. Chu could explain it to you in more technical terms, but it won't change the fact that the shuttle is not usable."

"We can't leave the shuttle. It is our only link to the station." Breanna continued looking at him with that challenge in her green eyes. "How far is it to the research-station?" she asked.

He sighed. "One thousand kilometers, maybe two, I'm not sure. The electric storm we passed through scrambled all the instruments."

"Do you at least know in which direction the station lies?" Dr. Liss asked.

"I think so, but again, I am not really certain of that either."

"I just can't believe this is happening," Rhea said for the second time. "To think, I actually volunteered for this mission."

"So did I," Monaca Vargas said, contempt in her voice. "I replaced Mabel who decided to join Dr. McClary at Alpha Colony."

"I still don't understand why they can't come and pick us up," Rhea said.

"There is a lot of disturbance in the atmosphere of this planet. Even if our communication system were operable, there is no guarantee the space station could pick up our signals. Getting a shuttle through the disturbance is already challenging. If we ever want to colonize this planet, we'll have to come up with designs that are more suitable. The electronic systems need to be isolated from the outer hull, for one thing, make them less vulnerable to electrical interference. I'm not an expert in these matters, my knowledge is limited. All of you were told there'd be a certain risk. There always is when landing on an unknown planet."

"No one is blaming anybody," Dr. Liss said, "at least I am not. It is just hard to accept our predicament. So, you suggest we move."

"I don't suggest it. I say we do. Our goal will be the valley below, we may have to spend the winter there, and then, in the spring, we can begin searching for the research station."

"We must wait for Dr. Banca and the others, and put it to a vote."

"It is not a question of should we or should we not," Striker said grimly. "We will move, if we want to survive."

"What gives you the right to decide what we do?" Remington challenged him.

Striker glared at him. This man will be trouble, he thought, I should have never allowed him to be part of this mission. He's belligerent, doesn't give a damn about protocol and cares only about himself. And he is armed. "I am the team leader," he said calmly, "and responsible for the safety of this team."

"You have no authority over any of us," Remington growled. "You and the pilot are the only military personnel here. Don't try to give us orders!"

"I am not giving any orders, Remington. I am only telling you how it is!" It was Striker's turn to growl. "You can stay behind, if you want to die. The choice is yours."

"Come on, you two. The last thing we need now is dissention." Striker was surprised at the sharpness in Breanna's voice. "We need a leader, somebody who is best qualified to judge our situation. I am behind Lieutenant Striker. I say we follow his suggestion. For now. Later, we can always choose another leader."

"I say we wait for Dr. Banca," Andrea Liss said. "He'll know what to do."

Chapter Eight
Alpha Colony

The two satellites were on their upward journey in the star-speckled sky. Tom inhaled deeply, aware of the strong, heady fragrance in the crisp air. He passed the recreational pool, walked over the narrow bridge that crossed the stream and headed for the women's bathing place.

Small waterfalls connected a series of ponds. One of these pools was hidden among thick, tall bushes. The women claimed it for themselves. There they would bath and swim nude, away from the men's prying eyes.

When Tom stepped into the small clearing, he heard gentle splashing. A naked female figure rose from the calm dark water and came toward him. He watched in fascination as she climbed onto shore, admired her slim body, the small cone-shaped breasts jutting from her narrow ribcage. When she turned he noticed her plump round buttocks. Black skin reflected the bright yellow light of the moons. She seemed to have seen him, because she started walking toward him.

"She's beautiful, isn't she?" a soft voice said beside him.

He turned, startled. "Sister Angela," he stammered, "I didn't see you when I arrived."

She laughed softly. "I was leaning against that big tree over there. I watched you come."

"This is Naomi," Sister Angela said, turned toward the girl and took her hand. "Come, step into the light, let Brother Thomas have a look."

The girl faced the pale light of the moons. Tom stared at her small juvenile breasts, the way they tilted upwards, the short brown nipples. His gaze wandered down her flat belly, it came to rest on her thick, curly black triangle. There was an odd stirring in his loins. "I don't understand," he said, looking at Sister Angela.

"Look closer. Touch her belly."

Tom reached out, gingerly put his finger against the girl's hip, and trailed it across the satiny skin of her belly. A tingling sensation in his finger made him jerk away.

"Go closer and look at her groin." Sister Angela's voice was tight. Tom felt her hand on his arm, it seemed clammy, hot.

He knelt in front of the girl, peered at the black, curly thatch of hair. There was a shiny, transparent film covering the girl's vulva, part of her belly and the inside of her thighs. He needed to put his face real close to notice the gently pulsating ripples.

"What is that?" he asked, perplexed, looking up at Sister Angela. The breath caught in his throat.

She had removed her black robe, stood naked in front of him. The veil of her blonde hair covered half her face, part of her shoulders. Like a serpent trying to escape, her pink tongue darted between her white teeth.

His numb mind registered the beautifully shaped full round breasts, her flat belly and gently flaring hips. He also noticed the thin gelatin film that covered her slim inner thighs, part of her lower belly, and the golden curls of her pubic hair.

"Touch it!" she commanded with a shaky voice.

He obeyed, didn't jerk back when he felt the soft vibration run through his fingers. Moving them in a circular motion around her swollen vulva, he wasn't aware when he began to rub her slit.

A moan escaped from Sister Angela's lips. "Oh, Brother Thomas." Her voice sounded husky, breathless.

His finger slipped into her, his lips touched her smooth white belly. Urgent hands began to tug on his trousers, pulled them down. He felt gentle fingers curl around his painful erection, stroking him gently.

"Take her," a voice whispered into his ear. "Go on and take her."

His lips moved up, fastened on swollen nipples, a soft neck and closed on a warm open mouth. He put his hands under her taut buttocks and lifted up. Slim arms went around his neck, strong legs wrapped around his torso. Then he slid into tight, hot moistness.

Sister Angela was light, but after awhile his legs began to shake. He moved toward the tree, pressed her back against the soft, resilient bark. She cried out softly when he thrust deeper into her. "Put me onto the ground," she breathed.

Sinking to his knees beside the tree, he fell forward, his penis still inside the woman's belly. Her legs opened wider, her buttocks lifted off the ground as she met his powerful thrusts.

Tom felt a warm body on top of him, felt it move with him as he rocked between Sister Angela's clutching thighs. "I can't wait much longer," the breathless voice of Naomi whispered into his ear, her hot breath caressing his neck. She slipped from him, pulled him off Sister Angela. Rolling onto his back, he watched the girl straddle him. Hovering above him, she grabbed his erect penis, guided it into her black curly thatch. Tight, moist softness slid over his swollen glans; for a moment there was slight resistance, and then with a cry he slid into another hot, incredibly soft and narrow sheath.

His eyes were glued to the young woman's small, but shapely conical breasts as she writhed above him. The light from the moons seemed brighter now, and her body became a black silhouette against the starlit sky.

Naomi, he thought, *her name is Naomi.* He'd seen her before, she was one of the young women in Sister Angela's small convent. He was having sexual intercourse with a future nun! And Sister Angela! He'd practically raped her, and after she trusted him. He was responsible for her breaking her vows. He was *The Great Despoiler*, the serpent in the *Garden of Eden*!

He would burn forever.

But it was pretty clear that neither Sister Angela nor Naomi had been innocent virgins. It also became clear that young Naomi was quite an expert when it came to using her body in the performance of the sex act. She let her inner muscles ripple along the length of his penis in a way that betrayed her innocence.

He heard a splash from the pool. Turning his head, he saw Sister Angela disappear in the black water. Then he felt Naomi leave him, freeing his stiff pole. She knelt beside him, plump buttocks facing him. White teeth flashed in her black face. Slapping her left buttock gently, she looked at him with large, brown eyes. Getting up, he moved behind her, put his hard mast against her soft buttocks and pushed it between her spread thighs. An electrifying tingling sensation ran through his body, and then he slid past her thick labia and entered her hot interior.

She clenched her inner muscles, trapping him inside her. Then she began milking him fiercely by pumping her lower body. He grabbed her slim hips, thrust deep into her demanding sex organ. It wasn't long before he felt the coming of a tremendous climax. He let it built up, and then with a hoarse cry he exploded, spilling his seed into Naomi's young womb.

She quivered in his grasp, arched her back and cried out as a spasm ran through her body. He sensed movement beside him. Gentle hands pulled him backward and pushed him onto his back. There were figures surrounding him. The pale moonlight reflected off naked female bodies. Young female bodies. Nubile breasts and slim bodies silhouetted against the sky.

He recognized a face above him. Sister Angela. "Do not be afraid, Brother Thomas. It is as it should be." Her voice was soothing, husky. "Tonight destiny will be fulfilled."

One of the girls approached carrying a mug; she pressed it against Tom's lips. He tasted bittersweet liquid.

"Drink from the nectar," Sister Angela whispered. Swallowing it, he became aware of the strong fragrance in the air, he also recognized the liquid. It tasted just like the herbal tea Ho Ling offered him. Not unpleasant, but it left a lingering, strange after taste. He became aware of the painful erection he started sprouting.

Sister Angela pushed him flat onto his back. "Save your seed for me, Brother Thomas," she whispered against his ear.

A slim body straddled him, soft hands grabbed his aching penis. Once more he felt the slight resistance as his organ entered a young vagina. Smooth, soft walls closed around his shaft and took him deep inside. Waves of pleasure radiated through his body. He wanted to dig his fingers into those flashing narrow hips, wanted to pull them deeper into his lap, but strong hands held his arms pinned to the ground.

Suddenly he was free, but only for a moment. Another pair of legs straddled his body, another tight, but incredibly soft vice enveloped him; smooth hips pumped violently above him.

They took turns. How many of those young demanding vaginas descended upon him he didn't know. There was continues pleasure. Finally there came a point where the built-up pressure grew so strong, he knew an eruption was near. "Now!" he called out hoarsely.

The girl above him lifted off, hands propelled him toward a woman who was lying on her back with her legs spread wide open. He fell between them, and with a loud sob he thrust into her soft sheath. She felt moist and warm and accepted him eagerly. After a few strokes he erupted with tremendous force.

A deep, bellowing sound blended with the ecstatic cries of a woman. He thought his climaxing would never stop. Fluid kept gushing from him, and his penis seemed enormous inside Sister Angela's slight body.

There came a low chanting coming from a dozen female throats, but he was only dimly aware of it. When it was finally over, he collapsed into the woman's arms. He lay there for a long time, his penis still hard, still tingling, still inside Sister Angela. When he began to move again, she struggled beneath him, gently, but forcefully pushed him off. "You gave me what I needed," she said, "tomorrow night you will put your seeds into another of my Angels. You are *The Chosen One,* Brother Thomas."

Suddenly he was alone, desire still strong, and unsatisfied. Between his legs his penis strutted into the darkening sky.

The two satellites once again finished their journey and disappeared behind the treetops. The pond went silent, but the heady fragrance lingered in the air. A tree-frog drummed nearby. In the distance, a swamp-tiger roared its challenge. A flock of *owls* crossed in front of the third moon's reddish disk.

Shaking his head, he lay there, staring at the placid waters. There was no evidence that anybody had been here. Did he dream the whole thing?

A sound from the direction of the nearby bushes made him turn his head. Someone started coming down the path, entered the clearing. It was Anina. She seemed startled when she saw him. "What are you doing here at the women's bath place?" she asked.

"I don't know," he answered, sat up, and wiped his forehead.

She saw his erection, smiled. "Who's that for?"

He grinned, suddenly embarrassed, shrugged. "I was having a dream."

"It seems to be going around." She slipped out of her robe, stood naked. She seemed younger, more vibrant. He stared at her breasts, they looked fuller, rounder. What made him think they were beginning to sag? "You're beautiful," he said.

She smiled. "I'm going for a swim."

He watched as she ran toward the water, watched her fleshy, but solid round buttocks rotate gently beneath smooth skin. She dove in, swam a short distance, and then sank under the surface. Her head bobbed up close to shore. She climbed out of the water, a beautiful naked nymph. Shaking her hair, she came running back toward him, laughing and dripping water.

Straddling him, she stood above him for a moment. Between her legs something glittered, reflecting the reddish light of the moon. Sinking lower, she impaled herself on his rigid mast. An electric shock went through him as her soft walls closed around his penis, waves of pleasure stabbed into his brain. A soft sigh escaped her open lips. She lifted her arms skyward, her face turned toward the pond, her smooth forehead creased into a frown and her eyes took on a far away look, as if she were listening to something only she could hear.

Tom watched her face, watched the frown turn into a smile, and then his gaze wandered down to her beautiful breasts, to her flat rippling belly and fastened on the spot where their bodies were joined. Her pelvis moved furiously in his lap, with every downward thrust she repeatedly took him deep into her.

His hands reached up, his fingers dug into her soft breasts. Then, as an orgasm shook her body, he emptied himself into her; and even though he came twice already, there was no diminishing of pleasure.

When they were finished, she smiled down at him, lifted off. He closed his eyes, heard her walk back to the pond, listened to the splashing of water.

"Come," she said after awhile, "let's go home."

Chapter Nine
Exploration Team Delta

Fortunately, Dr. Banca proved to be a reasonable man and saw it the same way Striker did. Remington grumbled, but acknowledged that it was in the best interest of everyone to move.

Since this was an exploration vessel, there were plenty of tools and equipment to give the shipwrecked a fair chance at survival.

Even though everyone carried a med-kit Dr. Liss insisted they take along the shuttle's Computerized Medical Doctor. The CMD would be able to diagnose and treat most medical ailments, including performing simple operations. Dr. Liss packed it onto the Air-Floater, along with some of the heavier equipment. Breanna and Monaca were put in charge of the floater.

The terrain was rough. Boulders, deep crevices, and ravines made traveling treacherous, and sometimes nearly impossible. Slippery lichens on the ground added to the danger. Low shrubbery and stunted, sprawling trees didn't provide much cover from the elements. They made good progress until late afternoon, when a thunderstorm hit. It roared unlike any storm any one of them ever experienced, except for Dr. Banca, who spent five years in a research station on the fourth planet in the Alpha Centaury system. That one had been, according to him, a savage, cruel world, much more rugged than this planet.

They found shelter underneath a rock shelf that looked almost like a cave, damp and cold, but it provided protection from the storm.

The temperature dropped, it began hailing, large chunks of ice-balls fell from the black, thundering sky. Huddling around a couple of small heaters, they made themselves as comfortable as possible. It looked like their first day came to an end.

The storm lasted all night and most of the next day. Torrents of raging water ran past them from above, and they considered themselves lucky to have found this protected place.

Looking out at the rolling, dark clouds Monaca Vargas turned to Breanna and said, "I can't imagine spending the rest of my life on this planet. I wish I had gone to Nu-Eden. My family will be wondering what happened to me if I don't come back in five years as I told them I would."

"Sometimes I wonder what it was that possessed me to want to go to the colonies to search out new frontiers," Breanna sighed.

"Why did you?"

Breanna shrugged. "I am a xenologist. I study alien life forms. You know I had a chance to go to Sirius V, but I didn't think it was adventurous enough, not enough excitement."

"I hope you're happy, now," Rhea Rosetti remarked sneeringly. "This should be enough excitement for you."

"Oh, shut up!" Breanna hissed. "I've just about had enough of your sarcasm."

"Ladies, ladies," Dr. Banca said soothingly. "We are all in this together. If we want to survive, we cannot afford to quarrel with each other. As a unity we have a chance, divided we may all die. Every member of this team is important, so, please, be nice to each other." He looked at Remington who was busy cleaning his gun. It was not one of those modern lasers the military used, but an old-fashioned pistol that fired titanium bullets. "Are you expecting to shoot someone, Mr. Remington?"

The big man looked up from his activity and grinned. "You never know. Let's just say, I like to be ready for anything that may cross my path."

"Just make sure you aim that antic thing in the right direction when you fire it. I'd hate to be hit by a stray bullet."

Striker, who had quietly been listening and watching, padded his own sidearm. "I think Mr. Remington should leave the shooting to the professionals," he said.

Remington made a sound in his throat. It sounded like the challenging growl of a large cat. "I *am* a professional, Mr. Striker," he said. "Just because you are military doesn't mean you can best me."

Striker smiled. "Who said anything about besting, Mr. Remington? There is no contest here. Dr. Banca is right, we have to stick together."

"Like some kind of family, I suppose," Remington growled.

"That's right," Dr. Banca said. "Like a big family, because that is what we are, a family of humans, a new tribe on an unknown, possibly hostile planet."

"Well." Remington grinned, pushed a full clip into the handle of his gun. "I am here to protect my family." He looked at Striker. "Against anything."

Striker walked away. He surveyed the water-drenched terrain. Studying the small rivers that the flood of water created, he decided against breaking camp. It would be too dangerous to start climbing now. So far, most of the way the decline had been gradual, but he didn't know what lay ahead, and they had less than four hours of daylight left. Not enough time to cover a lot of distance and to find adequate shelter for the night.

He turned back toward camp to see Breanna watching him. She smiled when she saw him looking at her. "Listen up, everybody," he said. "We'll stay here tonight, no sense to leave now. Any objections?"

His gaze lingered for a moment on Remington. The big man smiled, but didn't say anything.

"All right," Striker said. "That's settled." He walked over to where Breanna was sitting, squatted down beside her. "How are you holding up?" he asked.

"Fine." She smiled. "Under the circumstances."

It remained cold and damp underneath the rock shelf. Light drizzle fell from the cloudy sky. Just before dark, a group of four-armed hairy creatures, the size of chimps, dropped from the top of the shelf. When they saw the humans, they uttered high-pitched, shrill cries, but otherwise didn't make any threatening moves.

"Don't!" Breanna called out sharply when she saw Remington draw his gun.

"I'm not taking any chances," Remington growled.

"They are not attacking us. They're only curious, and probably just as surprised as we are," Breanna said.

The creatures had flat, almost humanoid faces, with protruding, shimmering eyes. No noses, just slits and round, puckered mouths. Their four arms were long and bony; their double-jointed legs quite thin, but muscular, with sharp-clawed large feet.

Of the eight that Striker counted two were larger than the rest. When he looked closer, he saw a row of small nipples on the chests of three of them. Then he saw that one of them had a tiny infant clinging to its belly.

Breanna must have seen it at the same time. "They're mammals," she said, excitement in her voice. "Perhaps even humanoid."

"Ugly critters," Remington said. "I wonder if they'll make good eating. Sooner or later we'll run out of rations, and we'll have to start eating local food."

One of the larger creatures bellowed, the others answered with high-pitched whistles, then they all took off with unexpected speed and agility.

Had they been aggressive they could have created a lot of havoc, Striker thought. *We might have lost some people today. From now on, we will post guards.*

They kept the two heaters on during the night, and not just for warmth.

"I'll take the first watch, Lieutenant," Chu said. "I'm not really that tired."

51

To Striker's surprise Remington volunteered to take the second watch. Striker took the third, and a man named Herm Woolf, one of the geologists, agreed to take the last shift.

It seemed he just fell asleep when Remington kicked him gently in the ribs. "Your turn, Striker," the big man said.

The pale light of the two satellites threw double shadows as Striker made his way toward the tree they picked as guard post, away from the camp. Striker sat in the darkness of the branches, one of the big laser rifles across his lap, his torchlight beside him, ready to bathe the immediate area around him with bright daylight.

The night filled with strange sounds. Chirping, barking, and soft, eerie hooting. So far, they didn't see any large life forms, except for those *monkeys*, but it was obvious, this planet was not dead.

Woolf joined him before it was his turn and Striker sat with him awhile. "So, what do you think, Lieutenant?" Woolf said. "What are our chances for survival?"

"As a group, not bad. As individuals?" he lifted his shoulders again, even though he knew the other man couldn't see him in the shadows. "Some of us may die. This is going to be a harsh place to survive in."

"Are you certain they won't come looking for us?" Woolf sounded hopeful.

"No, I'm not certain, nothing ever is." Striker chuckled grimly. "Captain Cunningham won't risk another shuttle or team, but sooner or later a ship will come from Earth. Maybe then."

"When will that be?"

"My tour of duty is supposed to be for five years. They'll send replacements then."

"That's how long I signed up for also, five years. That's a long time," Woolf mused.

"It will seem even longer here." Striker rose, stretched. "I think I'll hit the sack again. Keep your eyes and ears open." He slapped the other man on the shoulder in a gesture of camaraderie. It would be good to have another friend.

He barely crawled into his sleeping bag when a shadowy figure knelt beside him.

"Are you sleeping already?" a female voice whispered.

"Almost," he whispered back and opened one eye to see who it was, but he couldn't see her face in the darkness.

"I'm cold," she whispered, "and I feel lonely. I need someone to snuggle up to."

He undid the seam to his sleeping bag, let her join hers with his, and then she slid into the bag. She must have taken off her heavier outer clothes. When he put one arm around her, he felt her soft breasts beneath her thin blouse. "No wonder you're cold," he chuckled. She laughed into his ear; her long hair tickled his face. Then she moved into his embrace, put her lips over his. Her hand snaked toward his chest and stroked it gently.

"Did you know that two naked bodies are much warmer than two clothed ones?" she asked.

"So I've heard. What are you telling me?"

Laughing into his mouth, she pulled on his pants. "Take them off," she whispered huskily.

Naked, she felt warm and soft. He had been a long time without a woman, and when he entered her, he tried to stop himself from moaning too loud. When they reached the peak of their passion he closed her mouth with his, top keep her from crying out. Breathing hard, they lay in each other's arms until they both fell asleep. He slept well. Dreamed of a soft bed and another willing woman he knew a long time ago. He woke early, slipped naked out of the insulated sleeping bag, trying not to disturb her. Breanna turned in her sleep, her body trembled slightly when the cold morning air caressed her skin, but she didn't wake up.

After dressing silently and quickly, Striker walked over to the tree where Woolf was keeping watch over the camp. He found the other man leaning against the thick, gnarled trunk with his head bent forward and his chin resting on his chest. Striker nudged him with his foot. Woolf yelped, startled. He looked up, reached for his laser, which had slipped from his fingers.

"Had I been a hostile intruder," Striker said, "you'd be dead now."

"I'm sorry," Woolf stammered. "I must have dozed off just before you came. What time is it?"

"Time to wake the others. We should get an early start."

Chapter Ten
Alpha Colony

The chanting started low and hypnotic then it rose like the sound of a drum every time he thrust forward. His thighs slammed into the fleshy buttocks of the girl who was kneeling in front of him in the tall grass.

He closed his eyes, let the chanting envelope his mind, concentrated on the waves of exquisite pleasure flooding his body.

The girl moaned loudly and pushed back against him. He felt the gushing of liquid, not his.

"Fill her vessel," a soft voice whispered beside his ear. Sister Angela. She pressed her naked body against his back, moved with him. Her breasts felt soft and spongy on his skin. He let go, erupted with a hoarse cry. The girl pulled away, another one took her place. Sobbing, he pushed his erect member deep into the offered orifice.

Young, they were so young. Yet, there had not been one virgin among them. They were women, all of them. Their vaginas were tight, but capable and eager to slide over his engorged organ. They had no difficulty taking it completely inside them.

"You are *The Chosen One.*" Sister Angela whispered. "You must fulfill your destiny."

He looked up at the bright disks of the satellites already separating. How long had this been going on? He didn't know. How many young wombs had he filled with his seed? Three? Four? It didn't matter. As long as that fire burned inside him, and as long as a pair of inviting thighs opened, he would sink his organ into the heavenly bliss they offered.

He realized that he wasn't kneeling anymore. Strong arms and thighs cradled him, soft breasts cushioned his chest. "The night is almost over." Sister Angela's breath came in ragged gasps. "I will take your gift once more, Brother Thomas."

He did not come immediately, he moved steadily between her soft slim thighs. She felt warm and yielding, covered his face with kisses and milked him with great passion and expertise. Not an innocent virgin either, this Sister Angela!

The chanting became louder until it reached a crescendo at the same time his orgasm peaked, and then slowly died away. Sister Angela cried out in a foreign language, her body jerking in great spasms as he filled her vessel.

They lay silent for moment, her long legs still wrapped around him, and then she released him. "Go now, Brother Thomas," she said, "we must end the ceremony. Without you."

He stumbled away like a man who couldn't wake from a dream. His mind was numb, his body weak, the chanting seemed far away now. He stopped on top of the narrow bridge, stared into the flowing water of the stream.

What happened to him? He, who never before occupied his mind with sexual fantasies, never held any great desires for other women besides his wife, now seemed consumed by lust. He did not know his sexual prowess. Even now, after exerting himself for hours, he could still feel the hardness of his penis.

His eyes searched the heavens, stared at the reddish alien moon. "Forgive me, Lord," he prayed silently. "I don't know what to do."

As he passed one of the small ponds, he heard soft cries. He stopped, looked toward the pond. He saw naked limbs entwined in each other. A naked breast. A pair of white buttocks moving between spread thighs. Without thinking, he moved closer, watched the copulating pair.

"Preacher man," a familiar voice said beside him. He turned to look into Orona's almond shaped dark eyes. She put her arms around him and pulled him down on top of her, her body wet, warm and soft. With a hoarse shout he went inside her, entered her deeply.

The pleasure came immediately and felt almost painful. She squirmed beneath him, pulled up her knees until they touched her shoulders. He put his hands under her buttocks, dug his fingers into the fleshy globes. She doused his mast with her hot discharge, but he couldn't climax, he was empty, yet, he kept on driving his rod into her tight, creamy sheath with furious thrusts. When she told him to stop he pulled out, rolled onto his back, his breath coming in ragged sobs.

"Take it easy, Preacher man," Orona whispered. "You'll drop of a heart attack." She touched his erection and giggled. "You're too much man even for me." He moaned, pulled her face against his. "Finish me," he begged, "I haven't come."

She shook her head. "I'm sore. You were like a wild man. Maybe tomorrow night, come back tomorrow night, but come earlier."

She stood above him. He stared at her naked body, the outline of her breasts against the sky, the dark shadow between her legs. "Go home to your wife," she said softly and walked away. His eyes were riveted to her rotating round buttocks, he wanted to run after her, grab them and squeeze them, but somehow it seemed too much of an effort.

The two beside him were still locked together, the woman writhing on top of the man. He watched her breasts as they bobbed up and down, admired her pumping plump buttocks, watched her quiver in the man's lap as he climaxed inside her.

Tom's and the woman's eyes locked. She looked familiar, but he didn't really know her. He gave her a foolish grin, pointed at his own stiff mast. She nodded, smiled, and then she lifted off the other man. Climbing on top of Tom, she impaled herself on his pole, slowly sank into his lap.

"I'm Myrna," she said, studying his face as she greedily sucked him into her belly.

"Tom," he grunted. "You feel good."

"So do you," she said, her lower body gyrating.

He reached up and dug his fingers into her breasts.

"Are you on something?" she asked. "You look strange."

"I don't know and I don't care," he almost shouted, "just fuck me!"

"All right," she said, shrugging. "I don't mind. As long as you can make me come."

She pumped tirelessly on top of him and climaxed a couple of times. He felt only half-conscious and just stared at her sweat-drenched naked writhing body. When he came, it rushed with the roar of a *swamp tiger.* The woman collapsed on top of him. When her breathing went back to normal, she said, "For an old guy you sure have stamina. I've never met anyone like you. I heard Orona call you *Preacher man.* Are you some kind of a preacher?"

"No," he said, "just a man."

"Some kind of man" she said thoughtfully.

Tom closed his eyes. He suddenly felt very tired.

* * * *

When he opened his eyes again, the stars and moons were gone. The alien sun began to rise in the west. Tom grew aware of something wet touching his lips. Then he realized that he wasn't alone.

Two large purple eyes stared into his. He wanted to sit up, but a weight on each of his arms prevented that. "What do you want?" he croaked with a dry throat.

There were three of them. The two who sat on his arms and the one who held a fruit against his lips. Tree-elves.

So far the humans had not been able to make contact with them, didn't even know if they should consider them intelligent. They were small, frail looking creatures, about a meter tall, with bald heads, large eyes, and pointy ears. The humans saw them flitting through the trees, like monkeys, mostly at night. Any effort at making contact proved unsuccessful. Until now.

The one holding the fruit said something in a soft, almost child-like voice.

Tom shook his head. "I don't understand you," he said.

The little creature took a small bite out of the fruit and again offered it to Tom. Tom opened his mouth, bit into it, hoping that it wasn't poisonous. It tasted sweet, with a tangy, but pleasant aftertaste. He

56

swallowed, took another bite. When the fruit was gone, the two holding him down stood up, and then all three turned and ran toward the trees. Like monkeys, they climbed the trunks, disappearing among the branches.

Tom lay there, staring up into the sky, his thoughts confused. He felt a warm sensation spreading through his body, his feet and fingers tingled. The feeling of lead in his veins disappeared. He sat up, wondering, flexed his muscles. *Amazing,* he thought, *I don't feel tired. I should be exhausted after last night.*

Images of naked young female bodies writhing and squirming above him flashed through his mind. He could still feel the heavenly pleasure he experienced as his hard penis penetrated their tight and soft, young vaginas, heard their cries of ecstasy echo inside his head when he filled their vessels with his discharge.

Had it happened? Had it been nothing but a dream? Or was all this just a figment of his sick imagination? What about the tree-elves? Surely, they had been real! He wasn't sure of anything.

He discovered that he was naked, the crisp morning air created goose bumps on his skin. His pants and shirt lay in a crumpled heap nearby, but his shoes were on his feet. He slipped out of them, waded into the lake and let the cool water caress his body. Rubbing himself with his hands, he dunked his head under water. The water looked quite clear and he could see something moving close to his face. He reached out and touched a jelly-like substance. Before he could pull away, it wrapped itself around his fist, like a washcloth.

He surfaced, lifted his hand out of the water. As he did so the spongy cloth slipped off his fist, lay for a moment on the surface. Tom studied it, puzzled. It was circular, about 30 centimeters in diameter, almost transparent and the color of pale translucent flesh. He felt a curious pulling in his head as he stared at the softly pulsing object. A shiver ran through the quivering mass, and then it transformed itself into an oblong ball and disappeared under water. Something about its appearance seemed familiar to Tom, but he couldn't remember what it was.

The sun climbed above the treetops. He pulled himself up onto land, used his shirt to dry his body. Then he headed back toward the settlement. As he walked down the trail, he heard voices. A group of young men came toward him. They were members of the small fighting force that accompanied the colonists. Even from the distance he recognized the big, beefy body of Sergeant Vicks at the head of the group.

"Good morning, McClary. You're up early."

Tom gave him a crooked grin. "It's a beautiful day, can't waste a day like that."

Chapter Eleven
Alpha Colony

The Mother-ship supplied the colonists with plenty of building materials. When Sister Angela insisted they build a place of worship, a church, they did. It even sported a steeple. The only thing it lacked was a bell. Behind the church, a small dwelling that served as living quarters for Sister Angela and her *Angels,* as she called her girls. There were fourteen of them, none of them over twenty years old.

It was hard to tell what Sister Angela looked like under that black, shapeless robe she wore, but flashes of her white, naked form kept popping into Tom's mind. He knew that her body was slim and lovely, and full of passion. At least he thought he did.

"Tell me about last night, Sister Angela," he said.

She sat behind a metal desk. It was plain and functional, like the room. Looking up from the book she had been studying, she gave him a curious glance.

She has beautiful eyes, Tom thought, so blue, so innocent and so angelic, just like her face. "Is Angela your real name?" he blurted out.

The gaze of her eyes never wavered. Suddenly, she smiled. "My, we are inquisitive this morning, Brother Thomas," she said softly. "You look troubled."

"I am troubled," he said exasperated. "Tell me about what happened last night."

"What did happen last night, Thomas?" Her blue eyes seemed cool, but her voice wasn't.

"I want to know if I am imagining things." He put his hands against his head. "Am I going insane?" He looked up, she came around the desk and stood in front of him. *She's so beautiful,* he thought and wanted to reach out, take her into his arms and kiss her sensuous full lips.

"Tell me what you think happened," she said softly.

He shook his head. "I can't speak it out loud. Maybe it never did happen. Where are all the girls?"

"They are sleeping. They need the rest."

"Why?"

"Last night's ceremony took a lot out of them, physically and mentally." She put a hand against his cheek. "You are *The Chosen One,* Brother Thomas, and you have a right to know." She took his hand. "Come into the garden with me."

They walked down a narrow sandy path. There were shrubs and wild flowers blooming all around them. Sister Angela led him to a bench made from tree branches and motioned for him to sit down. "I have not always walked the *Good Road,*" she began, joining him on the bench. "Neither have my *Angels.* You see, I come from a mining planet. I grew up in harsh surroundings. My parents were both killed when I was ten years old. I survived the only way I could. I sold my body. Asteroid miners pay good money and most of them don't care how old you are.

"I became very good at my profession. Once I was old enough I picked young girls off the street. I taught them everything I learned the hard way. I gave them protection and a place to stay. My *House of Angels* became well known and I amassed a fortune.

"But I also attracted the attention of a certain criminal organization, and when it became clear that my business might be taken over, that my life might even be in danger, I decided it was time to get out and move on. I took my *Angels* and boarded a ship headed for the colonies."

Tom listened silently. He looked up when Sister Angela paused. "So the church and all this is just a lie!"

Sister Angela shook her head. "No, it isn't. My father was a preacher. He taught me everything about *The Good Book.* When I boarded that ship I vowed to change my ways. I would teach my girls everything my parents taught me. They would become good and faithful wives to some hard working colonists. They would live a harsh, but fulfilling life."

"Looks like you failed."

"No, no, I didn't fail. Everything is happening the way it was ordained." She put a hand on his arm. "Not long ago I had a vision. You were in it, Brother Thomas. I was told that my *Angels* and I were the *Blessed Vessels* and you were *The Chosen One.* Whatever happened these last two nights is part of a great plan. You and I, we have no control over it."

Tom laughed harshly. "*I* have no control over it, that much is true. But you, you lured me to the pond where you fed me some kind of drug, and all that chanting, those naked girls! You! It just made me crazy." He looked at Sister Angela. "You know, I came here to ask your forgiveness for what I did. But now, I don't know anymore."

She touched his cheek with a soft hand. "There is nothing to forgive, Brother Thomas. It was all ordained," she said gently. Then she put her lips on his. They were warm and soft. He wanted to take her into his arms, but resisted the temptation.

"I better get back to my chores," he said, getting up. "That generator is still not working properly." When he walked away, she called after him, "By the way, my name really is Angela."

He left the garden, his mind in turmoil. How did he know if Sister Angela really had a vision? She had been a prostitute for so long, probably done drugs for years. It was quite possible that her mind was so warped she actually conjured up a vision.

The drink she gave him, he held no doubts that it had been drugged. He coupled with girls younger than his own daughters. On some planets, he'd be thrown in jail for what he did, on others, he might even lose his life. *They are prostitutes, whores*! his mind shouted. *All of them, including Sister Angela*!

"Good morning, Preacher-man," a voice said behind him. He turned, saw Orona trying to catch up with him. She reached him, gave him a bright smile.

She wore a coarse brown robe, like most of the women, but in his mind he saw her slim naked body. He knew now that he had not been dreaming; what he remembered about her was true.

Her almond eyes sparkled with mischief when she looked at him. "What I said last night about you coming down to the pond tonight, I meant it," she said. "You sure know how to please a woman."

Tom felt awkward, was lost for words. "I'm not sure," he finally stammered. "If my wife finds out…"

Orona laughed. "Your wife! I wouldn't worry about her. She's been fogging Stephan Tilus every night."

Stunned by what she said Tom stared at her. "She doesn't know what she's doing," he said, "she thinks she's dreaming."

"She does?" Orona's expression became thoughtful. "That might explain why she acts so crazy. She seems like a wild, sex-starved nympho when she's out at night, no inhibitions what so ever, none. But during the day she's reserved and doesn't want to talk about anything but her work." She turned to leave, over her shoulder she said, "So don't forget about tonight. I'll be waiting."

Tom didn't answer, changing his mind about the generator. It could wait. He headed for the hospital station instead.

There was a nurse on duty behind the desk in the small front office.

"Is Dr. McClary in?" he asked.

The nurse smiled. "Good morning, Mr. McClary. Your wife is in, but she's busy with a patient."

"That's all right, maybe I'll be back later." Tom turned to leave when the door to one of the examination rooms opened and Anina walked out.

"Tom?" she said, puzzled. "Something wrong?"

He stared at her; she looked good in her white lab coat. He noticed that her hair hung loose around her shoulders. "I don't know," he said, "can we talk?"

"Sure, come into my office."

They walked down a short corridor, entered another small room. "They don't give you much space," he commented.

She smiled. "It's big enough. I just use it to make some notes." Her eyes were thoughtful when she looked at him. "What is it, Thomas? You seem agitated. Are you ill?" Concerned, she laid a hand against his forehead.

He shook it away, sat down in one of the two plastic chairs. "Are you fucking Stephan Tilus?" The words came out unbidden, harsh. Under usual circumstances, he would never say it like that.

"What?" She put a hand to her mouth. Her eyes were large. She looked frightened.

"Are you having sex with Stephan?" he asked again, choosing his words more carefully this time.

"How can you...how would you...?"

"How I know? It doesn't matter. Are you?"

She sank into the other chair and stared at her hands. They were shaking. "Am I talking in my sleep?" she didn't wait for him to answer. "These dreams I've been having, they seem so real, but they are only dreams, nothing more. They fade as the day goes by."

"They are not dreams, Anina. What you experience is real," he said gently.

"No, you are wrong!" she almost shouted. "I would never do those things in real life. They are fantasies, just crazy dreams. They mean absolutely nothing."

He reached out, took her shaking hands into his and pulled them against his lips. His tears fell on them. "It's all right, honey. You have no control over it. None of us have."

She pulled her hand away. "What do you mean? What have you done?"

He stood up, pulled her close against him. "My dreams were as bad as yours," he said, "only now I know that I was not dreaming. You're the doctor. Tell me, has anyone come to you to talk about his or her dreams?"

"They wouldn't come to me. I'm only a GP. Maybe you should ask Dr. Rodriguez, he's the psychiatrist. I can't talk about my patients, but you are my husband. Yesterday Rob Cameron came into my office; he's one of the geologists. He was gone for a couple of weeks. He didn't look too good. He told me about the nightmares he's experienced when he camped out in the bush. He talked about alien life forms, babbled on about this beautiful woman in the lake. I sent him to Dr. Rodriguez."

She was composed again, almost cool. "Was Orona in your dreams?" she asked.

"Yes," he said, "but only very briefly."

The light in the ceiling flickered. Anina's eyes were on his face; they seemed shiny with moisture. "You still haven't fixed the generator," she said.

"I know," he nodded. "I'll get to it right away."

"That's good." She began fidgeting with her hair. "I think I'll start wearing my bun again, what do you think?"

Smiling, he nodded. He could see a tear rolling down her cheek, and on an impulse, he took her into his arms. "I love you," he whispered into her ear.

"Me too," she said and gently pushed him away. "You better go now. I have a patient waiting."

"So do I," he grinned. "Except mine can't tell me where it hurts."

When he walked into the front office, he saw a tall, blond woman in a white outfit bending over the desk. She looked up when he went past her. "Oh, hello Tom," she said, "what are you doing here?"

"Good morning, Mabel." Tom was surprised to see her in such friendly spirits.

She straightened up, brushed down the front of her coat. He couldn't help but notice the swell of her breasts and wondered what she looked like naked.

"Do you have a moment, Tom?" she asked.

"I was going to check out the generator," he said, "but it can wait."

She grabbed his arm. "Let's go outside."

To escape the searing heat of the blazing sun in the bright sky they headed for the shadows of a tall Corander tree. It was cooler under the thick low hanging branches.

"Another beautiful day," Tom said, for lack of anything else to say.

"It sure is," the woman said, she seemed to hesitate, looked at Tom with pale, blue eyes. "The days have been beautiful, but what about the nights?"

Tom stared into her pale eyes. *Those eyes,* he thought, *no wonder they call her 'The Ice-cube'.* He never seemed able to warm up to her. "The nights can be very beautiful, too," he said.

"Yeah," Mabel nodded. "Listen, Tom, we never really talk much, you and I. I'm not much for small talk, and I don't have many friends, you know. But you seem like a nice guy, with you helping out at Sister Angela's church and other stuff. People trust you, so I thought, maybe I could talk to you."

She started talking fast, under her breath, as if afraid, someone might hear.

Tom smiled. "I am a good listener, Mabel. If I can help, I will. And don't worry, I'll keep it confidential."

She sighed. "You know Ted Cameron. I've been having sex with him for three nights in a row now."

A little embarrassed Tom held up a hand. "Your love life is your business, Mabel. You don't have to explain to anybody."

"I know, but Tom, think about it. Ted Cameron? I've said *no* to guys that are more attractive. Ted is a bore, during the day I can't stand him, at night I can't get enough of him. I am like a sex-starved nymphomaniac. That is not like me."

Tom smiled. "I can't comment on that, Mabel. I don't know you well enough."

A rosy tint colored Mabel's cheeks. "You're funny, Tom. In case you don't know, I've had my fantasies too, and you've been in them." She put a hand over her mouth. "Sorry, Tom, I don't know why I said that. It just came out. You are married, for heaven's sake. I must be insane."

"I'm flattered, Mabel." Tom was still smiling, but then he became serious. "You've been frank with me. You have a right to question your sanity. I've been questioning mine. What if I told you I've had sex with Sister Angela?"

"You and Sister Angela?" Mabel's eyes widened. "When?"

"For a couple of nights now. Always at night, all night long. I am out of control, can't stop. And not just Sister Angela. I've had sex will all of her *Angels*. Three nights ago, I discovered my wife with Stephan Tilus. Now you're telling me this about you and Ted. Here comes the crazy part, Sister Angela thinks she is having a religious experience, you think you are going insane and my wife thinks it is nothing but a dream. There is something weird going on."

"Your wife and Stephan?" There was a strange expression in Mabel's face. Her eyes were on Tom. "In that case I wouldn't feel too bad if you and I..." she caught herself. "I mean I'd rather do it with you than with Ted." Her eyes grew large, she closed them for a quick moment, and then looked at him with a crooked smile, "I don't know what I'm saying

64

anymore."

Looking into her pale eyes, he thought, *She's very beautiful and attractive, and she wants me. She's right, with Anina screwing Stephan it would make it just fair. If she gets pregnant, I'd just be doing my share in the continued existence of our colony on this planet.*

"Say yes, Tom," she said with a husky voice, "I don't know why, but I have the sudden urge to be with you tonight. It's like a vision. I see you making love to me and it seems right. Maybe I'm having a religious experience, too." She laughed and touched his hand. "I have a good feeling about this. I'll be waiting for you tonight by the women's bathing place."

He watched her walk away as she headed back toward the hospital; his mind was spinning. This was the second woman who had propositioned him. He had no intentions meeting her or Orona, tempting though it might be.

No, this night he would spend with his wife.

Chapter Twelve
Exploration Team Delta

A spine tingling roar was the only warning, and then the cat-like creature was upon Kendrick, who brought up the rear. Striker turned when he heard the man's scream. Man and beast were both rolling on the ground, the animal snarling and Kendrick yelling for help.

Before Striker could act, Remington casually walked up to them, pulled out his antique gun and put a bullet into the body of the cat. With a defying scream, the beast let go of Kendrick and swiped at Remington with a huge paw. He jumped back, fired another shot between the snapping jaws. Spitting and snarling, the beast advanced toward Remington, dragging its large body along the ground. Remington emptied a whole clip into the body of the animal, until it stopped kicking.

Kendrick was still screaming, holding his bloody arm. Dr. Liss rushed to his side. "Someone help me," she called over her shoulder. Striker reached them, to look in horror at the man's torn arm.

Rummaging through her bag, Dr. Liss pulled out a strip of leather, wrapped it around the injured arm and tightened it. "I've stopped the bleeding," she said to Striker, "that's all I can do. I hope the CMD can save his arm."

Breanna and Monaca set up the portable medical unit. Dr. Liss hooked it up to Kendrick, who by now was only half-conscious. He relaxed, when the CMD pumped his body full of painkillers.

"Is he going to be alright?" Breanna asked.

Dr. Liss shrugged. "This unit is the best modern science has produced so far. It will disinfect the wound, mend torn muscles and ligaments, and graft artificial skin. He has a good chance."

Striker wondered what would happen once the medical unit ran out of drugs and supplies. Dr. Liss seemed competent, but she could never handle surgeries or serious injuries and illnesses. He studied the body of the dead creature. It was large, covered with shaggy hair, its six legs ending in huge four-digit paws, which were equipped with long, sharp and wicked claws that were capable of inflicting terrible wounds. Pointy canines protruded from the long snout, and the long tail was tipped with a hard, spiny ball. There was no question, this was a savage, deadly predator.

"Let's hope there aren't too many of these around." Breanna, who came up behind him, voiced his own thoughts. He turned, smiled at her. She leaned against him. "Andrea says Kendrick will be all right. His arm

66

will be useless for a while, but it will mend. He's lucky he didn't loose it."

"We'll have to be much more aware of our surroundings from now on," Striker said. "Next time we may not be so fortunate." He looked at Breanna. "About the other night…" he began.

"What about it?" Her green eyes were large when she looked at him.

"I don't want you to think that I took advantage of the situation," he said. "I mean…it was you who climbed in with me…" he hesitated, "maybe I misunderstood."

She laughed softly. "You didn't misunderstand. Actually, I should be the one apologizing. Maybe it was I who assumed too much."

"Well, well…" said a deep voice behind them. "The two lovers."

Striker turned his head to look at the big man. "I guess you're the hero now, Remington. Kendrick owes you his life."

"Just doing my job." Remington grinned.

"You'll be out of ammo if you don't practice a little restraint," Striker said.

"Don't you worry." Remington padded his backpack. "I am well stocked."

"Not my worry, as long as you are the one who carries it."

Remington prodded the carcass of the large cat with his foot. "Sooner or later we will have to look for food, those rations won't last forever. Wonder what this critter tastes like." He tipped his broad-rimmed hat in a mock-salute. "Since everybody seems to look upon you as the team-leader, Striker, what are your orders regarding this animal?"

"We'll leave it for the carrion-eaters." The man's sarcastic attitude annoyed Striker. He knew Remington was trying to rile him, but he refused to take the bait. "If you want to make yourself useful, Remington, why don't you sweep the area and see if there are any other dangerous animals around. Pick yourself a couple of men. Make sure they're armed."

"Yes, sir, lieutenant!" Remington tipped his hat again and walked away. That was the first time he called him by his rank, but Striker knew Remington was just mocking him. One day they would be butting heads, and it would not be a good day. Remington was a big man, with bulging, corded muscles, not an adversary to be underestimated.

Striker looked at the rest of the group. Ever since the attack on Kendrick, they stayed close together. The mood was subdued, most of them were beginning to show signs of weariness.

It was already late afternoon, but they couldn't stay here, it was not an ideal place to set up camp, with no protection against attackers. The thorny shrubs and the large boulders were ideal hiding places.

Even the air was not safe. They saw flocks of winged creatures, and on a couple of occasions, several large shapes circling above them. Too high to make out clearly what they were, but Striker wasn't prepared to take any chances. This environment was hostile and it would breed hostile animals. "Let's get a move on, people," he called out. "We'll have to find a better spot to spend the night."

Grumbling and cursing, the group began moving again. Woolf helped Kendrick with his pack. The injured Kendrick seemed to be in better spirits than most of the others. Remington walked in front of the group. Chu and a man named Acram Mian took the rear. Mian was a trained survival expert, ex-military. He kept mostly to himself, didn't talk very much. Striker spoke to him only a few times and got the impression that the man didn't care much for people. He was dark-skinned, like Ashim Sirski, the meteorologist, and Concitta Sanchez, the geophysicist, but his facial features were different.

He carried a big hunting knife strapped to his waist and a small, but powerful laser-pistol. There were a number of gadgets hanging on his belt; Striker recognized one of them, a *Guard-Dog.* This device, when activated, would alert the carrier of approaching life forms. It wasn't very effective in a crowd of people, that's why Mian usually slept away from the others.

Striker stayed close to Remington. He didn't fully trust the big man. He was too cocky and too sure of himself. Remington seemed to be in a talkative mood. He fell back and walked beside Striker. They finally reached a flat plateau, the vegetation was sparse, except for the tall trees. "Can't you contact the research-station with your personal com?" he asked.

Striker grunted, shifted his pack on his shoulders. It was beginning to get heavy. Carrying the big laser-rifle in both his hands made it awkward to balance his pack. They all carried more than was comfortable. "All I get is static," he said. "The station is hidden inside a small valley, surrounded by mountains, which are blocking the signals."

"Damn!" cursed the big man. "It would have been nice if they'd send that land rover to pick us up." He stopped, stared ahead and cursed again.

Striker saw it at the same time. A deep chasm, too wide to cross even with a temporary bridge made from cut tree-trunks. He lifted an arm. "Don't walk any further," he warned the others, then approached the chasm carefully, with Remington right beside him.

It looked deep and stretched in both directions. The walls were smooth; they would need ropes to get to the bottom, but Striker ruled out that possibility. "It can't go on forever," Remington remarked, looking first in the left direction, then to the right. "Which way to go?"

"We'll figure that out tomorrow," Striker said. "Tonight we camp here." Nobody complained when he told the team, some even cheered.

The area lacked any natural shelter, so they decided to pitch their tents. It didn't take long until they erected all five tents. Five flimsy looking silvery structures, like halves of giant eggs protruding from the rocky ground.

Acram Mian came up to Striker. "We're running low on water," he said. "I saw a small creek about 15 minutes back."

Striker nodded. "Take Chu and Woolf with you," he said. "And watch your step. Where there is water there usually are animals. And don't get lost."

Mian grinned, touched a black finger to his flat nose. "Don't worry, lieutenant. Survival is my business." His teeth flashed white between thick, large lips.

"I know." Striker smiled. "Just the same. Watch out for Chu, he is good at survival in space and in the air. On land, I'm not so sure."

"Like you, sir?"

"Like me. I am also out of my element."

"We'll be back before dark," Mian promised.

Striker watched the three walk back the way they had come, each of them carrying a couple of inflatable water-containers. They should have filled their canteens when they passed that stream. He shrugged and made a mental note to put Mian in charge of anything that had to do with survival, like water and possibly food.

The sun started disappearing behind the mountain ridge, it would be dark within an hour. Striker decided not to sleep in a tent. He would be just as comfortable in his sleeping bag under the stars and in the open. He didn't need the illusion of safety, which the thin material of a tent provided.

Mian, Chu, and Woolf came back shortly after dark. It took longer than expected. Striker was already sitting at his guard-post when Chu joined him. "Any problems back there?" Striker asked.

Chu sat silent beside him. "We found something you might want to look at in the morning," he said after awhile.

"What did you find? A way to get us out of here?" Striker grinned.

Chu chuckled. "I'm afraid not, but I think you should bring Breanna McGuiness."

69

Chapter Thirteen
Alpha Colony

After supper in the mess hall, Anina excused herself. "Sorry, Thomas," she said. "I know you had plans for us, but I have a couple of patients coming in tonight."

"This late?" Tom asked, surprised. "Why don't they come during the day?"

Anina shrugged. "It's Lin Wong, she is having some problems with her pregnancy. I want to do a more thorough examination." She smiled. "Maybe tomorrow night."

Tom went home alone to their sleeping shelter. There wasn't much to do after dark. Never an avid reader, he already read the few digital books they brought. Lighting wasn't a problem, the light in the ceiling from the solar power and the batteries would last all night, if necessary.

He went to bed, naked, dimmed the light and stared at the darkened ceiling. Maybe Anina would be home soon, he could wait. He closed his eyes for a moment, concentrated on the images flashing through his mind.

When he opened his eyes again, he looked at the empty spot where his wife should be lying. He must have drifted off to sleep, the remnants of a dream still lingered in his mind, but all he really could remember were the tree-elves.

He got out of bed, opened the door, and without realizing it, started walking toward the ponds. Crossing the narrow bridge, he stopped to look at the sky. The pale moons were high in the zenith, flooding the land below with their eerie light.

When he reached the women's bathing pond he found a woman leaning against the thick trunk of a tree. She saw him, came toward him. It was Mabel, she was completely nude. He stared at her voluptuous body, noticed her full, solid breasts.

"You came," she said and opened her arms.

He stepped into her embrace. She pressed her warm body against him, her hand slid down his belly, found his already reacting organ. Then she pulled him into the tall grass, spreading her thighs, as he fell on top of her. She was ready for him, he slid with ease into her wet sex-canal, entering her deeply. The waves of pleasure immediately began to wash over him.

A passionate woman, she urged him on as he labored on top of her. It wasn't long before she experienced her first orgasm. She came with ecstatic cries, her fingers raked his back as she rode the crest of her climax. "Let me be on top," she whispered.

They uncoupled, Tom lay on his back and watched her straddle him. He noticed that her pubic area was shaved. Her vulva was thick and smooth. Slowly she let herself down, hovered above his swollen member. Her labia touched his slippery glans. With a loud sigh, she sank into his lap, swallowing his aching organ to the root.

He couldn't see her face in the shadows, but he knew that her pale blue eyes were upon him. "You are a passionate woman, Mabel," he said and moaned as she began to rotate her hips.

"Thank you, Tom," she gasped, whipping her lower torso back and forth. "Contrary to what people say about me, I am not an ice-cube."

"You're hot," he grunted, his eyes glued to her beautiful breasts. "You are certainly hot." He came inside her with a deep cry in a long, shattering climax.

When he finished, she lifted off. "I'm taking a dip in the water," she said and ran toward the pond.

He closed his eyes, waited for her to return. When she didn't come back, he sat up, searched for her in the pond. He saw a slim, female form in the water, but she swam in the shadows of a tree with branches that stretched far into the pond. He got up, walked to the water's edge.

The woman in the water had long, black hair; he only saw her back, but he knew it wasn't Mabel. *Orona, it must be Orona!* Wondering where Mabel disappeared to, he jumped into the water, approached the woman from the back.

He didn't know if she heard him coming because she suddenly began moving away from him, toward the shore on the other side. *She wants to play hard to get,* he thought and followed her. He caught up with her just as she climbed up the embankment. Putting his hands around her, he cupped her breasts, his stiff pole touched her soft buttocks, slipped between them. Then he slid into her creamy sex-organ. She pushed back against him, struggled, but he held her tight. Her struggling drove him crazy, like a berserker he moved in and out of her. She kept silent all that time, didn't utter a sound.

Letting out a series of satisfied grunts, he erupted inside her with explosive force. He slipped out of her; she turned around in his arms. When he saw her face, he stepped back with a surprised cry. "You are not Orona!" he croaked dully, his mind in turmoil.

Her large, round eyes sparkled with dark-green iridescent colors in a beautiful and delicate, but alien face.

She smiled suddenly, displaying a row of small, sharp teeth. Then she slipped by him, disappearing in the water.

He stared after her, but she never surfaced again. Slowly he climbed onto dry land. Looking around, he realized that he was on the other side of the pond. A rustling sound in the tree above him made him look up to see half a dozen small shapes drop from the low branches, circling him.

He looked into their elfin faces, he couldn't read their expression, but he didn't sense any menace from them. One of them beckoned, turned around and began walking away. The others herded Tom. He followed them down a narrow path, for a while it ran parallel to the creek.

* * * *

After walking for a long time, about two hours in Tom's estimation, they made a sharp right turn. Tom noticed the rocky wall of a steep cliff to his left. The path ended suddenly, they stepped into a small clearing. There was a large pool of water, a waterfall cascaded down the cliff, sending sparkling streams gently into the pool of water below.

The group of tree-elves stepped into the water, motioned for Tom to do the same. The pool wasn't very deep. The small creatures began to swim, but the water reached only to Tom's chest.

They headed for the waterfall, walked into it, through it and down a dark tunnel. There was a lush valley on the other side, ringed by high cliffs. Tom suddenly remembered an old Earth legend. "Shangri-La," he whispered.

The two moons bathed the valley with their pale light. Their bright disks were reflected by the calm water of a large lake. The creek widened into a small river that emptied itself into the lake. Tom saw a cluster of grass covered huts at the mouth of the river; he realized that in all likelihood he was going to meet the inhabitants of this planet.

The tree-elves and Tom started walking again. They followed a wide, well traveled path. Tom noticed that the trees in the valley were not as tall as the ones outside. The fruit trees looked trimmed, cultivated.

They passed the huts, entered a grove of larger trees, inside the grove was a grass-covered glade with a small pond in its center. A giant flower grew in the middle of the pond. It reminded Tom of a giant water lily. On the flower stood the most beautiful woman Tom had ever seen.

She was nude. Flaming red hair hung past her buttocks, strands of it covering her full, round breasts, her flat stomach. She looked human, except for her large round eyes. They glowed with green iridescent colors and looked straight at Tom.

There were other female shapes on land and in the water, but Tom ignored them. His eyes were glued to the tall, beautiful vision on the flower.

"Welcome, traveler from another world," said the voice. It held a strange quality to it, as if it came from all around him.

"You speak my language," he said, astonished.

There was the sound of tinkling laughter. When she smiled, she became even more beautiful. "I didn't speak at all," the voice said. "My words are inside your head."

Telepath, Tom thought and said aloud, "You can read my thoughts?"

"Only when you speak them, but I can feel you. I receive your emotions, not your words."

An empath, then, Tom thought, not a true telepath.

"I sense that you understand," the woman said, laughing again. "You find me beautiful, and you desire me."

"Very much so." Tom found himself in the water, it wasn't very deep. The flower was huge, thick leafs grew mostly under water all around it, a carpet of purple petals covered the surface of the flower. Tom hoisted himself onto it.

The alien woman in its center opened her arms, she was even more beautiful this close. He looked into her strange luminous eyes and stepped into her embrace. Her body felt warm and soft against his skin. He kissed her fiercely. She opened her mouth and let his tongue enter. She tasted of flowers and sweet honey, and he swallowed the fluid that flowed into his mouth. An unstoppable desire came over him, between his legs his organ seemed to swell to enormous proportions.

Kissing her neck, he put his hands on her round buttocks, pulled her closer to him. His lips fastened on her long nipples, suckled until they shot their sweet nectar down his parched throat.

She flowed onto her back, her long legs opened; gently moving tendrils beckoned him to enter the dark orifice between her smooth thighs.

Falling to his knees, he moved on top of her, and when he entered her, he roared his pleasure into the night, like a swamp tiger after a kill. Never before had he experienced such softness, such exquisite bliss. Her sex-organ seemed to have a life of its own, it pulsed around his penis with gentle movements, contracted and expanded with a steady rhythm that sent waves of almost unbearable pleasure through his entire body. He climaxed without loosing any fluid.

She fed him more of her nectar, he moved between her soft thighs with untiring, steady strokes. Nothing else existed in his universe but this beautiful, alien woman underneath him. He didn't remember leaving her embrace.

Lying in semi-darkness, he stared at the crisscrossed hollow reeds that formed the ceiling above him. Looking around him, he noticed that the walls were of similar construction. The room he rested in was not very large, but big enough to hold a small group of people.

A flood of light entered the room suddenly, and he squinted to stare at the opening door. A naked female figure was silhouetted against the bright light. She came closer, knelt beside him. She looked like the alien girl he encountered by the women's bathing place, her large green eyes studied him silently. "Where am I?" he croaked.

She said nothing, just laid a hand on his forehead Smiling, she put her hand behind his head to indicate for him to sit up. In her other hand she carried a small bowl, which she held against his lips. His throat was dry and he drank the offered liquid. It was cool and sweet, tasted like sugar water with a tardy after taste. When he emptied the bowl, she stood up and walked out of the door.

Tom sat for a moment, staring at the bright opening. Everything seemed so unreal. The happenings of the previous night were blurry, fragmented memories. It was obvious that he stumbled upon an indigenous life form. But what about that woman on the flower in the pond? He remembered what Anina told him about Rob Cameron, the geologist. He had mentioned a woman in a lake.

Who was she? What was she?

He got off the grass bed he lay on and stepped outside. The sun was already high in the blue green sky, and the clear water of the lake reflected its bright light. He stood in the shadow of a tall tree, one of many surrounding a cluster of huts.

There were people splashing in the water, some walked among the huts. All were females. All looked young. And all of them were naked. A couple of them walked by, they carried fruit in woven baskets. When they saw Tom they smiled, but walked on without stopping.

He ran after them. "Who are you people?" Tom asked, but they only looked at him out of large green eyes. "Can you understand me?" They just looked, smiled, and walked on.

He walked toward the lake. Gentle waves were washing over purple sand; his bare feet left shallow impressions that filled quickly with water.

One of the alien females watched him as he walked toward her. Looking closer, he noticed that most of them were wearing necklaces made from small shells around their necks. Some wore belts made out of long strands of grass, with colored stones and shells woven into them.

The one who was watching him smiled when he came close to her;

she reached out, offered him something. It looked like a fruit. When he hesitated she took a small bite out of it, then, smiling, she held it out again. This time he took it, bit into it. It tasted delicious and he wolfed it down, realizing how hungry he was.

She laughed. It sounded like a high, musical chime. It was the first sound he heard from them. Then she spoke something in a soft, chirping language.

"I don't know what you're saying," Tom said, "but it sounds beautiful. You have a lovely voice."

She cocked her head, seemed to be listening to something. Suddenly, she turned and ran toward the lake and dove into the clear water.

Tom watched her disappear under the surface, watched for her to come up for air. She finally did and came running back. Droplets of water dripped from her beautiful body, smooth muscles rippled under soft skin. She was laughing when she stood again in front of him, her eyes large and shining with bright green fire. "Come, join me in the *Water that gives Life*," she said and reached for his hand. Her words came clear and without hesitation.

"So you do speak my language," Tom said, somewhat perplexed.

"I speak through the *Mother*," the girl said.

"I don't understand."

The alien girl touched her neck. Tom looked closer, saw the shiny thin film of a transparent substance around her neck.

"This is part of the *Great Mother*, and through it I can communicate with you. The Mother knows everything."

"This *Great Mother*, is she the woman in the pond?"

The girl nodded. "She is that and much more." She smiled. "You are the *Chosen One*. The Great Mother is very pleased with you. Tonight, when the night suns are high, you will give the seed of life to my sisters and me. There will be much happiness. I know, I already felt your seed-giver inside me, and it was pleasurable."

Tom stared at her. "Are you the one I met by the pond the other night?"

Laughing, she nodded. "Yes, I was the one. The Mother sent me to you."

"She did? Why?"

"To make new life, what other reason could there be?" The girl shrugged and pulled on his hand. "But now you will swim with me in the *Water that gives Life*."

Tom followed her into the water. It felt pleasantly warm.

A small group of alien girls swam toward him, crowded against him. With pearly laughter they touched him, stroked him. One touched his genitals, curled her fingers around his penis.

They all looked the same to Tom; he couldn't tell which one was the girl who talked to him. Only when she spoke did he know who she was. "They are all eager for tonight," she said, her green eyes sparkling. "They have never collected the seeds of a male before. I told them how you felt inside me."

"Where are your men?" Tom asked.

"Our men?"

"Yes, the males of your species. Men, like me?"

"There aren't any." She dove away.

One of the girls was licking his belly, her soft lips moved down to his penis, sucked it partially into her mouth. Tom could feel himself react to her sucking. He fought the urge and gently pulled his swelling member out of her mouth. He felt sharp teeth graze his skin. Suddenly he was angry, he wanted to scream at them and tell them to leave him alone, but when he looked into their innocent eyes, his anger subsided.

"You are children," he said softly and ran his fingers through silky hair. "Innocent children."

He looked across the calm water of the lake, noticed the large number of broad-leafed plants floating all around the lake, like water lilies. They were smaller versions of the one he had seen in the pond, the one that carried the beautiful woman with the flaming hair.

The vision of her appeared suddenly in his head. She was laughing, and his heart ached for her. *Tonight,* a silent voice seemed to whisper in his mind. Then the vision was gone.

One of the girls rose up in front of him, shook water out of her long purple hair; she laughed, pressed her full breasts against his chest.

"Are you the one who speaks?" Tom asked.

"I am," she said, looking up at him.

"If there are no males, how do you get impregnated, fertilized?" he asked her. "Who puts the seed inside you?"

"Oh that! It is no great mystery. When the night suns meet in the sky the Great Mother summons the *Ugly Ones,* the misfits, you call them tree-elves. They are not very smart, but they are very good seed-givers."

"So they are your males, these tree-elves?"

"Oh no, they are of a different species."

"I don't see any children."

"Children? What are *children?*"

77

"Little ones. What about babies, small cuddly babies?" Tom began to feel frustrated. So many questions and no real answers.

"I don't understand the concept." The girl frowned, genuinely puzzled.

Tom grabbed her delicate shoulders, stared into her luminous eyes. "You must remember being small, being a child?"

She laughed. "I was never small. I was always like this."

"What about your mother and father?"

"Mother, father? I don't fully understand the meaning of those words. I perceive *father* as the one whose seed made me, is that correct?" She seemed to listen again, nodded. "There is no way to know who that is, just one of the *Ugly Ones*. It is not important. My mother is the *Great Mother*. She is mother to me and to all of my sisters."

She wrinkled her forehead. "My head is beginning to feel strange from all these new ideas and new concepts. I must leave you for a while. My sisters will keep you company." She swam away, splashing him with her feet.

He shook his head and watched her disappear under the surface.

So child-like and grown-up at the same time. Her body certainly was the body of a full-grown woman. What about her mind, though? It seemed totally alien to him.

The other girls splashed around him, they put their arms around his body, pressed their soft full breasts against him and licked him with velvet tongues. He disengaged himself gently and walked back to shore. Sensing that he wanted to be left alone, they did not follow. He lay in the smooth, purple sand and watched them frolic in the water.

"Children," he murmured to himself. "Little girls in mature, sexy bodies, products of a young man's wet dream."

* * * *

He must have dozed off. When he opened his eyes it was dark, the two satellites were rising above the high cliffs. He heard footsteps in the soft sand. Looking up, he saw one of the alien girls standing in front of him.

She smiled. "It is time," she said and held out a hand.

Taking her hand, he let her pull him up.

"Where are we going?" he asked.

"To fulfill your destiny," she answered, looking into his eyes. "Come!"

Chapter Fourteen

Captain's Log
August 22, 2985

Our horticultural team did a fine job with the garden. However, it outdid itself with the park it created on the 18th floor. There are of course no trees or shrubs, but we have grass and a small pond with a waterfall. The pond is not very big, only about ten meters across, but it is good for the soul. Where they got the water lily from, I don't know; it is enormous, maybe two meters in diameter, and quite beautiful.

Chapter Fifteen
Space Station

Captain Cunningham stood at the porthole, staring out at the crescent of Nu-Eden. The planet seemed to call to him. He turned away when the transparent material of the porthole began to darken. In a few moments the light rays of the primary would hit this side of the station as it rotated around the planet below.

Nighttime fell over the station, but he couldn't sleep, so he decided to go for a walk. The elevator took him up to the 18th floor. When he entered the garden, he inhaled the humid air deeply. *Almost like being on the surface of a planet,* he thought and began his slow walk on the narrow gravel path that circled the garden along the outer wall. It was a nice long walk, nearly 180 meters until he returned to where he started.

After walking it a couple of times, he decided to rest on one of the benches close to the pond. Sitting down, his eyes fell on the plant that floated in the center of the pond. It looked larger than the last time he saw it. A carpet of purple flowers covered its surface, and thick green leaves on the outside created the illusion of a comfortable resting place.

His eyes adjusted to the semi-darkness. A single light in one corner threw long shadows across the garden and the calm water of the pond. Water cascaded down a small waterfall on the other side, keeping the pond in motion, and from becoming tepid and stale.

The gentle splashing sound made him drowsy, and he closed his eyes for a moment. When he opened them again he was surprised to see someone kneeling on the water lily. Startled, he blinked his eyes a few times to clear them. The figure on the plant moved, rose. He caught a glimpse of naked breasts, partially covered by long strands of hair, a flat belly, and between her long legs a small, red triangle.

There was no doubt that he was looking at a woman.

Her head turned. She looked at him out of large luminous eyes. When she saw him, she smiled. "Hello, Captain Cunningham," she said softly, but with a clear, melodious voice.

He felt a strange pulling in his head. Then she disappeared.

Shaking his head, he wiped a hand across his eyes and forehead. He could feel beads of perspiration trickle into his eyes. Looking around he saw that he was alone. The plant was empty. The petals looked undisturbed.

When he heard the whispering of the opening elevator doors he turned his head, watching the caretaker of the garden walking toward him across the grass.

He was elderly, almost as old as the Captain.

"Good morning, Mr. Jackson," Cunningham smiled, wiped his forehead again, hoping the other man wouldn't notice his discomfort.

"Good morning, Captain." Jackson returned the smile. "Can't sleep?"

"How did you know?"

Jackson chuckled. "Why else would you be here? All by yourself." He hesitated. "I won't be long, Captain. I'm just making my rounds."

"Go right ahead. Don't worry about me. I'll be leaving shortly, anyway." He watched the other man walk to the pond, stick his hand into the water and bring it back up to sniff it.

"Something wrong?" Cunningham asked.

Jackson shook his head. "Nothing I can pinpoint. The water is clear, smells alright."

"But?"

"We've had a nice school of fish in here, brought'm up from the planet." He scratched his head. "They seem to have disappeared. Can't figure that one out."

"That is peculiar." Cunningham rose, walked closer to the pond. In its middle, the huge plant floated placid and silent. For a moment he caught the fleeting impression of a slight movement among the petals, but when he stared at it, everything remained quiet. "Have you seen anyone or anything ever sitting on top of the water lily?" he asked the other man, feeling a little foolish for asking it.

A frown flickered across Jackson's forehead. Avoiding the Captain's eyes, he said, "No, never."

Cunningham did not miss that slight hesitation, and pressed the issue. "Ever seen a beautiful naked woman in the water, or anywhere in the park?"

Jackson stared at him for an instant, his jaws clenched. Then he shook his head. "I'm not that old, Captain. My mind is fine, and I don't suffer from delusions, neither do I see beautiful naked women where there aren't any."

Cunningham smiled. "No offence, Mr. Jackson. I wasn't suggesting you were delusional, but it can get lonely up here, and sometimes we daydream. We may see things. Things our mind conjures up. Nothing to be ashamed of." He patted the other man on the back. "If you ever want to talk to me about anything, feel free to visit me in my office." He winked. "We Old-timers have to stick together."

Jackson nodded, smiled tightly. "Like I said, we're not that old. Our minds are still crystal-clear. There is still a lot of juice left in us. Right?"

"Right. One more question. Has anyone set up a holo projector in this garden?"

"Not that I know of. Why?"

"Just wondering. Well, I must leave you. Have a pleasant day, Mr. Jackson, and try to find out what happened to those fish."

Cunningham walked slowly back to the elevator, deep in thought.

Had he been hallucinating? Who was the woman he saw? Was he going senile? He didn't think so, especially after talking to Jackson. Obviously, the man was hiding something. Something he seemed afraid to talk about. The Captain couldn't blame him, after all *he* wasn't going to mention the incident to anyone.

Checking his watch, he noticed that it was nearly five o'clock. No sense going back to bed, he wouldn't sleep anyway. Therefore, he decided to visit the conservatory.

He chose a table close to the outer rim, the wall that faced the sun. Now darkened, it reduced the fiery ball to a still glaring, but harmless bright disk. The view as spectacular as ever. He could never get enough of it.

Only a couple of tables were occupied. Not many people were up this early in the morning.

A redheaded man at the table nearest to him watched him sit down. Before he could get comfortable, the man got up and began walking toward him.

A young man. Cunningham recognized him as one of the technicians who were responsible for the cryogenic chambers.

"May I have a word with you, Captain?"

Cunningham nodded and indicated the chair across from him. "Take a seat."

"Thank you." The young man sat down, fidgeting. "I hate to bother you, Captain, but I am worried."

"Worried? About what?"

"My sister. Have you heard from Research Team Delta on the fifth planet?"

"Sorry. I wish I could say I have." Cunningham shook his head. "What's your sister's name?"

"Breanna McGuinness. I'm Bret."

"Breanna McGuinness. She's the xenologist, right? A bright, young woman. She was excited to go. Last night I received a report from the research station, Mr. McGuinness. As you probably know there is a lot of interference in the atmosphere, they can't always get through. Professor Tennenboum reported the discovery of ruins. He didn't go into details, because the connection turned bad. He seemed quite excited. He also told us that the research team is still missing. We have to assume the ship crashed, but that doesn't mean our people aren't still alive. Just stranded."

"Stranded? You have to send a rescue team, Captain!" Bret became more and more agitated.

"It's not that simple. We don't have another exploration ship."

Bret leaned forward, stared at the Captain. "You can't just forget about them. Surely something can be done. We have a number of shuttles."

"Shuttles, yes. For transportation. They were never meant for use as exploration vessels on wild worlds, like the fifth planet in this system. If the team shows up at the research station, we can pick up anyone who wants to come back to the space station. But remember, all the members on the team went down to that planet because they wanted to explore a new world. They knew the dangers, and they were prepared to spend some time there. Your sister included. Give them time." Cunningham tried to put the young man at ease, pretended there was nothing to worry about, when in reality he was greatly concerned.

"Why aren't they reporting in?" Bret asked the question Cunningham kept asking himself. He shrugged. "I don't know. There could be a variety of reasons. The ship's com might have broken down, for instance. They may be in a region where there is a lot of magnetic activity."

"A lot of speculation, Captain Cunningham. You should never have allowed them to go down there. If anything happened to my sister…"

The Captain's eyes narrowed. "What then, Mr. McGuinness?"

Bret stared at the Captain for a moment, his green eyes burning, his hands curled into fists. He opened his mouth to say something, then his shoulders sagged and the gaze of his eyes dropped. "Nothing, Captain. I'm sorry I bothered you. You're probably busy with more important things." He rose, turned to walk away.

"Everything that happens on this station is important to me, young man." He spoke sharply. "Your sister wasn't the only one who went down to the fifth planet. There were nineteen others. I care about every member of that team, do you understand?"

"Yes, sir." Bret looked back at Cunningham. "But I only have one sister. She's all I have. Do *you* understand?"

The Captain watched the young man walk away, toward the elevators, anger welling up inside him. Why did everyone blame him when things went wrong?

I need a holiday, he thought. *Maybe I'll break all the rules, go down to Nu-Eden and go sailing.*

He had no intention of being in the elevator with McGuinness, so he leaned back into his seat and stared at the planet that started to create more and more of a mystery. The psych-team he sent to both colonies hadn't reported back, yet. They were due back in one week. He didn't expect much, if something were amiss, at least one of the teams would have contacted the station by now.

Half of Nu-Eden was bright, the other half, the continent where the two colonies were located, lay in darkness.

Wonder if Father Champain finally succumbed to the seductress he claimed to have seen, Cunningham thought fleetingly, chuckling to himself. Seductress, indeed! Then he remembered his own experience in the park, and a sobering thought hit him.

What if there was some kind of virus that infected the settlers? What if someone brought it back to the station?

This was not something he could easily dismiss. He needed to question Jackson again. Suddenly there seemed to be a heavy weight settling on his shoulders.

Maybe I'm getting old, he thought. *Perhaps it is time to retire.*

Chapter Sixteen
Exploration Team Delta

"What is it?" Breanna asked, starring at the crumbling, moss-covered ruins.

"You're the expert," Striker said.

"Alien life forms are my specialty, not ruins of their habitat." Breanna touched the weathered stones gingerly. "These are old," she said.

"How old?"

She shrugged. "I don't know. Professor Banca is the one to ask."

"Then let's bring him up here."

Herm Woolf coughed beside Striker. "Maybe I can be of help, after all, I am a geologist. I have studied ruins on Sirius V."

"Sorry," Striker said, smiled. "With all the experts on this team it is easy to forget what everyone does."

Woolf climbed through the oval opening in the wall, his laser in his hand. "Sometimes animals take up residence in these places," he said, sweeping his scanner as he stepped into the room. "It seems all clear," he called back.

Striker followed him, with Breanna close behind. A lot of debris cluttered the room, mostly branches, dried leaves and broken stones. In one corner lay a pile of bones, evidence that some animal had been in here. The roof was gone, only a couple of blackened, rough timbers remained.

"Be careful," Striker warned, pointing up. "Those things look rotten."

"The walls are older than those timbers," Woolf said and stepped through an opening into another room. "This is interesting," he said as Striker joined him. "Look at that fire-pit."

Striker looked, seeing charcoal logs. "They had fire," he observed.

"That's right, but what strikes you as significant here?" Woolf sounded suddenly like a lecturer.

Striker shrugged. "They had a fire-pit."

Woolf smiled patiently. "These ruins may be old," he said, "but these charcoals are not."

Striker had never really been interested in old civilizations. They were dead, that's all he worried about. Dead civilizations didn't pose a threat. He gave Woolf a sharp look. "What do you mean?"

"Someone used this place as recent as maybe five years ago," he said with a triumphant smile.

"That would mean there are people on this planet, living people," Breanna said, her breath coming fast with excitement. Then she smiled. "I don't mean humans, but beings with some intelligence."

"I don't really know if I can share your enthusiasm," Striker said. "They may well be hostile." He scanned the room with different eyes, suddenly aware that they may be facing a new threat to their survival.

"This will be of great interest to Professor Findlay," Breanna said.

Professor Findlay was the anthropologist, Striker recalled. He also had a degree in paleontology. Striker surprised himself when he remembered that, but then again, maybe it wasn't such a surprise after all. Professor William Findlay was the oldest member of the team. When Striker read the files on every member on this mission, he tried to familiarize himself with the profession of every one of them, and it struck him as befitting, the oldest man studying things that were old. "I'm sure he will be quite interested," he said, "but I'm afraid we can't waste time studying these ruins. Our survival is at stake here, and right now our enemies are time and the weather."

"Surely we can spare a couple of days," Breanna begged.

Striker shook his head. "I'm sorry. My greatest concern is the safety of the team, and in the light of this new discovery I'm even more concerned now." Scanning the room again, he saw another pile of bones buried under some debris. Suddenly those bones seemed to take on a greater significance. "Let's get out of here," he said. "I have a feeling these are not the last ruins we'll come across."

They walked back in silence, with Breanna sulking and Striker anxious to get back to the rest of the group. "Let's keep what we found to ourselves for the time being," he told Breanna and Woolf.

"Why?" Breanna asked. "They have a right to know."

"And they will know, when I decide to tell them." Striker said firmly. "But first I want to put some distance between those ruins and us."

He decided to call Chu on the com. "We're on our way back," Striker told him. "No word to anyone about what you saw. Tell Mian!"

"Understood, sir."

Striker knew he could count on Chu; after all, Chu was military, used to minding his own business, used to obeying orders without question. Mian as an ex-service man would still be bound by the code.

They left for the ruins at daybreak. When they entered the camp, most of the group were still in the tents. Remington and Gregorchuck were standing by the chasm, apparently studying it.

"Out for a stroll, Striker?" Remington said, watching the three of them approach.

Gregorchuck gave Striker a long stare from under bushy eyebrows. "Where the hell have you three gone this early in the morning?" he bellowed.

Striker patted the water bag he carried. "We thought we should get some more water. I took Breanna along. She wanted to study the fish Chu thought he saw yesterday."

Remmington grinned hugely. "If Woolf wouldn't be with you I'd say you wanted to have some time alone with each other. Or maybe you did. Just the three of you."

"You have a filthy mind, Remington!" Breanna fumed and stalked away.

"She's got fire, that redhead." Gregorchuck laughed and winked at Striker. "You may not be able to keep her for yourself, lieutenant."

"She belongs to herself," Striker said, "not to me."

"You two can play house. I don't care." Gregorchuck punched Striker on the arm. "I was young once." His eyes twinkled.

Striker had to smile. Maybe he misjudged the big, beefy man. Under that belligerent attitude he seemed to hide a jovial personality. His wild graying beard made him look older. Striker knew that Gregorchuck was only eight years his senior. "Have you two figured out how we can get to the other side?" he asked.

Remington shrugged. "You're the leader. You come up with an idea."

"Maybe we can use the floater," Gregorchuck suggested.

"I'll discuss it with Kendrick. He is the engineer." Striker said. He looked across to the other side of the chasm. It was wider here, but about a hundred meters to the left it narrowed to a gap only ten or twelve meters wide. *Gregorchuck might just have a valid idea,* he thought. "Stay alert," he told Remington and walked away, looking for the engineer.

Striker located Kendrick rolling up his sleeping bag. "How's the arm?" Striker asked.

Kendrick grinned. "Healing, I hope." He stood up. "Thanks for asking. I wish I could be of more help around here."

"You can. Gregorchuck suggested we use the floater to get across the chasm. Maybe you can think of a way that lets us achieve that. After all, you are an engineer."

"I design buildings, not bridges." Kendrick smiled. "This will be a new challenge for me."

In the afternoon, they started building the *bridge* Kendrick designed. With the lasers they cut long, sturdy saplings and branches and built a tripod on their side of the chasm. Woolf, who turned out to be quite handy, took the floater across the chasm and built another tripod on the other side.

Balancing the floater over emptiness was chancy and dangerous. The floaters were designed to float only a meter or so above solid ground. However, Woolf strapped himself onto the flat surface and very slowly and carefully, he crossed the ten meters of open space, pulling a rope with him to the opposite side. With a rope tied to either end of the floater, they pulled it back and forth until Woolf accumulated enough cut timbers to build the second tripod.

Then they tied two ropes to the top braces of the tripod and two to the bottom braces. Woolf pulled the ends of the four ropes across the chasm and tied them to the tripod on his side.

Four short pieces of rope fastened to the floater secured it to the guiding ropes, providing a safe platform that could easily be pulled from one side to the other. Loaded going across, empty going back to be loaded again.

It took the rest of the afternoon to finish the construction and they decided to wait until the next day to cross the chasm.

Breanna joined Striker in his sleeping bag that night again. "I thought you were mad at me," Striker said as she pressed her naked warm body against his. She laughed softly and let her hand travel across his belly. Touching his penis, she whispered, "I said that I would back you as the leader of this team. You made a decision and I accepted it. Now be quiet and make love to me."

Striker moved between her opening thighs, his penis hard and solid. He slid it easily into her soft, moist vagina and pushed deep. She moaned and slammed her hips against his. Even in the confinement of the sleeping bag, she managed to move under Striker with great passion.

Spent and satisfied they lay in each other's arms, listening to the sounds of the alien night.

"Do you think we'll ever get back home?" Breanna asked.

Striker looked up at the still unfamiliar constellations. Only one of the two moons was visible above the treetops. "I don't know," he said. "But we can't give up hope."

"What if we can never leave here?" Breanna shuddered in his arms. "What then?"

"Then we will try to survive as best as we can," he told her softly. "We humans are a tough breed. We will survive."

She snuggled against him. He held her tight, glad that she chose him.

89

Chapter Seventeen
Space Station

When Beringer entered the captain's office, he found him studying his computer screen. "What's so urgent, Jeremy?" Beringer pulled up one of the chairs and sank into it. He smiled. "This is comfortable. Unlike my own quarters. I guess being a captain does have its benefits."

Cunningham returned the smile and said, "Some." Then he became serious, touched a control on his desk and let the screen rotate slightly. "Look at this, Les."

Beringer stared at the three-dimensional image of a room with a door at the other end. Three blinking lights above the door drew his attention. "What am I supposed to see?" he asked.

"You are aware that I have a team of experts exploring this station, right?"

Beringer nodded.

"Well, they're five levels down right now. So far, they haven't discovered anything alive. I'm talking about machinery or equipment that works. Until they found this. Apparently, those lights began blinking soon after they entered this room. Other changes have also taken place. For instance, the door that led into this room stood open. After the team entered it, the door closed and breathable air filled the room."

"The team is trapped?"

"Oh no, the door can be opened. That room is an airlock, fully operational now."

"There is more, I assume?"

Cunningham nodded. He couldn't hide his excitement. "Behind the door is a large chamber, filled with electronic equipment and air."

"Any life signs?"

"No life signs of organic origins. But our scanners are detecting functioning machinery."

Beringer shook his head. "How could anything be alive down there? This station is ancient."

"We don't know. I told Dr. Wong, the team leader, not to proceed until I can get a few armed men to them, in case there is danger."

"You've made the right decision, because now it is the responsibility of the military. I will take a couple of my men and get down there as fast as possible." Beringer rose. "I will need the exact location of the team."

"I have a guide standing by," Cunningham said. His eyes were grave.

"Let's hope our presence here will not be challenged by the owners of this station. This whole thing could have major ramifications. I'm counting on you to handle this situation with extreme caution. Much depends on it."

Beringer smiled reassuringly. "I have a well-trained team. We ask questions first, before we shoot. Don't worry."

Cunningham's expression was serious. "I do worry, Les. This is no time to crack jokes. Be careful."

"I will." Beringer left, headed for the elevator, which took him to the third floor.

The elevator sank slowly down to the lower level. While standing inside the fairly large cabin he studied the strip of blinking lights beside the elevator door. Someone attached numbers beside each of the lights. The technicians, who brought the elevator back to life, managed to figure out the function of the colored circles beside each of the blinking lights, but they failed to decipher the alien letters, or numbers.

He wondered what they would find behind the door he saw on the screen. Possible answers to many questions?

The elevator stopped with a gentle rocking motion, and the door opened. He stepped into the cold looking corridor that separated the sleeping quarters of the officers from the single room where the enlisted men were bunked. His boots made a harsh sound on the hard metal floor as he crossed the short distance to his room located at the end of the corridor.

While most of the living areas in the tower had been modified to create comfortable surroundings for the crew, Beringer insisted that the two floors, which the military occupied, be left in conditions that are more Spartan.

Recognizing his brain pattern, the door to his small suite opened as he approached and closed behind him automatically. Once inside, he activated the personal com in his earlobe. A series of short beeps let him know it was ready.

"Lieutenant Wang, acknowledge," he said, and within moments the lieutenant answered the call.

"Wang here."

"I'll see you in my quarters in 30 minutes. Bring two marines. Full battle gear. And Lieutenant, do it quietly."

There was a moment of hesitation, and then Wang asked, "Is this a drill, sir?"

"No drill, Lieutenant."

Again, that short hesitation, then, "Understood, sir."

Beringer touched a spot behind his ear, a gesture that de-activated his com. Opening a closet he pulled out his combat-uniform. He didn't know what kind of weapons they might be facing, if any, but the material of the uniform should deflect the burst of a conventional laser.

After dressing, he strapped on his sidearm. He'd be wearing a spacesuit, and the sidearm would be useless, but he felt better with the comforting pressure of the laser against his hip.

He also chose a bulky laser-rifle, hoping he didn't have to use it.

30 minutes later, he heard the sound of boots in the corridor, and he told the door to open. Lieutenant Wang saluted as he walked through the door, followed by two marines. The visors of their helmets were up. Beringer recognized Cruz and Sisco, both of them capable men, and he nodded his approval. All three carried heavy laser-rifles.

"Permission to speak, sir." Lieutenant Wang's black, almond shaped eyes were narrow slits. Beringer knew Wang well enough to know that he wasn't happy. "Speak," he said.

"Why the secrecy? If there is a threat, shouldn't the other men know?"

Beringer smiled. "So far, I'm not aware of any threats to anyone's safety. There is no reason for alarm. A discovery has been made on the fifth level of the station, and our presence is required, in case there is a threat."

Wang relaxed visibly, so did the two marines. They were as anxious as the lieutenant to find out why they were here.

"If you gentlemen are ready, let's go."

They met their guide by the airlock that separated the tower from the station. After donning spacesuits, they entered the airlock and then boarded an elevator, which took them to the floor of the huge docking bay.

Beringer was familiar with this section of the alien space station. As part of their military exercises his men would get into spacesuits at least once every three weeks, board the small battle cruiser and take it out into space. Sometimes he made them walk on the surface of the giant station. It was like walking on a small asteroid.

Now he squinted up at the two micro-suns 30 meters above. In their harsh light he could see the immense size of the docking bay. Not for the first time he wondered what kind of people built this incredible vessel. He was not an engineer, but he could appreciate the knowledge the builders of the station must have possessed.

Maybe he would soon find out who they were.

A number of black oval spheres were lined up against the far wall, like giant eggs, sinister and mysterious. Since this was a docking bay for space vessels, it was assumed they were shuttles. So far the engineers failed to gain access to them. In fact, most of the space station proved inaccessible.

"I don't know if you've been briefed," the guide's voice came over the communicator. "You won't be able to take off your suits until we get down to the fifth level."

"We are aware of that," Beringer said.

"Alright, then follow me."

Walking in the bulky suits was not difficult in the low gravity. Beringer adjusted the level of his magnetic soles so he could lift his feet without effort.

They reached a door at the other end of the bay, not far away from the alien shuttles. When the guide opened it, Beringer looked into a huge duct. Stepping across the threshold, he realized they were entering a staircase. In the harsh light of a micro-sun, he saw the staircase that wound itself around the outside wall, leaving an open tunnel in the center. A platform supported by ropes from the ceiling turned out to be a temporary elevator.

"It is quite safe," the guide assured them. "We've been hauling men and equipment without any problems. Beats climbing these stairs."

The platform took them down one level. Leaving the staircase through a gaping hole in one wall, they came out in a large corridor.

The guide noticed Beringer turning around to look at the huge hole, then at the closed door beside it. "We had to use lasers to gain access to this level. Without power we can't operate these doors. And even with power we couldn't, because we haven't been able to figure out the controls." His tone almost sounded apologetic.

"Too bad," Beringer said. "It would make things a lot easier."

"This way," said their guide, and headed for yet another large hole, into another staircase, and then onto another temporary elevator.

"You'd think they would have built a staircase, which connects all the levels in the station, but for reasons only the builders know it isn't so." The guide chuckled. "Who knows how aliens think."

Beringer didn't comment. He felt tense, anxious to get to their destination. Gripping his laser-rifle tightly in his gloved hands, he hoped that there would be no reason to use it.

When they arrived on the fifth level a wall that was clearly not part of the original design blocked off the corridor they entered.

"We've installed an airlock," the guide explained and opened the door that led into the small chamber. Once inside they waited until the room was filled with air. Beringer saw the guide open the faceplate of his suit. "We have air in here," the guide said. "It's fresh and clean."

"I'd rather take no chances," Beringer said, leaving his suit sealed.

"As you wish." The guide opened the door in the opposite wall. They walked down another corridor. This one was wider and higher then the others, and longer. It was packed with tools and other equipment useful only to a construction crew. He also saw bedrolls, small metal tables and benches. A large door at the end blocked their way, above the door a series of lights blinked in rapid succession. After they crossed the threshold, the door closed behind them. They were in another small room. Beringer heard a sound, like a chime ringing.

When the chime stopped, a door in the opposite wall slid open. The room behind it looked familiar; Beringer recognized it as the one he saw on the Captain's screen. It looked larger than he expected it to be. He found the rest of the exploration team inside. He counted eight people, five men and three women, all without spacesuits. He saw the suits piled up in a corner, along with other gear and equipment.

"I'm Dr. Wong," said an elderly man. "Glad you're here, Commander. We're anxious to carry on."

"Are you sure all of you should be here when we open that door?" Beringer asked. He knew they could all hear him over his external speakers.

Dr. Wong smiled. "This is a big moment, Commander. Nobody wants to miss it."

Beringer shrugged inside his suit. "Well then, carry on." He moved to the back of the room, his marines beside him, weapons ready.

"Obviously, we haven't opened this door, not yet. So let's hope this works." Dr. Wong touched a large blue-shimmering oval groove in the doorframe. The moment he touched it the blue light became brighter and began blinking rapidly. A series of chimes rang out, and then the door started to slide into its frame.

Before anyone could move, Beringer stepped forward. "Nobody enters until I say so!" he said, his throat dry and rough. Slowly he walked through the door, entered the room on the other side. Cruz and Sisco were close behind him.

Somehow, he felt disappointed when he looked around. There was nothing to see but a number of semi-transparent cylinders standing upright in the center of the room. Softly glowing circles of light and dials covered one wall. A long bench with levers and blinking lights in front of the cylinders completed the décor.

He and his men spread out, searched the rest of the room, but they found nothing that could be considered dangerous. No alien beings with terrible weapons, no monstrous creatures hiding in dark crevices or corners, ready to pounce on them.

A couple of doors in one wall, with faintly glowing lights above them, caught Beringer's attention. He checked one door and found it locked. He didn't touch the blue oval in the frame. "I think it is safe to enter," he said into his com.

The eight members of the exploration team streamed into the room. He heard their exclamations as they looked around. They seemed to be excited about something.

His job was done. The adrenalin flow slowed. He felt suddenly tired, and thirsty. Opening his faceplate, he walked up to one of the women. "Do you people have anything to drink?" he asked.

She nodded, while she was staring at the tall cylinder closest to her. "In the other room, with our gear," she said absentmindedly.

Beringer looked at the cylinder that seemed to captivate her attention. There was something inside. He looked closer. The image was blurred, but Beringer suddenly understood why everyone was so excited. There was a body inside, the naked body of a human being, unmistakably female.

"What am I looking at?" he asked in a harsh whisper.

"I don't know. Possibly one of the original inhabitants of this station."

Beringer heard the tremor in the woman's voice. His own heart suddenly started beating faster, and he knew his palms were sweaty inside their gloves. It wasn't fear he felt. He was a soldier; his mind and body conditioned never to feel fear. However, that didn't mean he couldn't experience emotions, like happiness, sadness, or excitement, and he realized that the exhilaration of the others also infected him.

He stood in the presence of a great discovery.

He walked around the cylinder so he could see the face of the being inside. The breath caught in his throat. Even the diffusing element that enveloped the body could not hide the haunting beauty of the face, too perfect to be human. He couldn't see her eyes, they were closed, but her lids were large, her lashes impossibly long.

"She looks as if she is just sleeping," Beringer whispered.

"She probably is," the woman said beside him, her voice not too steady. "This is a cryogenic chamber."

Chapter Eighteen
Alpha Colony

He drank from the half shell, let the liquid linger on his tongue, swallowed. It tasted sweet and tangy.

It's a drug, he told himself, but he didn't care. The reaction came immediately, between his legs his erection grew. The girl, who held the shell, smiled at him. Her alien eyes were huge and luminous, he put his hand on her soft round breast and squeezed it gently.

She dropped the shell, put her slim arms around his neck and pulled him down on top of her. Her thighs opened wide and his penis sank into her soft vagina. He cried out as the pleasure began to build inside him. She caressed his back with soft, gentle hands, worked her lower body against his, but she never uttered a sound.

It didn't matter to him, she felt warm and yielding, and his pleasure peaked in an explosive climax. He pulled out of her, looked at the circle of naked bodies surrounding him. Open thighs beckoned, green, luminous eyes watched him. He fell between a pair of satiny thighs, entered another soft vessel, and filled it with his seed. Then another one.

Someone offered him a shell filled with sweet nectar. He gulped down its contents, felt strength flow through his veins. Warm and creamy alien vaginas closed around his aching organ repeatedly, soft yielding bodies pressed against him, smooth satin skin rubbed against his. When he spilled his seed, it rushed with great, explosive force. He was untiring, he climaxed in each one of them, leaving his gift behind.

How many? He didn't know.

When the last one received his gift the alien females crowded around him, lifted him up, then they carried him into the water, toward the giant plant floating in the center of the pond.

The woman with the flaming hair suddenly stood there.

A smile crossed her beautiful alien face, her green, luminous eyes reflected the pale light of the two moons. Water droplets sparkled like diamonds on her white skin. She opened her arms. He stumbled into her embrace, pressed his body against skin as smooth as silk, breasts, soft and warm. Long nipples thrust into his mouth and he began sucking, swallowing the sweet, pungent nectar. She pulled him down onto a bed of soft petals, her thighs parted and he entered heavenly bliss.

His bellows echoed across the pond, as never ending waves of pleasure raced through his body, enveloped his brain. After riding the crest for a long time, he collapsed inside the alien woman's cradling arms and thighs.

"I have chosen well," her velvety voice said inside his mind. "You have performed beyond my expectations. Your seed is strong and will be instrumental in the continued existence of my daughters."

Tom felt suddenly drained, tired to the point of being ill. Falling into a deep stupor, he grew oblivious to the things that happened around him.

When he awoke, he found himself back in one of the huts on a bed of dried grass. One of the girls brought him a woven basked full of fruit and a gourd filled with a sweet liquid. After he ate and emptied the gourd, he could feel strength seep back into his tired body.

He felt the need to get up and walk around. He went down to the lake and washed himself. It was quiet at the beach, there was hardly a ripple on the lake. He looked around to find he was alone. He sank down, stretched out on the soft sand. Breathing deeply, he detected a musky fragrance in the slight breeze coming from the direction of the pond that lay hidden somewhere among the tall trees.

His memory of the night before remained sketchy.

Flashes of naked limbs and satiny thighs. Warm bodies pressed against his. Round buttocks moving in his hands. Tight liquid sheaths sliding over his penis and hips slamming into his. The alien woman on the giant flower; the feel of her soft breasts against his chest. Her kisses. The flowing nectar.

He wiped his forehead, closed his eyes to bring the memory of her closer. Like a beautiful dream, it eluded him.

Who was that woman? What was she? Was she the one the girls called *The Great Mother*? She referred to them as *my daughters*.

A sound made him look up. It was one of the alien girls. "It is time again," she said softly, smiling down at him.

He studied her slender form silhouetted against the sky; admired her perfect figure, her full breasts, the narrow waist and flaring hips. Long silky hair framed her beautiful face, and her large, alien eyes only enhanced the beauty of her delicate features.

His gaze traveled down her long shapely legs. Without seeing them, he knew that she possessed round, firm buttocks, just like all the other girls. Yet, her beauty paled against that of the one they called *The Great Mother*. "Are you the same girl that always comes to me? I can't tell you apart."

"I am, but come now," the girl said, holding out a long-fingered hand.

"Where are we going?" he asked, as he walked beside her, but he knew the answer already. "To the pond, right?"

She nodded. "The Mother is very pleased," she said. "We must hurry, time is growing short. The *Two Companions* will soon be meeting in the sky. The secret rites must then be performed to be successful." She pulled him into the grove of tall trees, guided him toward the pond.

They were waiting for him, young alien girls, naked and beautiful. Their slim bodies all looked the same, and so did their faces. In the middle of the pond floated the giant flower, a number of smaller versions all around it.

"Where is The Great Mother?" he asked.

"She'll be here."

"I must talk to her," he said. "I am very confused. I need some explanations."

"I speak for the Mother. There is nothing to explain," the girl said patiently. "You are *The Chosen One*. You have been sent to us by the *Star Gods* to give us your seed."

"Damn it!" Tom cursed. "I am a human being, not some kind of mindless male animal that exists only to breed."

"You are angry." The girl touched his cheek. "Do you not find us desirable? Have we offended you in some way?" Her large eyes looked into his. "Do we not give you pleasure?"

He grabbed her hand. "That's just it. I desire all of you, but most of all, your Great Mother. I've experienced pleasures I never knew existed. But this is all wrong! We are of different species, I don't even know if we can ever produce offspring." He put his hands over his face. "For God's sake, I am a married man. I love my wife and yet, here I am, a wild beast lusting for something that looks human, but is not."

"You are distressed." The girl ran her hands over his chest, and then she put her lips on his, her small tongue sneaked into his mouth. She tasted of fresh flowers and sweet honey.

One of her hands touched his penis, which began swelling against his will. The lustful feeling inside him grew overwhelming. Groaning, he let her pull him down into the grass.

"Remember the first time you put your seed-spiller into me?" she whispered into his ear. "Let us do it like that again."

She got to her knees, presented her buttocks to him. Between her slightly spread thighs the puffy lips of her sex organ beckoned. Kneeling behind her, he guided his stiff mast between her pale cheeks, and with a shout, he pushed it deep into her welcoming sheath.

As he moved his hips back and forth behind the kneeling girl, he became aware of a strange, humming sound. He looked up to see the ring of alien girls. They were kneeling all around him, hands locked and rocking to the rhythm of his movements. From their open mouths came this eerie sound.

Aware of the built-up pressure in his loins he let it roll over him, climaxing with great force. He felt the girl's sucking motions around his jetting penis. Digging his fingers into her pumping hips, he pulled her tightly into his lap. When she left him, he looked expectantly at the watching girls; below his belly, his penis stood erect, ready to be plunged into another willing warm sheath.

Even though he climaxed only once, he felt drained, tired. As if sensing it, one of the girls knelt beside him, offered him a gourd. He drank from it, savoring the sweet taste of the liquid. The expected surge of power and strength came almost immediately.

"Let's get on with it," he growled, pushing away any feelings of guilt or wrongness. All he wanted was to put the giant thing that sprouted between his legs into as many of these hot, soft alien sex organs as he could.

This was a gift, every man's dream come true. All these willing beautiful young virgins, waiting just for him to fill them up with his seeds. No worries, no consequences, just heavenly pleasure! Who was he to question that? He moved behind the second girl, entered her. His hands grabbed her soft hips, held her while he pounded away between her soft buttocks.

A gentle breeze brushed over him, bringing with it the sweet, musky fragrance from the pond. Looking at the pond, he saw the silhouette of the *Great Mother* illuminated by the two bright moons overhead. Her long flaming hair was moving softly in the breeze.

I am pleased, came a ghostly whisper in his head, and then he heard her silent laughter. Staring at her beautiful silhouette he cried out as another orgasm raced through his body and brain.

He was still aware when he entered the silky vagina of another girl, and then his mind seemed to cloud over. Even though he heard the increasing eerie sounds from the mouths of the alien girls, he became unable to form any clear thoughts. His body moved untiring, without direction from his conscious mind, his climaxing penis spilled his seed into sucking vessel after vessel.

* * * *

He awoke with a dull humming in his head. Between his legs, his penis looked shrunken, chafed.

101

Again, his memory of the previous night remained a blur. He remembered soft round buttocks, his belly smashing into them, his penis milked by velvety vaginas. Ghosts of unimaginable pleasure danced in his mind, but that's all they were, ghosts.

"I have to get home," he murmured, "they'll be wondering where I am. Anina will be worried." He got up, crawled outside. The sky looked slightly overcast, clouds shadowed the sun, but his eyes ached when he looked up.

There was nobody around. The place seemed deserted. He walked up the trail, came to the narrow opening in the cliff. The gentle splashing of the waterfall on the other side echoed through the tiny cavern. Stepping into the creek, he entered the dark tunnel.

The large pond on the other side looked different in the daylight. There were tall trees all around it. He spotted the path and waded through the water toward it. The path was not very wide and slightly overgrown, it probably didn't receive much traffic.

Running parallel to the cliff for a while, it suddenly made a sharp left turn. He remembered that turn and with confidence he walked on.

When the sky darkened and he walked for what seemed like hours, he knew that he was lost.

Chapter Nineteen
Beta Colony

"This is just so massive," Mandy shook her black curls. "Think about it, at night we are screwing ourselves to exhaustion, and on top of that, we are screwing older men, married older men. It seems so unreal. I can't even remember everything very clearly." She stared at Rosanha with her big brown eyes. "Sometimes I think I'm dreaming."

"You're not. I remember things quite well." Rosanha screwed up her eyes. "Except when I did it with that guy from Alpha Colony. I wonder about him, I haven't seen him since."

"Maybe you made him up." Lillith sat down her basket, began picking out the small leaves that fell between the berries.

"Who then, took my virginity?" Rosanha challenged her. "I didn't dream that."

Lillith shrugged. "Maybe it was your Mr. Ranson, what does it really matter? You are a woman now. That is what's important."

"It matters to me. I'd like to know what happened to that young man." Her eyes took on a dreamy look. "You should have seen him, he was so good looking and he knew everything about making love."

"What's there to know?" Mandy's teeth shone white in her black face. "You open your legs, he puts it inside, how hard can that be?"

Lillith giggled. "It's hard if it isn't hard. Get it?"

"Oh, you're such a comedian," Mandy said. "Hey, Rose, maybe us three should go to the lake tonight, maybe your *Mr. Good-looking* will be there."

"I don't know." Rosanha felt uncertain. "What if he's shy?"

Lillith laughed. "I like shy guys."

"Since when?" Rosanha asked. "I wasn't even sure till now if you liked men."

"I like'm. I'm just picky."

"Right, you like them married."

"Children, children!" Mandy picked up an empty basket and resumed picking the small yellow berries. "This is not the time to argue. The mystery still stands: why are we so horny at night? Why do these men go crazy as soon as it gets dark? I bet you anything, if you would go to Mr. Ranson right now and say, *want to fogg me*? He would be shocked, maybe even embarrassed. He wouldn't do it."

Rosanha shook her head. "You can be so crude sometimes. I don't believe I know you, Mandy."

Lillith and Mandy laughed. "You think I'm crude, you should hear some of the guys talk, now there's crude."

"I know how they talk. They don't impress me. You should have heard the young man from Alpha Colony, he was so polite."

"What's the difference?" Lillith threw a berry at Rosanha and giggled. "He got what he wanted, didn't he? I can just hear him say, *Lovely lady, would you mind terribly if I put my seed-maker into your delicate flower?* Maybe that's his style. Would you have let him if he said, *Let's fogg?* Would you? What exactly did he say?"

"Nothing, it just happened. And he would never talk that crude, you'll see. I'll go with you tonight. He'll come." Rosanha tossed her long braids over her shoulders. "You'll see."

They continued picking their berries in silence. The sun began to throw long shadows, it was almost time to get back to the small settlement.

"Oh, oh!" Lillith jumped up suddenly, startling the other two girls. "Did you forget? Father Champain called a special meeting tonight, before supper. Let's hurry or we'll be late."

They delivered their baskets to the kitchen. The cook glared at them. "Is this all you girls picked? What have you been doing the whole day?"

Mandy stuck out her tongue at the older woman. "You're never happy. Maybe you should come down to the lakeshore at night."

"What do you mean by that?" A streak of color crept into the woman's cheeks. "Have you girls been snooping around where you're not supposed to?"

"We have to go to the chapel." Rosanha said and pulled on Mandy's arm. "Are you coming too, Mrs. Armesto?" Without waiting for an answer, they ran out of the door and headed for the small church building.

The chapel was almost full, some latecomers joined the three girls as they rushed through the door. They took their seats in one of the last rows. Father Champain already stood behind his pulpit. An imposing figure, dressed in a black cloak, and with his long beard and burning eyes, he looked like the archangel himself. When he looked up Rosanha had the feeling that he was looking directly at her.

"Evil and sin have befallen our small community!" he thundered. "The time to take measures is now." He paused, glared at the congregation. "I have seen with my own eyes, down by the lake, the evil things being done under the cover of night. I have seen whores and fornicators. I have seen the *Demon-woman from Hell* appear out of the water. I have seen her naked breasts and thighs, and her belly that is

104

without a navel. She has tempted me with her dark *Triangle of Sin,* but I resisted the evil seductress." He lifted his fist and shouted, "I resisted the temptation of the flesh. And so must you!

"This is a new frontier, a new planet, we've named it *Nu-Eden,* and like in the Garden of Eden there is a snake in this new paradise."

Rosanha's attention began to drift. She bent over to Mandy. "What's a fornicator?" she whispered.

Mandy shrugged. "Who knows. Someone who fornicates, I guess."

"You're a big help." Rosanha looked around the chapel. It was not a fancy building, not at all the way she remembered the churches back on Earth. It really looked like no more than a large, rectangular structure, very plain inside and outside, large enough though to hold about 250 people. Half the colony. Not all of the 500 colonists belonged to Father Champain's church, only about 200 of them. However, sometimes non-members came to listen to the sermon.

By now Rosanha knew most of the settlers, some better than others. She spied her mother sitting beside Eileen and Roger Ranson. Not too far from them sat Francesca and Franco Geomez. She watched Roger for a few minutes. Even in daylight, he was a handsome man. A couple of times he would glance over at Francesca.

Rosanha stifled a giggle. I guess he is the fornicator and Francesca is the whore, she thought and had another, more sobering thought. And that makes me also a whore, I had sex with Mr. Ranson!

"I realize that some of you think the laws of Earth don't apply here anymore," thundered Father Champain, "but remember this, the laws of God supersede every law made by man. God's laws are still valid here on *Nu-Eden.* Satan is alive and thriving in this New World. He appears in many forms. Beware!"

Rosanha wondered if that young man from Alpha-Colony came here. In a crowd of over 200 people, it was not easy to find someone you were looking for. She didn't even know his name.

Thinking of him made her thighs tingle, and she couldn't wait for nightfall. She glanced over at Mandy, who, it seemed quite obvious, was lost in her own daydreams. *Wonder who she is thinking about,* Rosanha thought, *Maybe Franco Geomez. According to Mrs. Geomez her husband was having sex with Mandy and Lillith.*

People were getting up, Rosanha realized that the sermon had ended. She followed her two friends out of the door. Outside she waited for her mother. When Roger Ranson and his wife walked by her, she said, "Good evening, Mr. Ranson."

He barely glanced at her. "Oh, hello there," he mumbled and walked by.

"Didn't I tell you?" Mandy whispered beside her. "He ignored you completely. There is something really weird going on."

"Rosie." It was Rosanha's mother. "I haven't seen you all day."

"Elder Helstrome assigned me berry-picking duty," she said hastily. "Come, I'll walk with you to the community hall."

They walked side by side without talking.

"You're awfully quiet," said the older woman after awhile. "Is there something bothering you?"

"Not really," Rosanha said, then, "well, yes, there is. Last night, down by the lake, I met this young man from Alpha-Colony."

"From Alpha-Colony? That's a long way from here. How did he get here?"

Rosanha shrugged. "I don't know, he didn't say." She blushed. "He was awfully handsome."

Her mother stopped, turned to face Rosanha. "Handsome, was he now? Did you have sex with him?"

The young girl blushed even deeper. "Mother," she exclaimed, "how can you ask me that?"

"Because you are my daughter, and I care about the things you do." The older woman sighed and ran her hand across her forehead to wipe little droplets of perspiration away. "Strange things have happened lately. People are coming into my office to tell me about unusual experiences. Most of them involve sex." She closed her eyes. "Something happened to me that I can't explain. A few nights back, when I walked along the shore of the river, I saw your father."

"You saw daddy?" Rosanha stared at her mother. "I thought he was dead."

"That's what I was told. I never saw his dead body. He just suddenly appeared. He came out of the water, dripping wet, and completely naked." The woman delicately dapped at her cheeks with a small piece of cloth. "When I saw him I just broke down, and when he undressed me, I let it happen."

Rosanha looked away, embarrassed. "Where is he? Where is my father?"

"Gone," her mother said. "I fell asleep in his arms, when I awoke he was gone. Just like your handsome young lover from Alpha-Colony, unless you've seen him since."

"I haven't, but I'm sure he'll be back."

Theresa took her daughter's face between her hands. "Rosanha, darling, he is not real, just like the man who said he was my husband, it wasn't real. This place we call *Nu-Eden*, it should be called *Hell*. There is evil here, like Father Champain said, and we'll have to be on guard." She put an arm around Rosanha's shoulders. "Come, daughter, let's go and eat something. Maybe Mrs. Armesto has cooked up another gourmet dish."

"Pah." Rosanha made a face. "That old woman just pretends to be a cook. Who knows what she did before she joined our colony."

"Now, now." Theresa chuckled. "Do I detect some resentment here?"

"I don't actually hate her," Rosanha said, "but she can be so mean. She's never happy with the stuff we bring, and sometimes we work so hard, just to please her."

"She's had a hard life. She lost her husband and two children only a month before our ship left Earth, so don't judge her too harshly. She is a good cook."

The community hall was another large building constructed from pre-fab materials. Here the council members held their meetings and it also served as the dining area.

Rosanha and her mother lined up at the long counter to get their food. One of the kitchen girls smiled at Rosanha. "Mrs. Armesto made a spectacular desert with the berries you picked today. She was quite pleased. You must have found a good spot."

Rosanha took the tiny tubers the girl handed her and put them on her plate. "She never told us she was pleased. She never does."

The girl shrugged. "She's not that bad once you get to know her."

"I told her that," Theresa said beside Rosanha. "How is your father, Hillary? I hear he had a successful hunt."

"Yes, he did," Hillary said proudly. "He shot a couple Rock-sheep; they'll be part of tomorrow's supper."

"They're good eating, if you don't mind the greasy taste," Rosanha said, smirking.

Hillary laughed. "Cheer up, Rosanha, tonight we're having your favorite, smoked tree-fungus."

"Phew, I hate those." Rosanha made a face. "We've had them once already this week."

"Hey, you two, stop the chattering and move on! I'm starving," someone said behind them. It was Franco Geomez. He looked at Rosanha. "You're Mandy's friend, right?"

Rosanha nodded. She admitted to herself that he was quite handsome. Black curly hair, dark smoldering eyes. Suddenly, a funny sensation started inside her belly. *He foggs Mandy and Lillith,* she thought, *wonder how he'd feel inside me.* She blushed and turned away, moved on down the line to pick up a ladle full of black spiny pieces of fungus. *What is the matter with me, I've never looked at a man like that before!*

The image of the young man from Alpha-Colony popped into her mind. He seemed to be smiling. He stood naked, his penis strutted like a log between his legs.

Rosanha brushed her hand across her eyes to wipe away the image. Stumbling to the table, she sat down on the hard bench. Theresa sat down beside her and began to eat, she didn't seem to notice her daughter's distress. Rosanha wasn't hungry anymore, the pungent aroma of the smoked tree-fungus rose up her nose.

Her thighs and pubic area itched. Her vagina seemed inflamed. She needed the hard flesh of a man inside her belly. She couldn't wait for night to come.

Chapter Twenty
Space Station

Captain Cunningham insisted that he be present when they awakened one of the *Sleepers*. He watched anxiously as Bret McGuinness examined the gauges and controls. "What do you think?"

The young man looked at the captain. "I wish my sister Breanna were here now," he said slowly. "She should be here. She's the expert."

"I know, son, but she isn't," Cunningham said patiently, but he felt like grabbing one of the levers and pulling it, just to see what would happen.

As if reading his mind, Bret said, "I'd like everyone to step back a little. We don't want anyone touching something by accident, even though, by the looks of it, there are plenty of safeguards in place to prevent accidental initiation of the reviving process."

"So you can do it?"

Bret ran a hand across his short-copped red hair, and pursed his lips. "I think so. The controls are more sophisticated than ours, but not that much different. Those levers you are staring at open a valve at the bottom of the cylinders, allowing the liquid inside to drain out. Each cylinder has its separate controls." He smiled when he saw Cunningham pull back his hand. "Don't worry, nothing is going to happen until I push the corresponding keys on that control board." He pointed at the wall with all the gauges and blinking lights.

"How will you know which ones?"

"Give me a couple of hours to study the controls and trace the circuits. It can't be that difficult. After all, this is what I do best." He turned his back to the Captain, ignoring him and the others who were watching him.

"Insolent red-headed bastard," Beringer murmured beside Cunningham. "No respect for authority."

The Captain chuckled. "Goes with the territory. I'm told he is a genius. The best there is."

"We'll see. I liked his sister much better," Beringer grumbled, and stalked out of the room.

Since he could do nothing in here, Cunningham followed him. He found Beringer talking to one of the women of the exploration team, a tall, wide-shouldered Blonde with large glasses. Nobody wore glasses these days, a fashion fad 20 years out of date. Only eccentrics wore them now. Cunningham chuckled to himself. That Beringer sure knew how to pick them.

"This is Dr. Crestin," Beringer introduced the woman.

"Captain," the woman said, and gave him a little smile. "I believe we've met."

Cunningham nodded. Of course they met. He knew everyone on the team. "Dr. Crestin," he said, "you must be very excited."

"Oh, I am," she beamed. "When I joined the team I hoped we'd find something. But this is beyond my wildest dreams. Everyone is excited."

"Maybe we'll finally find out who these people are, where they come from, and what happened on this station."

"Too bad Breanna McGuinness isn't here," Dr. Crestin said. "She is a xenologist, also a linguist. I hope we will be able to communicate with these aliens."

Cunningham smiled. "One problem at a time. Let's hope her brother can awaken at least one of them." He looked at Beringer. "I don't want any weapons visible, but at the same time, let's not take any chances."

The Commander nodded. "I'll have my boys standing by, discreetly. If you don't mind, I'd like to be there when it happens."

"I want you to be there." Cunningham glanced around him, took in the people who were crowded in the corridor. He tried to keep the discovery quiet, but he'd been unable to keep the news from spreading. Almost everyone at the station asked for permission to be present when the first genuine alien of a space faring race was brought back to life.

Of course, there had not been enough room to allow everyone to be here. As it was, there were too many now. He shouldn't have been so generous.

Surprisingly, most of the people present spoke with a hushed voice, as if they were afraid they might awaken too many of the Sleeper at once.

"Excuse me," he said to Beringer and the woman. He spotted Professor Romanof among the crowd. The professor was hard to miss. With his seven-foot frame, he towered over everyone. On top of that, he was not soft-spoken.

"I'm telling you, we'll be disappointed, after all this time they'll all be morons!" Professor Romanof spoke to a short, balding man. Dr. Reinhard, a physicist. Professor Romanof was a mathematician.

"You don't know that, Professor. You know nothing about the human mind, much less about these aliens." Dr. Reinhard saw the Captain first, and lifted a hand. "How long, still, Captain?"

Romanof turned around, gave Cunningham a nod.

"Not long, I hope," Cunningham said and smiled. "I see you two are at it again."

"Everyone has a right to his opinion, but there are times when certain things are just obvious," Romanof growled. "My esteemed colleague here will not even allow himself to consider that these aliens most likely will have lost their cognitive abilities and will not be coherent."

"He calls them morons," Dr. Reinhard cut in.

"They may not even be that." Professor Romanof threw up his hands. "Mark my words, we may be able to revive their bodies, but their brains will be nothing but dead matter."

Cunningham chuckled. If he didn't know better, he would have thought that Romanof and Reinhard hated each other's guts. However, these men respected each other. Both were famous for their theories on multiple universes and back holes. Neither agreed with the other, of course, but they grudgingly admitted that both theories had their merits.

"Why waste time arguing?" Cunningham said. "We should know soon, one way or the other."

"Would you like to wager a small bet, Captain?" Romanof asked.

"I'm not a betting-man, Professor. Why don't you ask Commander Beringer? I've heard he's not above playing the odds."

"By the way, Captain," Professor Romanof said, "have you heard from the team on the fifth planet?"

Cunningham shook his head. "Nothing."

"I miss my discussions with Professor Findlay. He developed some interesting theories about the correlation between ancient civilizations and alternate worlds." Romanof shrugged his shoulders. "I didn't always agree with his views, but he understood numbers. Instead of studying anthropology hc should have become a mathematician."

"You talk as if he is dead," Reinhard said, accusingly.

"He's missing on a hostile planet. That is as good as dead. We should have heard from them by now."

"It's only been three weeks," Cunningham said. "If their shuttle crashed, which we have to assume, then it may take them a long time to reach the research station."

"Unless they get killed by the severe conditions on that planet, or eaten by wild animals." Romanof nodded and smiled smugly when Reinhard rolled his eyes. "I know what I'm talking about. I took the time to study the initial reports. That fifth planet is not human-friendly."

"I think I'm going to check up on Mr. McGuinness," Cunningham said. "I'll leave you to your discussion." *Scientists*! he thought, as he made his way back to the room with the cryogenic cylinders. *They're like little children. Always arguing.*

McGuinness looked up when the Captain approached. "You have an eerie sense of timing," the young man said and smiled. "I believe I've cracked it. I'm already starting the thawing sequence. The process will take about three hours until he awakes." He pointed at the only cylinder that was in a horizontal position. "That one is programmed to be the first."

"They *told* me you were a genius," Cunningham said.

McGuinness grinned. "Actually, it wasn't that hard, once I understood the basics of this whole installation. I can't take credit for everything. These people expected to be revived, and made it quite easy. It is just a matter of getting the process started. Now their computer will take over. All I can do is watch."

The Captain smiled. "Don't be too modest, young man. Take the credit." He stood, stroking his chin, while watching the blinking lights for a while, then he said, "Three hours? Hmm..." He didn't feel like being cooped up in the corridor for that long, making small talk with scientists he didn't understand. "I'll be going back up. Notify me when he's coming around."

He walked out, stopped to talk to Beringer. "Listen, I'll be back in three hours. Keep the crowds away from the alien until I'm back."

Chapter Twenty-one
Exploration Team Delta

"These ruins are ancient." Professor Findlay picked up a crumbled piece of stone. "Looks like some kind of cement. Wonder what happened to the builders?"

"Probably dead by now," Remington said.

"I certainly hope so." The Professor chuckled. "They'd be over a thousand years old if they were still alive."

Remington growled something, stalked passed Striker, leaving Findlay standing, shaking his head. "He's an idiot. No sense of humor," he said to Striker. "Of course they're dead."

The lieutenant smiled and sat down on a moss-covered rock. "I think you need to know, Professor, a few days ago, up in the mountains, we came across similar ruins."

Findlay lifted his head, stared at Striker. "You didn't tell anyone?"

"Besides Woolf, Mian, and Chu, who found them, only Breanna and I know."

"Why wasn't I told?"

"Because we needed to get off those mountains. Right now our priority is survival."

"You should have let me have a look, at least," Professor Findlay said angrily. "You can't make those decisions alone, Lieutenant. You might have put all of us in danger."

"You said it yourself, Professor, they're dead."

"The builders are, but there may well be descendants. You disappoint me, Striker."

Striker grinned tightly. "You and how many others? Being a leader is not always easy. And sometimes lonely."

"You volunteered for the job, Lieutenant, so don't cry on my shoulder."

"Nobody is crying, Professor." Striker rose, brushed off the seat of his pants. "I better go and talk to Remington about the possible danger we may be facing. You might just be right about living descendants." He didn't tell Findlay about the charcoals in the fireplace. No need to upset him more.

He found Remington talking to Woolf. Both men looked at Striker when he approached. Remington with an accusing look on his face. "I told him," Woolf said. "He was insistent."

"Keeping secrets only breeds mistrust, Striker," Remington growled.

"Well, you know now," Striker said coldly. "I'm appointing you Chief of Security, Remington. It will be your job to ensure the safety of our team." Striker knew the other man didn't like him, but by giving him responsibilities, he could be kept in line and might even make an ally.

"I'd like Woolf to be my deputy," Remington said and looked at Woolf. "If it's all right with you, Herm."

Woolf nodded, smiled. "I would have liked to have another look at those ruins, but I guess they won't run away. Besides, Professor Findlay can get a little overbearing, sometimes."

"I hope you don't say that about me," said a loud voice beside Striker.

Remington laughed. "Gregorchuck, one look at you and everyone knows you're an obnoxious son-of-a-bitch. You can't hide it."

"I guess that's why we get along so well. You know what they say about birds of a feather…" The bearded marine-biologist punched Striker on the arm and laughed. "How do you fit into this little group, Lieutenant?"

Striker smiled, rubbed his arm. "You tell me."

"A diplomat, that's what I like about you, Striker." Gregorchuck stroked his beard. "I saw Professor Findlay poking around in those ruins, and Professor Banca has gone off again on his treasure hunt. I wouldn't mind going down to the lake and do a little of my own research."

Striker looked at him sharply. "When did Professor Banca leave the camp?"

"About fifteen minutes ago. He took Sara and Concitta, his two favorite students, with him." He grinned. "Wonder what they're actually studying."

Remington laughed and scratched himself. "That Concitta Sanchez, she's hot. What do you think, Herm?"

Woolf shrugged, grinned foolishly. "She's hot. I guess. I wouldn't know." He looked at Striker. "What kind of danger exactly are we expecting, sir? Are we talking about hostile alien life forms?"

"Hostile? I don't know. Possibly."

"You want me to go look for Professor Banca?"

Striker shook his head. "No, I'll do it myself." He looked at Remington. "Your job begins now," he said, and turned away abruptly. He just didn't like the man, and he may have to change his opinion about Gregorchuck. Those two could have each other.

He stalked through the knee-deep grass, away from the ruins, toward the tents. They'd decided to set up camp near the lake, under the protection of a group of wide-spreading trees.

The valley they were in was huge, and so was the lake. Everything they needed was here. Tall, straight trees to supply the lumber for building a solid shelter, plenty of small animals in the forest to provide food for them to survive. The lake harbored a variety of aquatic creatures, and a wide, fast flowing stream brought fresh water from the mountains. Chances for survival were excellent, so far.

The ancient ruins testified that others once chose this place to live in.

He found Mian gathering rocks and throwing them into a pile. Nodding toward Striker the black man said, "We need a fire-pit for warmth and for cooking."

Striker smiled. "You're the survival expert, Acram. Can you cook, too?"

"Depends. Meat roasted on a fire tastes different." Grinning. "A little charcoal is probably good for you."

"Probably." Striker looked toward the forest, scanned the surface of the lake to the west, and then studied the expanse of prairie to the south. When they were still up in the mountains, they sighted numerous forests and small lakes and rivers, now he could only see the edge of another forest about a kilometer away. There were no signs of Professor Banca and the girls.

"Did you see which way Professor Banca went?" he asked.

Mian pointed south. "Last I saw he was following the lakeshore."

"Come with me. I'm not good at tracking," Striker said. "And bring your weapon."

Mian padded his hip and grinned.

"I guess everyone else is washing up." Striker scanned the lake again. A southern wind created small whitecaps, and he could hear the waves lapping against the rocky shore. He felt edgy, his nerves were raw. Somehow, this place seemed too peaceful. Out of the depths of the forest he could hear some large animal bellow a challenge then another one answer. Instinctively, his hand went to touch his laser. How he wished to be inside the safety of a spaceship, somehow those cramped quarters didn't seem so bad.

When he came to the small sandy beach he found it littered with heaps of clothing. He saw Chu sitting on a rock, a laser rifle in his lap. The pilot saluted when Striker and Mian walked up to him. "Lieutenant."

Striker returned the salute. "I'm glad to see at least one person with a level head."

Chu smiled. "I've never had much use for water; I prefer a sonic shower."

"Better get used to it." Mian grinned. "I'm afraid this is all we have to offer."

Striker spotted Breanna's red hair in the water. She waved when she saw him. He got a quick flash of her naked white breasts. Another woman, Rhea Rosetti, emerged out of the waves in front of her and started walking toward him.

She possessed small breasts and a thin, but muscular body, and he couldn't help but notice the thick dark bush covering her genitals. Most women he knew preferred to keep that part of their body clean-shaven.

She saw him looking, but pretended not to notice. She smiled when she stood in front of him. "Well, Lieutenant, aren't you going to take a dip?"

"Good morning, Rhea," he said, trying not to stare at her extremely long nipples. "Maybe later. Right now I'm concerned with Professor Banca."

"Why?"

"I don't like anyone going off by himself."

"He wasn't alone, Sara and Concitta went with him."

"I mean unarmed. They shouldn't go off unarmed."

Her brows knitted together in a frown, her gray eyes searched his face. "What are you trying to say, Striker?"

"This planet may not be as empty of intelligent life as we thought, at least that's what Professor Findlay suggests."

"We haven't found any evidence, yet."

"Actually, we have. Up in the mountains, a few days ago."

"Are you talking about those monkey-like creatures?"

"No, I'm talking about the ruins Mian and Chu discovered."

"Ruins like those?" Rhea pointed a thumb at the crumbling walls of the ancient village. "Nobody lives in them."

"We found remnants of a fire, which was made by someone as recent as five years ago. Fire means intelligence."

"That's surprising news." Rhea stared at Mian. "Is that true?"

Mian nodded. "Like the Lieutenant says."

"Why haven't we run across these people?"

Striker chuckled. "Who says they're people?"

"You know what I mean." She looked at the ruins, then into the forest, shivered. "We could be in danger."

Striker looked past Rhea, watched Breanna coming out of the lake. She squeezed the water from her long hair, shook red strands out of her

116

face. Her lovely body glistened wetly in the morning sun, and he realized again how beautiful she actually was.

"What are you three talking about?" she asked, laughing, her green eyes flashing. Then she planted a wet kiss on his lips.

"I told Rhea about the fire pit."

"Oh." She glanced at the small woman.

"She knew?" Rhea asked.

Striker nodded, feeling guilty about not telling everyone. "I thought it best to keep it quiet for awhile. I may have been wrong."

"You certainly were! Who knows what dangers we may have encountered." Rhea looked upset.

"I already had this discussion with Professor Findlay, so let's end it. It was my decision." Striker spoke sharply, and then turned to Mian. "Let's go and look for Professor Banca." He stalked away, angry with Rhea and with himself. *Damn it! He was the leader and shouldn't have to explain himself to everybody who questioned him.*

Mian walked ahead of him, slightly stooped over, his eyes searching the ground. "Shouldn't be hard to follow them," he said to Striker. "The soil is relatively soft and the grass is still bent where they walked. But we better hurry. Looks like we'll get some rain soon." He pointed at the dark clouds gathering in the west.

They walked close to shore, where the grass wasn't quite as high, but small rocks and boulders didn't make walking much easier. Striker looked back in the direction of the camp; some people were still in the water, but a few seemed to be gathering around Breanna and Rhea. He smiled grimly, it wasn't hard to guess what they were discussing.

When he turned to follow Mian, he saw the black man standing still, his laser in his hand. Making a motion for Striker to stop, he stared at a clump of nearby trees. Striker followed his gaze and saw a large dark shape partially hidden by the thick trunks of the trees. The shape moved. A shaggy head with long tusks appeared. Between the tusks swung an appendix slowly moving back and forth, like a giant snake. The animal stepped into the open, revealing a huge hairy body.

Striker recalled seeing holograms of similar creatures. They lived a long time ago on Earth. He couldn't remember what they were called.

The big animal stepped out of the trees; it trumpeted once, then it began to trot away from them and headed toward the forest in the south. A few moments later three more appeared, all smaller than the first one.

Mian waited for Striker to catch up with him, before they walked on. "I think they're herbivores," he said, "but they still could be dangerous."

"They're certainly large enough," Striker commented.

They watched the animals disappear into the forest, heard them trumpet one more time, and then it was quiet again. The tracks they were following led them into the forest not far from where the shaggy animals entered. A narrow trail wound its way through the thick underbrush. Striker could see the footprints of the three they were searching; he also saw prints of other creatures that came this way before.

"I think I need to have a long talk with the Professor. What in hell is he thinking, entering this forest," Striker cursed loudly.

The trail ended abruptly in a small glade. Everything looked peaceful, until Striker and Mian walked further into the glade and saw the bodies. Striker moaned in anguish when he saw the lifeless body of a woman.

Sara Golman, was his first thought. Her face was hidden behind long, black hair, and her naked body was spattered with blood. Somebody mutilated one of her breasts. Not far from her lay the body of a male, but it wasn't Professor Banca, it belonged to a younger, more muscular man.

Striker bent over the woman, gently turned her head. Breathing a sigh of relief, he studied the alien face. It was humanoid, but not human.

"Looks like we found the inhabitants of this planet," he said to Mian who was bending over another dead body. He saw movement at the far end of the glade; someone came running toward them. It was Concitta Sanchez.

"Lieutenant," she called. "Over here."

Not knowing what to expect Striker and Mian drew their weapons and walked slowly toward the black woman. They found Professor Banca and Sara Golman kneeling in the grass; between them lay the body of another one of the aliens.

Sara looked up. "This one is still alive," she said.

The alien turned his head; there was blood seeping from a wound close to his temple, but it was beginning to clot, forming a dark crust. He stared at Striker with large purple eyes. His lips moved and he spoke a few words.

Sara stroked his forehead. "We're not going to hurt you," she said soothingly. "You are safe with us."

Striker studied the stranger; he seemed fragile, his thin body not very tall. He was dressed in a short kilt and vest; both made from animal skins.

"Any others alive?" Striker asked.

"None." Professor Banca rose to his feet. "We counted seven, including this one. Two females, five males, all older. He is just a boy."

"How did they die?"

"Violent. Most of them had their heads bashed in."

"Wonderful. It seems whenever we find intelligent life we also find violence. Whoever did this is still around, maybe even close by." Striker turned to Mian who had been checking the dead bodies. "Did you find any weapons?"

Mian shook his head. "If they owned any they're gone now, along with any other possession they may have had."

"Robbery and murder. How long ago did this happen?"

"Not long. Maybe three hours."

"They were murdered in their sleep." Concitta stared at Striker. "We'll have to bury them."

Striker nodded. "I'll…" A clap of thunder interrupted him and then a few drops of rain began to fall. "We better get back to camp. I'll send a team, after the rain."

With watchful eyes he scanned the trees around them, expecting to see a horde of screaming, club swinging aliens spilling into the small glade.

Chapter Twenty-two
Space Station

Before Captain Cunningham entered the cryogenic chamber again, he asked Professor Romanof, Dr. Reinhard, Dr. Wong, Dr. Crestin, and Commander Beringer to join him, then he closed the doors to the chamber, under the protest of the people who remained behind in the corridor.

"How are things coming along?" he asked McGuinness.

The technician looked up from the gauges he had been watching and smiled. "You're just in time. I think he is about to awaken."

Looking at the alien man, Cunningham noticed the difference in his complexion. Now he looked like someone sleeping. His chest rose gently with every breath he took. As Cunningham watched he saw the large eyelids twitch, then they snapped open, revealing shiny purple eyes.

Beside the Captain, Dr. Crestin heaved a deep sigh. When he looked at her, he saw a tear running down her cheek.

The alien sat up, looked around with his large eyes. His gaze came to rest on the Captain, who stood closest to him. He smiled and said something with a soft, melodic voice. It was definitely a question.

Cunningham's throat felt tight, he cleared it loudly, feeling compelled to say something witty, before the stranger assumed these grunts were a language. "I don't know what you are saying," he said, "and you probably can't understand me either, but I welcome you."

The alien seemed to listen intently, a frown creased his smooth forehead, and then he smiled again. "Welcome you," he said slowly, his tongue stumbling over the words.

"He speaks our language," Dr. Crestin said breathlessly.

Pointing at himself, the alien said, "Arel."

"I'll be damned!" Dr. Reinhard exclaimed.

"I'll be damned!" the alien repeated, still smiling, still pointing at himself. "Arel," he said again.

"I think I'm winning the bet," Professor Romanof said. "He's a goddamn parrot. Just repeats what you tell him."

"There you go again!" Reinhard burst out. "Jumping to conclusions, as usual. I think he's telling us that his name is Arel."

"Arel," the alien repeated and nodded. Then he pointed at Reinhard, his head tilted slightly.

"My name is Joseph Reinhard," Dr. Reinhard said slowly.

"Joseph Reinhard," the alien said and nodded. "My name is Arel," he added. He looked at the Captain, pointed, then at Romanof, Dr. Wong, and

Dr. Crestin.

"My name is Cunningham," the Captain said and indicating the professor he said, "Romanof, and this is Dr. Wong." Before he could point at the woman, she said, "I am Amaya Crestin."

Arel nodded his head. "Cunningham, Romanof, Dr. Wong, Amaya Crestin."

"Amazing," Dr. Wong said and looked at Romanof. "I'm aware of the wild theories you've dreamed up. Forget them. This man is in possession of all his faculties, and quite intelligent."

"He's not a man, he's an alien," Romanof countered.

"Pah!" Dr. Reinhard exclaimed, "you'll never admit that you may be wrong, Romanof. You're such a hothead. I'm siding with Dr. Wong."

"All I'm doing is analyzing what he says, and so far he has said nothing intelligent." Romanof looked at the alien. "Say something intelligent!"

"I am alien man. My name is Arel. You are Joseph Romanof." Arel smiled. "You are a hothead."

"What?" Romanof stared, and then he laughed. "Like I said: a parrot. He doesn't know what he is saying."

"I understand," Arel said. "What is 'goddamn parrot'?"

Everyone chuckled, except the professor. "I still say he is a moron. A moron with a good memory," he growled. "You'll see."

Cunningham cleared his throat again. "Gentlemen! I suggest you stop arguing. And please, choose your words carefully when you speak. Obviously, our new friend here does have an excellent memory."

The alien had been listening to the Captain. "Memory," he said and pointed to a spot behind his ear. "You speak. Arel good memory."

Cunningham turned when he heard the pounding against the double doors. Beringer, who stood by the doors, grinned at the Captain. "I think they're getting impatient. My men are having a hard time keeping the crowd from breaking down the doors." The Commander was the only one with his communicator in standby mode.

"Let them in," Cunningham said. "But they better be civilized." He didn't listen to what Beringer told his men outside, turned back to the alien man, who was just climbing out of the half-open cylinder. Naked and apparently unashamed, he stood in front of the humans. He spoke in his own language, shook his head when they didn't understand him.

McGuinness held out a robe, which the Captain brought with him. Arel looked at it for a moment, then down at himself. Smiling, he took it from McGuinness and draped it over his broad shoulders. Then he walked over to the wall with all the gauges and blinking lights. He busied himself throwing tiny levers and touching the lights in a sequence that made only sense to him.

Bret McGuinness stood beside him, watching with apparent great interest. Neither of them turned when the first of the crowd came through the opening doors.

Cunningham watched them walk in, suppressing a smile when he noticed that they seemed almost reluctant to enter the room. He glanced at Beringer, who gave him a little grin. Then he saw the laser in the Commander's hand.

Beringer shrugged when Cunningham raised an eyebrow. *That's the problem with these military types,* the Captain thought, *they always have to play with their toys.* However, he was relieved to see the orderly conduct of the scientists and the crewmembers who were allowed to be present. All of them were eager to meet the first intelligent alien humanoid the human race had encountered. This was history in the making.

He turned when someone tugged on his sleeve. Staring at the young woman who looked shyly up at him, he searched his memory to find out who she was.

"I am Tiana Ling," she said, smiling. "I hear you need a linguist."

He remembered her name. He also remembered that she was a psychologist. She had been part of the psych-team that he sent down to Nu-Eden. "Yes, I do," he answered. "Do you have someone in mind?"

"Yes, me." Her smile widened when she saw his skepticism. "I used to teach children with speech problems," she explained.

"Well, you may just be of help to us. Later. Right now Arel, that's his name, is busy with his controls."

"What's he doing?" the young woman asked.

"I'm not sure." Cunningham hesitated to make a guess.

"He's reviving the rest of his people," Dr. Wong said from behind the Captain and pointed at the transparent cylinders.

"They're glowing!" Tiana exclaimed. "Oh, this is so exciting. Thank you, Captain, for letting me be here."

Arel turned away from the blinking lights and walked over to one of the cylinders. The liquid inside it was beginning to drain away. When the alien man reached up to touch a control at the top of the cylinder, he stood facing the watching crowd, his robe fell   open to reveal his naked body.

Beside Cunningham, Tiana sighed audibly. "He looks human," she whispered. "And he's so perfect."

Dr. Reinhard, who stood close by, chuckled. "You think he is perfect.

122

I can't wait to see the females," he said. "I took a peek at one of them inside her tank. Her face was almost angelic."

Listening to their comments made up Cunningham's mind. He knew there would be protests, but he was the captain, and this would be his decision. He turned to face the people who were standing in the back of him, lined up against one wall. Seeing their anxious faces, he hesitated momentarily, almost changing his mind, but he knew this was in the best interest of everyone, especially for the aliens.

"Listen everybody," he said with a loud voice, "I know you're all eager to see what happens next, but it will be a while until some of the others wake up. You've seen Arel, he seems to be all right. There has been some communication with him. Right now, there is no reason for anyone to be here. I think it is best if everyone leaves now, and I mean, back to the tower. You all have jobs to perform. We'll keep you posted. Thank you for your co-operation."

As expected, there were outcries of protest, but when Beringer and his three marines began herding them back into the corridor, they left reluctantly.

"You too, please," Cunningham said to Dr. Reinhard and Professor Romanof.

Romanof opened his mouth, but one look at the Captain made him close it again.

"You want us to leave, too?" Dr. Wong asked.

The Captain shook his head. "You and Dr. Cristin stay. After all, you're part of the team." He looked at Tiana Ling. "You can stay, also. I hope you're as good as you say."

Her almond eyes twinkled. "No confidence, Captain?"

"These are not little children with speech problems, Miss Ling. They may look human, but who knows how their minds work."

Tiana smiled. "I am also a psychologist. It may be of some benefit."

"I hope so." Cunningham turned to Beringer. "Maybe you should also stay, Commander. But keep your boys out of sight. We don't want to give these people the wrong impression."

"I understand, Captain."

Cunningham smiled and padded Beringer's arm. They were only formal in public; privately they used each other's first name.

Out in the corridor people were getting into their spacesuits. It would take some time to get everyone out of here. He walked over to one of the tables where a couple of the maintenance men sat on a metal bench. "Mind if I join you?" he asked.

Both men stood up. One of them cleaned the table with his sleeve. "Have a seat, Captain. Would you like a cup of coffee? We've got a pot going."

Cunningham sat down, dabbed his brow. "I think I could use a cup, thank you. Please, sit down."

They both sat. The one who wiped up the table filled a cup with the black brew, offered it to the Captain. "We don't have any whitener," he apologized.

Cunningham waved him off, took a sip from the cup. Both men watched him eagerly. "Is he awake?" one asked.

Swallowing, Cunningham nodded. "He is, and he is awakening the others."

The younger of the two drummed his fingers against the tabletop. "Do you think it's wise, Captain?"

"Wise? What makes you say that, Mr. Aranson?" The name of the young man had finally popped into his mind.

"There are fifty aliens in there." Aranson hesitated. "What if they are hostile? What if they want their station back? They could evict us, you know. We are the intruders."

Cunningham smiled, downed his cup. The caffeine seemed to calm his raw nerves, even though the stuff was supposed to be a stimulant. "You have some valid points there, young man, but I believe there is no reason for panic. We'll work it out." He rose. "Thanks for the coffee. I think I'll get back to my office. But first I'll have to go and see how things are progressing in there."

Chapter Twenty-three
Alpha Colony

Tom stumbled on in the darkness, panic gripping his chest. Low hanging branches and thorny shrubs cut his skin; once he tripped over a vine and fell. He lay there, gasping, listening. The sounds of the forest suddenly seemed menacing. The challenging roar of a swamp-tiger made him bolt to his feet. It sounded so close. A shaft of light broke through the treetops. The two moons were beginning their journey across the sky. Soon he would be able to see where he was going, maybe he'd find himself in familiar territory. He never liked the darkness, it brought back too many childhood memories, things he tried hard to forget.

Movement in the upper branches of the tall trees caught his attention. Looking up, he saw the dark shapes of tree-elves against the night sky. A couple of them descended, jumped down in front of him. They stood for a moment, studying him out of large purple eyes. One of them said something in their high-pitched language, then they turned and began walking down the path. Tom followed them. He had nowhere else to go.

It wasn't long before the path ended. They stepped into a large clearing, similar to the one close to the human's settlement. To one side there was a pond, a huge flowering plant floating in its middle. Tom saw a small group of alien females under the trees. They sat in a circle, watching something within the circle. Tom stared, it took him a moment to realize what was happening. Two of the girls were lying on their backs, between their wide spread legs moved two of the tree-elves.

The two with Tom let out a sharp high-pitched whistle, and then they ran toward the circle of females. Tom seemed forgotten. They never looked back. They jumped into the circle and stood waiting.

The two moons suddenly illuminated the clearing, and Tom was surprised to see the enormous size of the tree-elves' penis. Two of the females in the group that were watching, got up, walked into the center of the circle and lay down on the ground, their knees up and their thighs open. The two standing tree-elves fell between their inviting thighs and without preliminaries shoved their huge organ into the females.

As Tom stood watching, a half dozen more tree-elves broke from the tree branches above him. Running into the clearing, sprouting huge erections, they fell upon the waiting girls, and soon all of them were engaged in what Tom could only call an orgy.

Tom watched fascinated, suddenly becoming aware of the eerie silence. There were no sounds of pleasure or even heavy breathing. He saw one of the tree-elves stop rocking, saw his small buttocks quiver as he emptied his seeds into the female. Then he pulled out, moved over to another waiting female. The female he had been with got up, ran toward the pond and walked into it.

She was quite close to where Tom stood in the shadows of the trees. As he watched her, she peeled a semi-transparent, quivering sheet from below her belly. It contracted itself into an oval ball. She dropped it carefully into the water. Groping under the surface, she pulled out another quivering sheet and put it between her legs. It flowed up her belly, around the insides of her thighs, and part of it went inside her vagina.

She swirled her hands in the water again, pulled out another transparent sheet, this she put around her neck. Lifting her head, she looked straight at Tom. Then she climbed out of the water and came toward him.

He watched her come closer, looked into her green luminous eyes.

"The Mother has chosen me to speak to you," she said, smiling. "Why did you run away? You are not done yet."

Tom moaned. "What does she want from me? Why me?"

The girl shrugged. "Because the Great Mother wills it so." She ran her soft hand over his chest. "She promises you great pleasures still."

"I must speak to her directly." Tom fought the impulse to grab the girl, throw her to the ground and enter her lovely body.

"Very well." The girl took his hand, pulled him toward the pond. She stayed with him until he climbed onto the giant floating plant. "The Mother will come," she promised and waded back to shore.

Tom squatted on the edge of the great plant and watched the girl walk away. "I just want to get back home. See my wife again," he called after her.

A hand touched his shoulder.

"Thomas," said a familiar voice.

Startled, he turned to look into her smiling face. "Anina," he stammered. "How did you get here?" He studied her lovely naked body. She looked younger, more beautiful. She opened her arms. He flung himself into her embrace, hugged and kissed her hungrily. "I've missed you," he whispered into her ear. "I've missed you so much."

"I'm here now, Thomas," she said gently and kissed him back. "Make love to me," she whispered. "Now." She pulled him on top of her.

With a stifled cry, he entered her, cried out once more when the waves of pleasure washed through his body. Silently they worked against each other. She was tender and passionate, different then he remembered.

126

She was the way he always wanted her to be.

"I love you, Anina," he said, looking into her green eyes. "You have beautiful eyes, I've always loved them."

His lips fastened on her nipples; they seemed to grow longer as he sucked on them. He swallowed the sweet nectar flowing from them. "Your breasts, they seem larger," he murmured.

She laughed. "That's because you like them that way. Everything to please you, Thomas."

His body stiffened as he erupted inside her. When he made love to her the second time, she seemed even more passionate.

"Do you like it this way, Thomas?" she asked, as she milked his stiff penis.

"You know I do," he gasped, trying to hold back, but his control was slipping. He came with a mighty roar. After that he lay beside her among soft petals, looking up at the, by now, familiar stars. Overhead the two moons were parting already, soon the third one would rise.

"This is a beautiful world," he said dreamily, "maybe some day we can call it *home*." He turned to look at the profile of his wife, reached out to move a strand of auburn hair from her face. "Do you like it here?" he asked.

She smiled. "I like it here. It is home."

"I'm beginning to like it too, now that you are back with me." He stroked her cheek, ran his finger along her slender neck, over her breast. "Your skin is so soft," he murmured, lying back. Closing his eyes, he asked, "Have you spoken to Sister Angela lately?"

"Sister Angela? Do you desire her?"

He was beginning to feel drowsy, his answer came out slurred, "She's quite beautiful, you know. She is very desirable."

A pair of soft lips touched his. He opened his eyes.

"Brother Thomas." Sister Angela lay half on top of him. Strands of long blond hair tickled his cheeks. There was a soft glow in her blue eyes, and her beautiful smile lit up her face.

"What are you doing here? Where is Anina?"

Her lips brushed over his. "Hush. My dear sweet Brother Thomas. You seem unhappy, so I came to make you happy." Her soft hand touched his penis, stroked it until it was hard and solid, and then she straddled him. Her vagina was soft and moist. It closed around his penis like a tight velvety sheath. While she moved slowly on top of him, her blue eyes stared into his. Then she offered him her breast; he took the long nipple into his mouth, began sucking. Sweet nectar flowed down his throat,

127

giving him strength and endurance.

"Bless me with your gift, Brother Thomas," she whispered into his ear.

He lunged upwards, released his spermatic fluid with a loud cry of triumph. Her vagina was a pulsating, living thing around his spurting organ.

"Thank you, Brother Thomas," she said, as she kept moving untiring above him.

As the waves of pleasure surged through his body, his mind detached itself and began to wander. When his eyes focused on the woman above him, he looked into a pair of almond eyes.

She shook her long black hair out of her face and laughed. "Preacherman," she said, her black eyes sparkling.

"Orona!" His voice was suddenly hoarse, "what happened to Sister Angela?"

She lifted her slim shoulders, rotated her hips lazily above him. "She left. You were asleep, but sprouted such a wonderful erection, so I took advantage of you. I didn't think you would mind. I just want to make you happy." She snapped her hips, making him climax inside her. Her vagina sucked his seed into her womb.

He put his hands on her round buttocks, squeezed. As his fingers probed her back, they closed around a thick ropey thing growing out of her lower back.

He gasped, sudden understanding dawning in his murky mind. "You are not Orona!" he cursed.

She never stopped moving, just kept milking him.

"Stop it!" he shouted, fighting the urge to climax. "You are not human. You are a *Thing*!"

"Do I not please you, Preacher-man?" she asked in Orona's voice.

"You are not Orona!" he almost screamed.

"I can be anything you want me to be."

He stared into the icy blue eyes of Nurse Mabel, her blond hair longer than he remembered. It covered her large breasts, only the nipples poked through. She looked the way he would have liked her to look.

Her hips moved furiously in his lap, he cried out as a forceful climax gripped him.

"You see," she said when he finished, "it doesn't matter what I am. You do love me."

"I don't love you. You are an alien. I don't believe you know what love is. I love my wife. I love my daughters. In a way I also love Sister

Angela and Orona, but I don't love you."

The outlines of her body wavered again and changed.

Then he looked into a pair of luminous, green eyes. Her long hair was flaming red, it moved as if it had a life of its own. "I know your deepest inner thoughts now," she said. "You and I are one."

"Let me go," he pleaded. "I want to be with my own people, with my wife."

She slid off, kneeled beside him. "Go," she said. "I will walk with you."

He jumped into the water, not waiting for her, and waded toward shore. The clearing looked deserted, the alien girls and the tree-elves were gone. Overhead, only the red moon shined, its pale red light throwing dark shadows among the tall trees. Reaching the shore, he climbed out of the water. He walked without looking back.

A dull, sudden pain gripping his bowels, like a weight pulling on his anus, brought him to a halt. His hand went between his legs, what he encountered made him curse with anger and frustration.

A strand of thin, but extremely strong fibers grew from between his buttocks.

"What have you done?" he shouted hoarsely, turning to the alien woman, who stood beside him now.

"You and I are forever joined," she said. "I can give you eternal life."

"This is not living," he groaned. "I am your prisoner."

"Give it some time. Soon you will get used to it and you will realize that you are not living in a prison. As our systems integrate, we will be two separate minds living in one body and you have no idea how vast this body is. I am everywhere. *You* will be everywhere."

"How can I be everywhere?" he shouted. "A rope coming out of my ass ties me to you." He dug his fingers into her shoulders. "You are not even real! What are you? This is not your body."

She smiled and pointed toward the huge plant in the pond. "That is my body," she said, "and so is every *water lily* on this planet."

"But they are separate plants," Tom protested.

"They are, but I am in each one of them. If you would destroy one, it wouldn't matter. I cannot be destroyed. I am forever. I was born from darkness and became the *Mother of Light*. I am the Xandra." She stepped closer, kissing him on the lips. "You and I, we will populate this planet with a new species. It will be superior to my daughters and to the humans. You and I will be worshipped as gods. We will be gods." She took his hand. "Come, and I will make you happy. We can make love without ever stopping."

"Love?" He laughed hysterically. "What do you know about love? If you think that copulating all day long is *making love,* you know nothing. What I feel for my wife and my daughters, that is love. I love my parents, my brother and my sisters. That has nothing to do with sex."

"What about Sister Angela or Orona? You said you loved them also. Are you saying that is not so?"

"They attract me sexually, and maybe I feel even a certain love for them, how should I know?"

Tom felt a ghostly finger touch his mind.

"I don't understand that concept of *Love,*" she said slowly. "I see it in your mind, but I don't understand it."

"It is an abstract idea," Tom said, "you either love or you don't. It is the opposite of *hate.* It is a feeling. I cannot explain it."

"Maybe if I look like your wife or your daughter, could you learn to love me? I can be any woman you want me to be."

Shaking his head, he looked into her large alien eyes. "Whatever form you take," he said, "I will know that it is just an illusion."

"I can make you forget that," she said, almost tenderly.

"No, I won't let you mess with my mind." He grasped the strands of fibers attached to him and tried to pull them out of his body, but cried out as sharp pain shot through his belly.

"Come," she said gently. Again, he felt that ghostly touch, like a feather, brushing across his thoughts.

"All right," he said, letting her pull him back to the giant flower.

They stretched out among the petals, she held him in her arms. "Sleep now, my darling," she whispered. "When you awake you will think differently."

Chapter Twenty-four
Captain's Log
September 2, 2985

Last night I saw my wife. I know it is impossible, but she was there. In the park.

I've been thinking about her a lot lately.

I was standing at the edge of the pond, staring at the water lily, when I felt a gentle tab on my shoulder. I turned, and there she was, smiling at me. She looked just like I remembered her, lovely and full of soft curves. Her naked breasts were round and solid, a trifle larger than I remembered; her belly was flat, and her black pubic hair shaved into the shape of a heart, just like the way she used to do it.

"Hello, Jeremy," she said with that gentle voice of hers. "It's been a long time."

"Forty years," I said and stared at her, dumbfounded.

She put her arms around me, kissed me. She tasted of sweet honey.

My mind was numb. I couldn't think straight. Part of me wanted to push her away. I knew it couldn't really be her, but I had been missing her so much. When she pulled me to the ground, I made love to her right there beside the pond. We kissed, I swallowed the sweet nectar that flowed from her mouth. It gave me strength, endurance. How long we made love I don't know, but it must have been over an hour.

She was passionate, tender, and her body felt soft and yielding. When I climaxed inside her, it came with such force I thought my penis would explode. I don't remember ever experiencing an orgasm of that magnitude.

I fell asleep in her arms. When I awoke, she was gone.

I couldn't sleep anymore, so I went up to the observation deck to look at the planet below. It seemed to be calling to me. I could feel the pull inside my head.

Later I went back to my quarters and fell asleep on the couch.

When the lights came back on in the simulated morning, I wasn't sure if it happened or if I dreamed the whole thing.

Maybe I did.

But it seemed so real.

Chapter Twenty-five
Exploration Team Delta

Sara Golman took the young alien boy into her protective care, and he seemed to feel safe with her. Maybe it was because of her dark large eyes. Striker didn't know.

She named him Adam, and he accepted that name. He talked a lot in his alien, strange language and became frustrated when he wasn't understood.

"Tree," Sara said and pointed.

"Tree," he repeated, and smiled when she clapped her hands.

"Very good, Adam." She lifted a finger. "One tree," then she held up her hand. "Five trees."

"Five trees," he said.

"Excellent." She made a sweeping gesture. "Forest."

He looked at her with his huge purple eyes, shook his head and said, "*Selura.*"

"Selura?" Sara laughed. "I have absolutely no idea what you're saying."

Adam looked at Striker who sat on a rock, his laser across his knees. He pointed at the weapon, touched his lips and blew air from his mouth. "*Bluva,*" he said, his face grave, then he lay down on the ground, closed his eyes. Sitting up again, he stared at Striker.

The Lieutenant smiled grimly. "I have a feeling you know what this is." He touched the weapon and said, "This is *Death.*"

"Death." Adam repeated it slowly, nodded. "Death."

Striker looked toward the lake, watched a flock of large gray birds circling above the water. One of them dove down, claws outstretched, broke the dive at the last moment and rose again, an eel-like victim wriggling in its claws.

Sara followed his gaze. "We should give some serious thought to our own food situation," she said.

"I know. Gregorchuck has been studying the sea-creatures. He says they're safe to eat." Striker looked at Adam. "I've seen him pick and eat berries the other day. His metabolism isn't much different from ours."

Sara laughed. "He offered me some. I declined. I think he felt offended, but I didn't want to take a chance."

"We'll discuss the food situation tonight; maybe tomorrow we will dine on real meat." Striker rose, stretched his legs. "I'm going to check on the construction crew. Remember, stay close to the beach, and don't

132

wander away. Same goes for him."

He walked to where Chu was standing guard. The pilot nodded as Striker approached.

"How goes?" Striker asked.

"All's quiet." Chu cast a glance at the forest. "A family of *Monkeys* came nosing around for awhile this morning. I counted nineteen who ventured out into the open, but they left again."

"I don't think we have to worry about them," Striker said. "So far they've never bothered us. Keep your eyes open." He was heading for the site where most of the men and women were trying to erect a permanent shelter for the coming winter, when a short, paunchy man stopped him. Asham Sirski, the meteorologist.

"May I have a word?"

Striker nodded, surprised by the other man's agitation. "Problems?" he asked.

"Well, I'm not an expert when it comes to building structures, but I know weather and weather patterns. Back on the station, I've studied the first survey reports. It was winter then on this planet, most of the reports were sketchy, since all of the pictures and readings were taken from space. The recent studies came from Professor Tennenboum's team, but they only reported local conditions."

"I'm somewhat familiar with those reports," Striker said.

"Somewhat familiar." Sirski took a deep breath, his teeth gleamed white in his dark face. "That's the problem with you brass. You seem to know everything, yet, you lack detailed information."

"We have experts for that. Experts like you." Striker smiled. "Come to the point, Sirski."

"The point is...we will never survive in that flimsy building they are constructing. We'll be buried alive under three meters of snow in the first month of winter. And if by some miracle we should make it till spring, the level of the lake will rise, flooding us out."

"So what do you suggest?"

Sirski shrugged. "We could maybe move into the ancient town. Its elevation is much higher than our camp. There probably is a reason why the ancient builders chose that place. Some of the buildings have strong walls that can withstand the brutal winter storms, and believe me, they will be brutal and ferocious. The walls will also insulate us from the bitter cold. I've seen one building with a still functioning fireplace and a roof that is almost intact. It wouldn't take much to make it livable. You should talk to Professor Findlay, he spends all his time up there. By now he should know every building and its condition."

"You've given this some thought, haven't you?" Striker studied the short man and wondered why they never talked before. Sirski usually stayed in the background, didn't talk much with anyone.

"I don't want you to think I'm trying to undermine your authority, Lieutenant, but this is a very important issue. Our lives are at stake here, and I don't want to die on this planet. I'll try my best to survive. When you decided that we should leave the security of the shuttle you made a judgment call, most of us went along with it." Sirski fidgeted. "This time I think you should take it to a vote. It should not be left for you to decide."

"I'll bring it up tonight. There are a few other items we all need to discuss."

"Thank you, Lieutenant." Sirski looked visibly relieved. "If you want me to, I am willing to explain it to the others."

"Sure, that might be helpful." Striker began to walk away. He stopped, looked back. "I appreciate your suggestion, Sirski. I am as concerned with our survival as you are."

A few of the men were just trying to fit a heavy log into place when Striker walked up to them. Three of the walls were almost high enough. One side of the large square building was still open. This would be the wall with the entrance and a couple of windows. None of the men had ever worked or even been on a construction site. The only one with some experience was Kendrick, but he had designed structures made out of steel and glass, not wood.

"Are you coming to give us a hand, Striker?" Remington put down the laser he was using to trim one of the logs, rubbed his hands on his trousers. "Or is it against the rules for military people to do manual labor?"

"If there are such rules, I've never followed them," Striker said, trying to keep his voice level and cool. The man kept rubbing him the wrong way, and it was not easy to stay calm in his presence. "Maybe you should all take a break, something has been brought to my attention and I'm calling a meeting for tonight."

"Bad news?" asked Monaca. She and Tamara Mogatas were just coming out of the forest, carrying a long, heavy log on their shoulders. Lowering her end onto the ground, Tamara stretched and rolled her neck.

"Whatever it is, it can't be much worse than this. Having the afternoon off will give me a chance to carry on with my studies. I've discovered some interesting beetle larvae on those trees."

"I'm going for a swim," announced Monaca and looked at Breanna, who was still busy stuffing moss into the cracks where the rough tree trunks joined. She looked up from her work. "I'll join you a little later. All right?"

"I'll come with you. I feel all sweaty and grimy. This is not my kind of work." Andrea Liss did a few limbering exercises. Striker noticed some of the men watching her and he couldn't blame them. She had taken off her top, and even though her breasts were not large, they were well formed and the rest of her body was trim. A pleasure to look at. And she didn't mind displaying it.

"A swim sounds good to me," said Fried Kramer. It was no secret that he had taken an interest in Andrea Liss. He wasn't the only one. Striker noticed Herm Woolf spending more time than necessary in the company of the good doctor.

"Do whatever you want. I want to see everybody tonight, after supper." He turned and walked away.

One of the other women, Melina Mohawk, a dark-haired thin woman with a broad, flat nose and thick lips, followed him, and grabbed his arm. "Well, Lieutenant, we haven't had much of a chance to sit down and talk, you've been brushing me off. Do you think this afternoon would be a good time?"

Striker looked into her brown eyes. She gave him a broad smile. He knew what she wanted. "I'm busy," he said and walked on.

She laughed. "You're always busy, sticking it into Breanna, the green-eyed goddess."

He stopped, stared at her. "There are plenty of other men, Melina. What's your obsession with me?"

"I find you attractive, and I am horny. I need a man, but not any man. I want you. Am I that ugly to look at?"

"I don't think you're ugly. Like I said, there are others. Have you asked any of them?"

Her laughter was mocking. "Others? Now let's see, there is Raymond Chu. He is not my type, his eyes are shaped the wrong way. Maybe some day I'll explain what I mean. Then there are Professor Banca, Professor Findlay, and Ewor Gregorchuck. Every one of them is too busy with their studies. Remington is not a man I want to *ever* find between my legs, and neither is Ashim Sirski. You've seen the way Woolf, Kramer, and Kendrick drool all over 'Smoldering Eyes' Dr. Andrea Liss. That leaves Marcel Girard and you, Poul. In fact, only you, because Marcel has no interest in women. He told me so. He prefers men."

It was Striker's turn to laugh. "I like the way you worked it all out.

Not very flattering, actually."

"I am a very passionate woman, Poul. What does Breanna give you that I couldn't? You'd never know the difference in the dark. My breasts are large, my vagina tight and soft. I'm easily aroused. What else do you want?"

"How about love, Melina?" Striker smiled.

"I can give you that. In time." Her fingers dug into his biceps, almost hurtful. "Does Breanna love you?"

They arrived beside the cluster of tents. Striker sat down on the bench someone built from rocks and branches. He looked up at the woman, who stared at him out of large brown eyes. It wasn't that he found her unattractive. She looked pretty enough, but his commitment was to Breanna, and he never cheated on any of the women he became involved with. There had only been two, but that didn't matter.

He admitted, the thought of having sex with two different women did actually turn him on. "Have you talked with Breanna about how you feel?" he asked softly.

"No, I haven't. Should I?"

"Maybe you should. Don't tell her I suggested it." *What the hell was he saying? What was he thinking?* He got to his feet. "Maybe we should forget this conversation ever took place."

She smiled. "I understand." She touched his hand. "I'm joining the others for a swim. Want to come?"

"I have things to do. Maybe later."

She turned and ran toward the water. He watched her take off her clothes. She did actually have a finely formed body, not hard to look at.

"What was all that about?"

Striker turned to look at Breanna, who came out of one of the tents. She was naked, looking extremely attractive to him, even though dark streaks of perspiration and dirt ran down between her full breasts, and her red hair was hanging in a tangled mess.

"You are so beautiful," he said.

She laughed and blew him a kiss. "You're just saying that so you can get me into your sleeping bag."

"Would you come if I didn't tell you that I find you beautiful?"

"Probably not. A woman wants to hear flattering things." She gave him a thoughtful look. "You never answered my question."

"You mean Melina?" He waved it off. "Nothing important. She was just venting."

"I see. Well, I'm going to wash up." She touched his nose and walked away. He watched her plump buttocks, the way they moved gently and suggestively under smooth white skin.

She never told me that she loved me, he thought. *Do I love her or is this just a sexual attraction? What is the difference between love and lust?* He shrugged and turned to find Ewor Gregorchuck standing beside him. The big man grinned and tugged on his beard. "She's a woman of fire, Striker. Hang on to her. I've seen others leering at her."

"You?"

"Perhaps." Gregorchuck laughed, then dropped his voice to a whisper. "Actually, I have my eyes on Tamara Mogates, but that woman is too damn busy with her bugs. Maybe I should look for someone else. By the way, I've had a conversation with Sirski, and he has a good point. I agree with him, we should try to move into the ancient site."

"We'll discuss it tonight," Striker said. "How about you and I taking a stroll through those ruins. I'd like to have some facts backing me when I bring it up tonight."

Sirski had been right; they could transform a few buildings into livable quarters. They found Professor Findlay digging inside a deep pit. He looked up from his work, waved a hand. "I think this used to be either a bathing pool or a pond where they kept fish," he called out of the pit. "Come on down and check this out."

Striker and Gregorchuck climbed down a makeshift ladder. "Are you sure this thing is safe?" Gregorchuck bellowed.

Findlay laughed. "It wasn't built for overweight people like you, but I believe it should support your weight. It's not that far down, should you fall."

Rocks and dead leaves littered the bottom of the pit. Deep crevices held water from the last rain.

"They were sophisticated people," Findlay said. "Look at this." He pointed at a deep crack that formed around a large, round hole. "It looks like a drain, at one time a removable lid probably covered it."

"I hope you keep records of all your findings," Striker said. "Maybe some day somebody will read them."

"I certainly hope so." Findlay wiped the perspiration from his forehead. "What brings you here?"

"There is a meeting tonight. We'll need your input, Professor. We're thinking of moving up here for the winter."

"I think it's an excellent idea." Findlay nodded his approval. "Even though they are old, some of these buildings are still very solid."

Deciding to take that swim in the lake, Striker went back to the camp.

He found Sara and Adam sitting on the beach. The alien boy was drawing something in the sand.

"I think he is trying to show me where his people live," Sara said. "I have a feeling he is homesick."

"Aren't we all?" Striker smiled at Adam who pointed at himself and then at the far mountains to the south. "A long way from home. Just like us. You have no idea."

He stripped and walked into the water. The lake was calmer than usual. Lying on his back, he let the gentle waves lap over his body. There were only a few clouds above. He remembered growing up at his parent's farm on Earth, remembered a day like this when he looked into the blue, cloudless sky and dreamed about going into space. In his imagination, he visited alien planets and met their exiting inhabitants.

This, he thought, *has not been in my dream.*

The touch of a hand ripped him from his daydream. Sitting up, he saw Sara kneeling in the water beside him, her naked breasts like two pendulums swinging in front of his eyes.

"Did I startle you?" she asked.

"A little. I was just thinking of home."

"Will we ever get back?" Her dark eyes seemed to study him, her gaze traveled down to his exposed penis. She smiled, rose out of the water. He stared at the small triangle of hair that covered her thick vulva. "I get very lonely sometimes," she said with a low and husky voice. "Breanna is a lucky woman." She dove into the water and swam away from him.

Later, when everybody was sitting around the campfire, Striker brought up the issue of food first. All agreed to start living off what this planet might have to offer. The suggestion to move the shelter into the ancient city was, at first, welcomed with protests. "You mean, after working so hard you want us to tear down our new building?" Rhea asked.

"It's either that or having it collapse on top of us later," Ashim Sirski said. "And besides, I wouldn't call it a building, yet."

Oddly enough, Breanna was the one who argued more than anyone else did. She seemed to blame Striker for choosing this site in the first place. "What about all these trees we cut down?"

"I wouldn't worry about that." Sirski defended Striker. "We will need a lot of firewood. It is going to be cold."

At the end of the meeting everyone agreed. Work on the new site would begin the next day.

Breanna didn't join Striker in his tent that night. Mian, who sometimes shared the tent with him, decided to sleep under the stars, as he did most of the time. It seemed to Striker that he hardly slept when someone unzipping his sleeping bag awakened him. Sleepily, without opening his eyes, he murmured, "So you decided to come, after all."

A warm naked body slid on top of him, soft breasts pressed against his chest.

"Did you expect me?" a female voice whispered.

"I was hoping," he said, took her into his arms. Hot lips touched his, a tongue snaked into his mouth. It didn't take long for him to become aroused.

She grabbed his penis and with a deep sigh impaled herself, sliding her moist sheath easily over his engorged member. Moving feverishly above him, she cried out softly when she experienced her first orgasm.

He turned her onto her back, slid his hard rod into her soft flesh. Lying between her cradling thighs, he rocked on top of her writhing body for a long time, making her climax several times. Finally, he couldn't hold back any longer. Suppressing a triumphant shout, he pushed deep and exploded inside her pulsing vagina, digging his fingers into her fleshy, clenching buttocks.

When it was over, she lay in his arms. She stroked his chest with gentle fingers. He held her tight, didn't know if he should be angry with her or with himself.

She laughed suddenly and sat up. "I better go. I wouldn't want to fall asleep in here."

"You're right," he said and kissed her gently. After her first climax, he had known.

"Thank you, Poul," she said, softly. "I enjoyed it very much."

He watched her shadowy figure leave the tent.

"So did I, Sara," he whispered.

Chapter Twenty-six
Alpha Colony

The tender touch of a pair of soft lips on his eyelids brought him back to consciousness. Opening his eyes, he felt disoriented for a moment. His perception of his surroundings seemed different. It was bright, and yet, the two moons were just beginning their journey. The air seemed different, too. He could distinguish a multitude of fragrances.

"Did you sleep well, my darling?" asked a soft voice beside his ear.

He looked into her luminous green eyes and smiled. "Thank you, I did. As a matter fact, I feel fabulous."

She was so beautiful. He admired her beauty, inhaled her fragrance. Her flaming hair cascaded in loose curls over her smooth shoulders; her lips were full and red, with a tinge of purple, and her breasts round and shapely. When he sucked on them, he drank from the sweet nectar they offered.

Soon he was locked in her embrace. She took him into her, brought him to a shattering climax. He shouted his joy with primeval savageness, filled her vessel with his seed. They would create a new race of beings, superior to anything on this planet. The first of the pods would soon split open. He lay in her cradling arms, content and happy.

"Close your eyes," she said. "I will take you on a journey through our kingdom."

He closed his eyes, the momentary darkness was replaced by bright images. Looking through her eyes, he saw a different place. Another pond, he recognized it as the women's bathing place.

He saw Sister Angela and her flock. Sister Angela stood with her arms reaching into the sky. Forming a circle around her, the girls stood watching two people on the ground. One of the girls was on her knees, behind her a young man. His naked buttocks snapped back and forth, clenching every time he lunged forward. Sounds of soft chanting filled the air.

Then the scene changed. There was a small group of people not far from Sister Angela, men and women locked together in various positions.

He saw Anina, his wife. She was straddling a man. Tom couldn't see his face, but he had a good view of the spot that joined him to Anina. She kept her face upturned, toward the rising moon. Her buttocks moved furiously in the man's lap.

The images were sharp and clear. Every time the man lifted up Tom could see his penis for a quick moment, then Anina's descending sex-organ swallowed it up again. As if looking through a telescope, Tom could almost see the puffy lips behind Anina's auburn pubic hair, saw them mold themselves around the man's thick penis, saw the rippling of her flat stomach.

One part of him felt outraged, the other indifferent. He recognized the thin film of transparent matter covering Anina's belly and pubic area. Tom felt strangely elated when Anina cried out and quivered in the man's lap, as she accepted his seeds into her.

Anina lifted off the man, ran to the pond and entered the water. Then she peeled off the jelly-like film, held it in her hands as it changed shape, let the oval ball with its precious seeds slide into the water. Soon a pod would form; life would grow inside it.

Tom watched her swoop out another seed pouch, saw her put it over her pubis. She went back to the man she coupled with. This time she dropped to her knees; her pale round buttocks were up, her back arched. The man moved behind her, guided his erect penis between her slightly spread thighs, his hips snapped forward and Tom could see the thick pole slide into Anina's sex-canal.

Tom had seen the man before, but he didn't really know him. He was one of the agricultural specialists, young and handsome. No wonder Anina picked him. And there was no doubting his sexual prowess. His lean buttocks moved with great vigor, his muscular belly slapped into Anina's soft buttocks with every forward thrust. Strong hands held her hips to keep her steady. Her belly rippled and her breasts shook as she pushed backward to meet the young man's thrusts, and her cries of pleasure blended with the man's loud satisfied grunts.

There were loud cries and moans echoing through the whole clearing.

Tom's view changed again. He saw a small, shapely young woman, her almond eyes small slits and her full lips open, as she was bouncing on top of an older man, heard her cry out when the man spilled his seeds into her.

Orona! Tom watched her plunge into the water of the pond to replace the filled seed pouch. Then she went back to straddle another man.

It was good to see the human colony create new life. Humans were vigorous. Their sexual activities were not influenced by seasonal cycles. The two genders, male and female, copulated not only for the species' propagation, but also for pleasure. Some members were governed by restrictive morals, but that could be overcome. They were basically animals with a certain degree of intelligence. Their sex-drive was strong, which made them relatively easy to control. The most important key was the pleasure factor. Humans would do anything for pleasure.

Tom experienced a momentary darkness, and then he was looking at a different scene.

He seemed to be floating in the water at the edge of a small lake. To his right loomed high mountains, in front of him were rolling hills, covered with short grass. There were trees on the land, but they were not as tall as the ones he was used to.

On the shore, underneath the trees, a large group of people was engaged in sexual activities. They were humans, but strangers to Tom. He guessed that these must be the settlers from Beta-Colony.

All were naked, except one. A man, wearing a long black cape and a black hat, stood watching the copulating men and women. His voice rang out suddenly, "This is wrong! You will all be punished, you sinners! The wrath of God is terrible!"

Nobody paid attention to him.

Why was this man not affected by the pheromones in the spores? Why did he not respond to the mental broadcast? This needed to be studied more closely.

A simulacrum grew out of a sister plant floating nearby. A woman. Her coal-black hair long and flowing, her skin as white as pure ivory. Climbing out of the water, she walked slowly toward the man in the black cloak.

The man held his hands in front of him, his fingers formed a cross. "Go back to the hell that has spawned you, *Demon-woman!*" he shouted. "I will not succumb to your temptation!"

"I am not a demon," the woman said softly. "Look, I am an angel." From her shoulders sprouted suddenly a pair of wings. She spread them and opened her arms. "I have come to give you a taste of heaven, Preacher. Come!" She stood in front of him, looked into his eyes. The thick mat of black curly hair that covered her genitals beckoned.

He stared at her, the epitome of all women. Perfect, tall and beautiful, with large round breasts, a smooth flat belly, and long slim legs.

Tom saw the fine strands of fibers that came out of the small of her back, the strands that connected her to the mother-plant.

The man in black groaned, lifted his arms high. "Forgive me for what I am about to do, but I cannot fight this battle any longer." With that he threw open his cape to display a huge erection. He fairly threw himself at the winged woman in front of him. She received him in her arms, slid to ground and spread her legs wide. With a shout the man entered her, moved like a berserker between her clutching thighs.

So much for religion and morality. These humans possessed weak minds.

Tom heard the silent laughter of the Xandra, then the scene went blank and he found himself looking at Sister Angela. She was standing in the water in front of the great plant. Beside him stood Anina.

"Great Mother," Sister Angela said. "I have done as you requested. My Angels have coupled with many men; they have filled a great number of seed pouches. You said that none of the girls would get pregnant, yet I find myself with child."

"Was it not your wish to have a child of your own?" The Xandra spoke softly.

"Yes, it was." Sister Angela hesitated, "but I don't know if it is appropriate. You see, I am single and the leader of a convent. I am supposed to be chaste. Sometimes, during the day, I feel great guilt for the things we have done, my Angels and I. I thought we left all this behind us. This new place, here, was supposed to be a new way of life for us."

"My child," the Xandra said, "you have done nothing wrong. This is all part of *The Great Plan* in which you and your Angels play an important part. You are living a new life. This has all been ordained, you will be the mothers of a new race of men. You have my blessing."

"Thank you, Great Mother." Sister Angela smiled happily.

"I have a problem also." It was Anina who spoke.

The Xandra's attention shifted to Anina. "Yes, my daughter?"

"I also have had sex with many men. I let them climax inside me so your seed pouches could be filled. It is not that I didn't enjoy it. I never knew sex could be so pleasurable. I am not a nun, I never promised not to have sex, but I consider myself a religious person. Besides, I am married. You said you would find my husband for me."

"That is what I told you, and it will be so."

Tom felt elated when he heard the Xandra speak, but his hopes were dashed when he heard the next words.

"Look to your right."

Through the plant's *eyes* Tom saw. On one of the smaller floating plants crouched a naked figure, a man. He stood up, smiled. He was tall, not young, maybe in his forties, but well built, with handsome features. The top of his head was covered with thick carrot-red hair. Tom had never seen him before, yet, he looked strangely familiar.

Anina let out a loud sob. "Thomas!" she cried, "where are you coming from?"

The man jumped into the water, waded toward her. "I was lost, but I found my way home again." He took Anina into his arms, hugged and kissed her.

"Oh, Thomas, Thomas, I've missed you so much."

"*That is not me!*" Tom shouted, but realized that he was not physically there, just his mind. "What are you doing?" he cursed. "Why are you doing this? She'll know it's not me."

The Xandra laughed silently in his head. "She'll never know, just watch."

"*You* watch! As soon as that thing reaches the end of the rope..."

Tom found his consciousness suddenly back in his own body. He stared at the alien woman with the flaming hair. She changed the form of her eyes, they were human looking, slightly slanted, but still green.

She knew him so well.

"How can that... that thing that looks like me fool my wife?" he asked.

"Thomas, my dear Thomas, you don't know the extent of my intellect. I am continuously evolving, changing. I have learned a lot from you." The woman smiled, touched his cheek. "Your wife will never be able to tell the difference between the real you and my creation. I have grown an exact double of you. That double has your memories, your knowledge, your likes and dislikes. He behaves just like you, because he is you."

"I don't believe you. You don't know everything about me."

She kissed him on the lips, gently. "I know you better than you know yourself, dear. Come, make love to me, it's almost dawn and I want to show you something else."

He tried to fight it, but it was useless. Between his legs, his penis became painfully stiff. She took over his mind and body. He entered her softness with a savage thrust, crying out as the pleasure overwhelmed him. Looking into her eyes, he moved above her. There was a sudden shift in his awareness, and then he cried out hoarsely.

The woman underneath him chuckled. "Easy, my husband, we have lots of time. These last few days away from me have done you good. You look younger, more muscular, and..." she giggled. "I think you've grown bigger and harder down there."

"Anina, I..." he said, but the next words would not come. "*This is not me!*" his mind screamed. "*This is an imposter!*" Instead, he heard himself say, "I love you."

"And I love you," Anina said and gasped as she experienced her first orgasm. He felt her body spasm, felt his own climax approaching, came with a roar of triumph. Still hard, he kept moving between his wife's spread thighs.

"Oh, Thomas," she breathed, "you have changed."

"This is not me!" he screamed again. "What is happening?"

He looked into the sky. Above the trees the red moon was rising.

A sudden wrenching and he looked around wildly. He was back in the alien woman's embrace, his pelvis thrusting furiously.

"Stop it!" he shouted, but his body wouldn't obey, he kept on thrusting into her clutching sex-organ.

"You see, you can be with your wife any time you wish, or at least when I let you. It will be just like being there yourself, you won't know the difference." She pulled his face down, kissed him, fed him her sweet nectar. He swallowed eagerly.

"I love you, Thomas," she whispered into his ear and in his mind.

"I love you, too," he said and cried as he spilled his seed into her.

Chapter Twenty-seven
Beta Colony

They were lying behind the concealment of some low shrubs, watching in fascination the couples on the shore.

"Isn't that Mrs. Armesto over there?" Mandy whispered.

Rosanha looked to where Mandy was pointing. An older woman, her sagging breasts bouncing up and down, was straddling a man who was hidden by some clumps of high grass. But they could clearly see his stiff mast for a fleeting moment as the woman lifted up. Her hand reached down to guide it back into her thick dark triangle.

Rosanha giggled. "That's our cook all right, churning up something." Her own vagina itched. She touched herself. *I can't bear to watch this much longer,* she thought. *What happened to me? I never felt like this before.* She looked up into the sky. The two satellites were bright in the clear night sky, moving toward each other.

"Look over there," Lillith said beside her. "That is Larry Tyvek. He is not much older than we are. I never knew he had such a huge trunk."

The girls watched the young man take position behind a kneeling woman. Her fleshy buttocks gleamed white in the moonlight. With deliberate slowness, the young man put his dark stiff penis between the woman's buttocks. She arched her spine, pushed backward, and took the thick pole deep into her. His lean hips moved slowly back and forth, every time he pushed forward her fleshy white buttocks flattened against his dark belly.

Not far from them, another couple was locked in deep embrace. The woman had her back against a tree; her legs were wrapped tightly around the naked body of a slightly chubby man. She turned her head, her face suddenly became clearly visible.

Rosanha gasped, beside her Mandy let out her breath with an audible sound. "Don't look, Rosanha," she whispered fiercely. "Ignore it!"

Rosanha couldn't take her eyes away and watched the man's buttocks clench every time his pelvis snapped forward as he pushed his penis into her mother's belly. His hands went under Theresa's buttocks, then he stepped back, lowered her to the ground. She kept her legs wrapped around him, her arms still tight around his thick neck. Lying on her back now, she opened her legs wider to let her knees touch the ground. The man moved furiously on top of her.

The girls were close enough to hear his labored breathing and Theresa's soft moans of pleasure.

"Look, look," Mandy called out, "there is Father Champain."

A tall, gaunt man with a long beard and dressed in a black cloak, strode among the copulating couples. "This is wrong. You will all be punished, you sinners!" he thundered.

As the girls watched, they saw a woman with long, flowing black hair rising out of the water. She walked toward the man in black. Father Champain made the sign of the cross with his fingers. "Go back to the hell that has spawned you, *Demon-woman!*" his voice rang out hoarsely.

"This is massive," Lillith whispered, "I think I'm going *Nova.*"

The black-haired woman spread a pair of white wings, stood in front of the preacher. Father Champain flung open his black cloak, ripped it off his shoulders; he was a thin man, his body gaunt and lean, but his huge penis shocked the girls.

"This is absolutely *Total,*" Mandy whispered. They watched, almost in horror, as Father Champain threw himself into the arms of the strange winged woman, watched him drive his large, erect penis into her. She laughed as she received him; her long legs were wide open, and her fingers dug into his lean buttocks. His hoarse shouts rang through the moonlit night, echoed across the lake.

"I am going *Nova,*" Lillith whispered again. "Father Champain! Who would have thought!"

"Where is that friend of yours?" Mandy asked Rosanha, her face flushed. Her chest rose and fell as her breathing became faster.

"I met him at the south-shore," Rosanha said, still watching Father Champain and the woman from the lake.

Who was that woman? What was she?

They changed positions. Father Champain turned onto his back, the woman moving on top of him. Her long black hair fluttered in the soft breeze that came from the lake. Her eyes glowed with a strange fire, but that could be the reflection of the moonlight.

Something didn't seem right, there were no wings sprouting from her shoulders, but Rosanha remembered seeing them. Had she been hallucinating? She rose to her feet. "Come. Let's go."

The girls ran through the shrubbery, past the naked moaning couples under the trees. The south shore was not far. There was nobody there. Panting, the girls stood on the sandy beach and stared at the slightly rippling water.

"Where is he?" asked Lillith.

"I don't know." Rosanha turned away, disappointed, and almost bumped into someone standing behind her.

"You brought some friends," said a familiar voice.

"It is you," Rosanha stammered. "I was hoping I'd find you here."

The young man laughed and pulled her close. "Are you ready to play?" he asked and kissed her on the mouth.

She kissed him back, hungrily as sweet honey trickled down her throat. Her mind began to spin, she forgot her friends. She let him put her onto the ground, let him push up her dress. She was naked underneath. Her legs opened to his touch, and then he pushed inside her. He felt hard and big, filling her completely. She cried out, the cause was not pain. His penis felt hot and wonderful inside her young vagina. He moved with steady, powerful strokes between her wide spread thighs. Waves of pleasure radiated from her groin area, spread throughout her body. It wasn't long before she experienced her first orgasm. He waited until she peaked, the he climaxed inside her. His hot discharge filled her young vessel to the brim.

When he was done he pulled out of her, looked at Lillith and Mandy, who stood dumbfounded beside them. "Are your friends just watching or do they want to play, too?" he asked, grinning.

Mandy gulped, looked at the young man's erection. "I'll have some of that," she breathed and pulled her dress over her head. Naked, she slid to the ground. On her knees, she whispered, "What do you want me to do?"

"Just lie back and pull up your knees," he said, laughing. "Haven't you done this before?"

Mandy did as he asked, watched as he moved on top of her. He put his hands on her breasts; they were firm and round, larger than what was normal for a girl her age. A gasp escaped her open lips. With large eyes she stared at his stiff pole. "You are big," she whispered. "I hope you fit inside me. I've never done it with someone this big."

He laughed again, guided his penis into her sparse golden fluff and rubbed the head gently between her thick labia. Mandy moaned, reached down to guide his organ. "Put it in already," she gasped and cried out when he pushed down and entered her.

Rosanha watched the thick pole slide into Mandy's vagina, listened to her friend's ecstatic cries as the young man *fogged* her with long, deep strokes. Her own body was still tingling, her sex-organ burning with desire.

"This is massive, so massive," said a breathless voice beside her ear.

Rosanha almost forgot about Lillith, now also completely naked.

"I need it now," Lillith moaned. She lay down beside Mandy, with her legs wide open. The young man quivered in Mandy's embrace, then he pulled out, still stiff, and moved over to Lillith. Without a word, he entered her, his hands on Lillith's small breasts.

A soft mewling sound came from Lillith's throat. Her breath became ragged as she moved her slim body with snake-like motions. "Fogg me hard!" she screamed and slammed her hips up against his. "Don't hold back. I can take everything you've got."

Rosanha and Mandy lay on their stomachs beside the pair and watched with breathless fascination as the young stranger from Alpha-Colony rammed his massive organ with untiring persistence into Lillith's demanding sex-canal.

"She's like a snake," whispered Mandy. "I never knew she was so... "

"Sex-crazy?" Rosanha said.

Lillith screamed and clawed at the ground, while her body shook in the grip of an orgasm. The young man held her tightly to him, his buttocks quivered between the girl's clutching thighs. He pulled out and rose to his feet. He wasn't even breathing hard. "I like this sex-game," he said and laughed. "Want to play some more?"

Rosanha and Mandy nodded, their eyes glued to his stiff member. Rosanha licked her lips. "Can I suck on it?" she asked with a breathless voice. He moved in front of her, she put her lips on the shiny head, let her tongue flicker across it. Then she opened her mouth wide and sucked the warm, rigid flesh into her.

He stood still, watching her from shiny black eyes.

Closing her eyes, she sucked gently and swallowed when she felt warm liquid filling her mouth. It tasted sweet and strange, but not unpleasant. Like nectar from an exotic flower. It ran down her throat, a hot flame that spread fire through her whole body. She opened her eyes, looked into his and shuddered. He seemed to look deep into her soul.

"Enough," he said softly and slowly pulled his penis out of her mouth.

Her mind was not clear, her insides burned, her vagina was inflamed. "I need you," she whispered.

He nodded. "Kneel down," he ordered her. Looking at Mandy and Lillith, he said, "You too."

The girls knelt side by side in front of him, their backs arched and their firm buttocks high. He entered Rosanha first, pushed deep into her. She cried out sharply, began bucking immediately. After a few strokes he pulled out, moved over to Mandy. She just moaned. Her face hit the ground as she lifted her buttocks higher. Then he left her, too. He put his pole between Lillith's white cheeks. Lillith went wild and milked his penis fiercely.

He didn't stay long inside her before moved back to Rosanha. This time she almost screamed as he slid into her inflamed tight canal. "Make me come," she sobbed, "please, make me come."

He laughed softly behind her, held her narrow waist and slammed his hips with steady rhythmic movements into her soft buttocks. This time he waited until she finished an orgasm before he pulled out.

Then he did the same to Mandy and to Lillith.

Rosanha lost track of time. How many times he came back to her, she didn't know. The two moons put a great distance between themselves when he asked them to join him for a swim in the lake.

Rosanha felt satisfied, her body still tingled when she followed him and her two friends into the water. She felt very tired all of a sudden and was quite happy when he suggested they rest on top of the giant floating plant. She lay down among the thick, soft petals and closed her eyes.

* * * *

When she awoke, it was daylight. She didn't remember falling asleep, but remembered strange dreams. Sitting up, she looked around, but didn't see Mandy or Lillith. The floating plant she sat on was much smaller than when she climbed onto it. She realized it was not the same plant. There were two other plants of the same size, and when she looked at them, she noticed movement in the center of the closer one.

Someone sat up, a girl. She recognized Mandy. She looked around as if to orient herself, then she waved.

Rosanha waved back. "Where is Lillith?" she called. Before Mandy could answer, Rosanha saw Lillith on the third plant. Lillith slid into the water, swam toward Rosanha.

"I feel quite strange," she said and climbed onto the plant, flopping down beside Rosanha. "What a night," Lillith said. "But everything seems kind of fuzzy. I don't seem to be myself this morning."

"I feel the same way," Rosanha said. "I know I am me and yet, there is this feeling of newness, like everything I remember is somebody else's memory and I was just born. I can't really explain it." She looked at Lillith. "Why are you laughing?"

"I wasn't laughing," Lillith said, "I thought it was you."

More laughter, a woman's laughter. It came from inside Rosanha's head.

"You exceed my expectations, daughters. I am very pleased."

"Who said that?" asked Lillith and pressed her hands against her ears. "It seemed to come from inside my brain."

"I am the *Xandra*," said the woman's voice, "and you are my daughters. You are of the *Xandra*."

Rosanha looked around, perplexed. There was only Lillith beside her. "Who are you?" she asked. "And where are you?"

"I am the plant you are sitting on, Rosanha. I am also the plant Lillith found herself on when she woke up, and I am the one Mandy is on right now. I am every *water lily,* as the humans call it, on this planet. I am the water that nourishes these plants. I am the *Xandra*."

"Why do you call us *my daughters*?"

"Because you are. I have grown you out of my body."

"You are wrong!" Rosanha protested. "I wasn't grown from a plant. I am a human being. I am Rosanha Wilson."

"Yes, you are Rosanha Wilson. You have her memories, but your body came from me. I made you."

There was a sudden flash of light inside Rosanha's mind as the Xandra tore down the mental barriers she temporarily erected. Rosanha understood, so did Lillith and so did Mandy.

"We are sisters now." Mandy laughed inside Rosanha's head.

"We are." Rosanha nodded. She had difficulties accepting what she knew to be the truth. She was not human anymore, and yet, she felt human.

The Xandra, who followed her thoughts, said gently, "Even though your body wasn't born from a human woman, you are nevertheless human. I made you that way, except, I made you better."

"What happened to the real Rosanha?"

"She is alive inside you."

"Where is her body?" Rosanha asked, but she knew the answer before she asked the question.

"It was only a body. Quite inferior to the one you now own," the Xandra said soothingly. "The mind is what is important."

Rosanha looked over to the giant plant that floated not far away and shuddered a little.

"I need nourishment, too," said the Xandra inside her head. "You will go back to the human colony. Nobody will know what you are. I have given you free will, I will not control you, but if you need me, I am never far away. Good luck, my daughters."

The presence inside Rosanha's head was gone, but she knew it was

just an illusion; the Xandra would always be inside her.
  Because she *was* the *Xandra.*

Chapter Twenty-eight
Space Station

He called himself Starfinder, his species Genaar, which, translated, meant *Above Animals*.

He smiled when Cunningham asked him about his name. "In my younger days I used to be a pilot," he said with his deep, resonant voice. "But that was a long time ago."

It was Captain Cunningham's turn to smile. "Couldn't have been that long ago," he said. "You look much too young for that."

Starfinder laughed. "Not counting the thousand years I was frozen, I am over 200 years old, your years. Our species is long-lived."

"And here I thought I was old," Cunningham said. "I am 90."

"An infant," Starfinder said and chuckled.

"I feel like an infant," Cunningham mused. "Compared with your species mine is still in its infancy. Your people were already exploring the Galaxy when we were still dreaming about the stars and wondering what was out there."

"That is so," Starfinder agreed, "but you have progressed quite rapidly, once you discovered space-travel. It took us longer than that to reach neighboring systems. Now you are beginning to colonize yours. Your home planet Earth is far away from here."

Cunningham nodded and studied the alien, trying to be discreet about it. He knew Starfinder also studied him. This was the first time they finally found a chance for a private meeting. Awakening the rest of the alien sleepers happened without any glitches. All were healthy and in good spirits. Twenty-eight of the aliens were women. Twenty-two were men. The men all looked young and handsome, and the women beautiful. Cunningham corrected himself. Not merely beautiful, they were gorgeous, with slim, well-formed bodies. Their purple eyes a trifle too large, but it only enhanced their beauty.

"Thank you for not destroying any of our equipment when you moved into our station," Starfinder broke into his thoughts.

"And I thank you for not evicting us." Cunningham smiled. "We assumed the station was abandoned. Even now, after a month, I have a problem accepting your presence here. I'm amazed at your ability to learn our language so fast."

Starfinder chuckled and touched a spot behind his ear. "Thanks to a tiny computer inside my head. It really is old technology. In our sector of space, we are dealing with thousands of different species, each with a variety of languages. To establish our superiority we needed to develop a way to communicate effectively with them."

"What part of the Galaxy do you come from?" Cunningham asked.

"Far from here, how far I don't know."

"How did you get here?"

Starfinder gave him a smile. "In this station, obviously. We did have interstellar travel capability, but not anymore. Something went wrong when we slipped through the rip in the space fabric, the portal that brought us here. We found it by accident. Unfortunately, it only works one way. There is no way back for us." He gave Cunningham a grave look. "I understand you have colonists living on the planet we are circling. Is that correct?"

"That's correct. We have one thousand settlers trying to make a new home for themselves."

"Any problems?"

Cunningham hesitated. How much could or should he tell the alien? Shrugging, he said, "Nothing they can't handle. Why?"

Starfinder's large eyes stared at the Captain. They glittered with purple fire. "Have you found any of our people?"

Cunningham leaned back in his chair. Suddenly, he felt icy fingers touching his brain. "You have people down there?" he asked with a voice like sandpaper.

"Two thousand," Starfinder said slowly.

"Where are they?"

"Probably dead."

"What happened?" Cunningham gripped the armrests of his chair with cold and clammy hands.

Starfinder shrugged. "We are not sure. In the beginning, everything seemed fine. We thought we found the perfect planet, until we discovered a sinister presence."

"You mean you found the planet was inhabited?"

Starfinder shook his head. "We never found evidence of inhabitants, physical inhabitants. But that planet is not dead. Something was living there, probably is still living there. At first, we thought it might be a virus. The colonists became obsessed with the pursuance of physical pleasures. Instead of working and building up the colony, they spent most of their time copulating. But no children were born."

"Perhaps they were working too hard and that was their way of coping with the hardship?"

"No, that wasn't it. People were beginning to change. They seemed to loose their individuality. Then they started to die. They weren't supposed to die, not yet. All were young. We performed an autopsy on one of the dead. Something was wrong. The DNA makeup of the dead was not Genaar. When we did more autopsies, we found the results to be the same with the others. By now most of the colonists on the planet were changed, and it was just a matter of time until all of them would be infected with the virus."

"So it was a virus?"

"No." Starfinder shook his head. "Not a virus. We discovered that the colonists had been replaced!"

"Replaced? By whom?"

Starfinder spread his hands. "We don't know."

Those icy fingers were still caressing Cunningham's brain. "When you asked me about our colonists I did not answer you quite truthfully," he said slowly. "They also are behaving strangely. I've sent a psych-team down for a few days to observe the colonists, and what the team found was quite disturbing, to say the least. I blamed it on the harsh conditions the settlers are facing, but what you are telling me scares the hell out of me." He didn't tell him about the Demon-Goddess Father Champain claimed to have seen, nor did he tell him about his own lucid fantasy in the park, when he had made love to his wife, a woman dead for forty years.

"Then it is beginning, again," Starfinder said. "You must take steps to protect yourself and the station."

"How can we do that? What did you do?"

"There is one thing we found out, the alien entity seems to live in the water. The water you are using, where does it originate?"

"We brought it up from the planet," Cunningham answered, a horrible thought popping into his mind. "There was also a plant someone brought up. A huge plant."

"You brought a plant onto the station?" Starfinder seemed horrified. "You must destroy it! And you must sterilize the water. We don't know what we are dealing with." He wiped a hand across his forehead. "It may already be too late."

"Why do you say that?"

"How many of your people living on the station have been down to the planet?"

"Half of the researchers have been at one time or another."

"Have you?"

Cunningham shook his head. "I am the captain. My place is here on

155

the station."

"You must have everybody who has spent time on the planet's surface examined." Starfinder said urgently. "Our scientists will assist you. They know what to look for."

"What else must we do?"

"The planet must be quarantined. Nobody on the station must be allowed to set foot on it. Nobody on the surface can get back to the station."

"Is that what you did? Quarantined the planet?"

The alien nodded. "We were scared. We've never run into an enemy we could not see. We didn't know what to do. Moving the station was impossible, so we decided to close it down and go into cryogenic suspension, hoping whatever was living on that planet would be gone by the time we awoke again. When you revived us I hoped our people had found us." He rubbed his forehead with his fingers and closed his eyes for moment. When he looked at Cunningham again, his expression was grave. "We might have slept for a thousand years, but for us only days have passed since we abandoned our people. Some may have still been alive, but we couldn't take the chance."

"That's why you asked me if we had found your people? You were hoping some had survived?" Cunningham gave Starfinder a searching look. "A good reason for us not to panic. I'm not abandoning the colonists. We will quarantine the planet, as you suggest, but we will keep in contact. I want to find out what it is we are facing here."

"You are probably right," Starfinder agreed. "Maybe we overreacted. However, I suggest proceeding with great caution."

"We will. I must say, I am surprised," Cunningham mused, "you claim to be an old race, with an advanced technology, in contact with thousands of different other races. Surely you have means to deal with all kinds of threats?"

Starfinder smiled. "If you mean: do we have superior weapons? We do. It would have been an easy task to destroy all life on that planet, but that was not an option. We are a peaceful people and do not kill wantonly. Yes, we are an old race, but with age comes caution, and sometimes complacency. We chose our own safety, instead of trying to find out more about the enemy." His large eyes rested on Cunningham. "And let there be no doubt, an enemy it is, more cunning and ruthless than anything you have ever met. Don't let down your guard!"

Cunningham looked at the perspiration on the alien's forehead, at the sudden terror in the large purple eyes. "Is there something you are not telling me?" he asked softly.

"You are perceptive," Starfinder whispered. "Yes, there is. I was on the planet's surface. I've met the enemy, looked into her face, tasted her passion…"

A cold hand squeezed Cunningham's brain. The gentle touch of her hand on his face. Her body soft and yielding, her kisses sweet honey. How could she be alive after forty years? "You're telling me the enemy is a woman?"

"Not a woman, not really. I told you, I don't know." He stared at the Captain. "You said you brought up a plant. I want to see it."

Cunningham rose from his chair. His knees seemed suddenly weak. "We can do that right now."

Chapter Twenty-nine
Alpha Colony

He stumbled down the overgrown path, came out in a clearing. It looked familiar. He recognized the women's bathing place. The alien sun was a bright blazing fireball high above, warming the cool morning air.

He was free!

He touched his buttocks, felt between his legs. There were no strands of fibers growing out of him. He didn't remember how he managed to get free, but it didn't matter. He looked at the pond, saw the giant plant floating in its center. It was sleeping. He ran down the familiar path, crossed the little bridge.

When he passed the grove of *peach-trees,* he slowed down. People were picking the ripening fruit, he recognized Orona among the pickers. When she saw him, she smiled and waved. "Hey, Tom, where have you been?" she called.

He waved back, began running again. Anina was not at home, so she must be at the hospital. He put on a shirt and a pair of pants.

When he burst into her office, she called out "Thomas!" Then she was in his arms, kissed him. "I've waited for you to come home." She smiled happily.

"So have I. I have learned a lot these last few days. This planet is not really ours for the taking, Anina. It is already inhabited by a powerful life form."

"I know," Anina said. "I have met the *Great Mother*."

"Not the way I have." Tom studied his wife. She seemed to look younger. Her auburn hair hung loose around her shoulders, her green eyes sparkled with a soft fire. "My, I have forgotten how beautiful you really are," he said.

She gave him a bright smile and looked at him with a strange and thoughtful expression. "How is your memory?" she asked.

"My memory is fine. As a matter of fact, it is quite clear, and I feel better than I've felt for a long time."

"That's good." She grabbed his arm. "Come, there is something you must be told."

They headed for Sister Angela's little church. Sister Angela was in the back, in the garden. Nurse Mabel sat beside her on the wooden bench. "Hello, Brother Thomas." Sister Angela smiled when she saw him coming down the narrow path. She got up, reached down and pulled her black robe over her head. She was naked underneath.

There was a small bulge in her flat belly.

Tom stared. "Are you pregnant?" he asked.

She nodded; her beautiful face lit up by a smile. "I am, and you are the father."

"Impossible!" he blurted out. "It hasn't been long enough." He looked at Anina. "I'm not the father."

"It's all right, Thomas." Anina smiled. "I know everything. I am very happy." She opened her white frock, slipped out of it. A warm soft body pressed itself against Tom's back. He felt gentle fingers unzipping his shirt and his pants, felt them drop down. A soft hand reached around to touch his penis.

Anina kissed him, broke away. She grabbed his shoulders and turned him around with strong hands. "Make love to Sister Angela," she whispered. "I want to watch."

His penis became a rigid mast between his legs.

Sister Angela lay in the soft grass, her knees up, her white thighs spread; the golden fleecy triangle below her belly was sparse, her pink slit beckoned. Anina pushed him gently. With a moan, he sank to his knees, moved between Sister Angela's open thighs. A soft hand grabbed his penis, guided it toward the waiting orifice. Sister Angela smiled. He stared at her firm beautiful breasts.

The tip of his penis touched creamy moistness. With a loud moan he pushed forward, soft walls molded around his hard organ. Shockwaves flooded his body and unbelievable pleasure seared his brain. He moved as if in a dream. In and out…in and out…

He wasn't aware when Sister Angela was replaced by Nurse Mabel, couldn't remember when they changed positions. Staring at the naked arching back of the nurse, he slammed his hips into her soft round buttocks.

Again… and again…

After climaxing he pulled out, stretched out on the ground, watched Anina straddle him. "We all love you, Thomas," she said and laughed throatily. Her full breasts bobbed up and down, her hips gyrated in his lap. Her tight vagina milked his aching organ, making him climax again.

Sister Angela kissed him, straddled his face. His tongue entered her cleft, she tasted like creamy honey. He felt Anina leave him, Sister Angela moved down, took him deep into her. Her blue eyes never left his face as she rotated her slightly swollen belly above him. She smiled and whispered softly, "We love you, Brother Thomas."

He dug his fingers into her soft breasts. She bent over him and let him suck on her nipples. Swallowing the sweet nectar, he forced his lips from her nipples. "This is wrong!" he shouted. "What are you doing to me?"

"Loving you." Nurse Mabel said as she straddled him. Her hairless thick vulva caressed his glans as she rubbed it gently back and forth. Then her soft sex-canal took him deep into her.

"We are all one," Nurse Mabel said, her light blue eyes shining with a strange fire.

"Yes, we are one," said Anina and Sister Angela, who were kneeling beside him. "And we all love you, Brother."

He lay without moving, his penis deeply lodged inside Nurse Mabel, waves of pleasure still cursing through his veins.

"What are you talking about?" he demanded.

"I am the *Xandra*," said Anina.

"I am the *Xandra*," said Sister Angela.

Nurse Mabel squeezed his penis. "And I am the *Xandra*."

He closed his eyes. "Let me wake up!" he screamed. *This is a nightmare*.

Soft lips covered his. *Don't be afraid, brother,* a voice whispered inside his head. *We are the Xandra, and so are you.* His lids snapped open; he stared into his wife's green eyes.

"I am Tom McClary," he said, "and you are my wife Anina."

I am the Xandra, she repeated. Her lips never moved, but her words echoed inside his head, as if she spoke them aloud.

"Where is my wife?" Tom screamed, pushing up to dislodge Nurse Mabel. She fell backward and lay there, her pale eyes looking up at him. He stood in a half crouch, facing the three women.

"Tell me this is just a cruel joke," he sobbed. He pointed an accusing finger at Anina. "I've known you most of my life, loved you most of my life. I know you intimately. You cannot be the Xandra. Say you are not her!"

Anina smiled gently. "I cannot, but I *am* your wife, Thomas. I have all her memories, her character. She was getting old. I am just a younger version of her. Look at me, look at my flat belly, my buttocks. Look at my breasts, they were beginning to sag." She turned around, presented her round, solid buttocks. "Look at them, Thomas! Aren't they lovely?"

He saw the difference. She was Anina, and she was not. He was beginning to believe. "How?" he asked. "How can you walk around free, without being chained to the mother plant?"

"We are the new generation," Sister Angela said.

Tom looked at her, he saw the slight differences. She looked more voluptuous, her face looked even more beautiful than he remembered. Her skin showed no blemishes. "You say you are with child. How can you be if you are not human?"

Sister Angela laughed. He always liked her laugh. "I am human. I am an exact copy of the old Sister Angela, just better. Some modifications were made, I am healthier, will never be sick, but otherwise I am Sister Angela."

"But you are also the *Xandra*."

She nodded. "Yes, I am, but I am an individual. We all are, with our own thoughts, likes and dislikes. The Xandra is with us. She is aware of everything that goes on. She is present now."

"In other words, you are a puppet, and she pulls the strings," Tom spat.

"Oh no, you are wrong. We are free. She only guides us."

"Same thing." He looked down at his hands, his feet, flexed his fingers. "What about me?" he asked in a low voice.

"You are Thomas McClary," Anina said, "just not the original."

"I don't believe you," he said hoarsely. "I know what I am, who I am. I am not one of her puppets. Tell me, why do you know that *you* are part of the Xandra, but I don't, if I'm supposed to be?"

He cried out when the voice spoke inside his head.

Hello, Thomas, my son. Why can you not accept the truth?

She stood underneath a tall tree, flaming hair blowing gently. Her green luminous eyes were large and burned with a soft fire. She was so beautiful.

He knew that she wasn't there, just in his mind.

My daughters told you the truth, my son. You are the crowning of my creation. I have given you free will. Maybe I made you too well. I don't know. But I had to do it so the humans could not recognize you. You are my champion, Thomas. In time, you will accept your true identity. I cannot influence you, not really, but I will always be with you. I love you.

Her vision began to fade.

"Wait!" he cried out, but she was gone.

He sat down on the bench, looked up at the tree women. Anina sat down beside him, took his hand into hers. "We all love you, Thomas." She put his hand on her breast. "Does my breast feel soft and warm?" Touching his penis, she smiled, "and does this not arouse you?"

"That doesn't make us human. If this is all true, we are freaks, clones, artificial humans. Where is my real, true self? Where is the real Thomas McClary?"

161

"He lives."

"Where?"

Anina shrugged. "What does it matter? In the valley. He's happy; he lives a man's dream, surrounded by all those beautiful and willing girls."

"A slave!" Tom spat.

"Not a slave. His brain needed to be adjusted a little for him to accept the situation, but he will be taken care of." Anina stroked his cheek. "What do you care, Thomas. He is an inferior being. You are his superior. You are the real Thomas McClary now. Accept that. You are a human, a better human."

"How many of us are there?"

"We are the only ones, for now. More humans will be replaced." Sister Angela said. "It has to be done gradually. We cannot arouse the suspicions of the observers in the ship. The humans do possess terrible weapons. Once all the colonists have been changed, we can start to reproduce. There will be a human population on this planet someday, and the true humans never need to know about us. If we differ they will think we have mutated, that's all."

"Why replace them at all? Why not let them flourish?"

"We are the *Xandra*. We cannot allow it. The humans would destroy us."

"You are probably right." A sudden thought popped into his mind. "What about the seedpods? Won't they be wondering about them?"

"The tree-elves will move the seedpods to an area where there are no humans. By the time the pods split open and the Xandra-humans are born all humans will have been replaced."

Tom closed his eyes. The knowledge was inside him, he knew she spoke the truth. "When was this body created? I remember being chained to one of the mother plants by fibers inserted into my body, but somehow I don't believe that was me, I mean, this body."

"No, it wasn't. That was still the original Thomas McClary."

"What about the other one, the one who was here before me?"

"That was the first proto-type, an inferior specimen. He would not have survived. The Xandra took him back. He was just an experiment." Sister Angela crouched in front of him. Her blue eyes sparkled. "We three were the first with individual identities, but the Xandra is still a part of us. You, brother, are the only one with a true individual identity. You were born this morning."

She rose in front of him, kissed him on the lips, then she said. "You are not alone. We are your companions, through us your are connected to

162

the Xandra. She loves you, and so do we. We are one."

"Where is the human Sister Angela? Where is my wife?"

"I am your wife." Anina said beside him with a gentle voice.

When he looked at her with a grave expression she said, "Tom McClary and the females were taken to the valley. They are happy there, they will not remember their former lives. It is the only way. The Xandra does have compassion, she will not extinguish life, unless it is necessary. Deep inside you must know this."

Chapter Thirty
Space Station

The plant had grown. It covered almost half the pond. The naked woman standing in its center smiled at the men watching her. Her green eyes glittered in the bright light of the artificial micro-sun.

"Who are you?" Cunningham asked.

"I am The Xandra," she said with a sultry voice.

"What are you?"

"A goddess." She lifted a slim hand to brush long strands of red hair away from her face.

"How did you get here?"

She laughed softly. "You brought me."

"Are you real or just a figment of my imagination?" Cunningham looked at Starfinder. "Do you see her?"

The alien man nodded. "I see her. But that doesn't mean she is real. This is not what she really looks like."

The woman on the plant laughed. She was still looking at Cunningham. "I can be anyone you wish me to be," she said. There was a subtle shift in the lines of her body, her hair moved like a nest of vipers, changing from red to black.

"Jeremy, my darling," she whispered across the pond, "come into my arms. Let me fulfill your desires." Her eyes were not green anymore, but a beautiful hazel.

Without realizing it, Cunningham stepped into the water. Rough hands pulled him back onto dry land.

"She is not who she seems to be!" Starfinder's voice said harshly. "She is evil! While she satisfies your bodily desires she takes away your soul, rips it to shreds." The alien's voice grew hoarse, high-pitched, not at all the soft baritone Cunningham was used to hearing.

The woman on the plant changed again.

Her hair was still black and long, but her eyes became overly large. Not hazel any longer, but purple. The outlines of her body seemed to blur; she became shorter, more slender.

Starfinder moaned. "Go away!" he cried out in anguish. "You are not she. I hate you!" His voice broke. "You took her away from me. I loved her so much. She was my life."

"I am your lost love. I am Starmist, your mate." She stepped off the plant, slid gracefully into the water.

"Do it now!" Starfinder almost screamed.

Cunningham tore his eyes away from the beautiful vision that flowed toward them. Swallowing the lump in his throat, he tried to still the beating of his heart. "Now!" he told Beringer, who stood silently beside them.

Beringer brought down his hand.

The blast from the lasers melted her lovely body. She didn't scream. Her smiling face was the last thing they saw. Another blast destroyed the great floating plant, burnt it into a black mass that left an oily film on the water. The smell of burning vegetation was unpleasant only for a moment, then the ventilators sucked it away.

Starfinder sank to his knees and put his hands over his face. Cunningham touched his shoulder in a gesture of comfort.

Beside them, Commander Beringer cleared his throat. Cunningham looked at him, and then at the two marines, who still stood with their weapons at the ready. "Your work here is done, Commander," Cunningham said.

Beringer nodded, saluted and signaled his men. Even though their faces showed no emotion, it was written in their eyes.

They were men, and they were young.

Killing a goddess in cold blood is no easy thing. It would haunt them for the rest of their lives.

There was a bench nearby. Cunningham walked over to it, sat down. He watched Starfinder rise to his feet. The alien man stared for a long time at the now dark water of the pond. Silence fell throughout in the park, except for the quiet noise of the ventilators. "I know it was not Starmist," Starfinder said after awhile, "but it was like watching her die all over again." He joined Cunningham on the bench. "I apologize for showing you my pain. I'm usually more controlled."

"No need to apologize. We're all human," Cunningham said and smiled. "You know what I mean."

Starfinder managed a small smile. "I appreciate your empathy. Seeing your own mate must have been just as painful."

"It was. She seemed so real." Cunningham sighed. "I haven't seen my wife for forty years, but I still miss her."

"Mine was taken from me only a few short weeks ago." Starfinder said. "Even though it has been over a thousand years for the entity who calls herself *The Xandra*, she still remembers my mate and me. What are we dealing with?"

"A goddess, as she claimed," Cunningham said. "Tell me how your mate Starmist died." When Starfinder hesitated, he added, "Unless it is too painful to talk about it."

"It is, but maybe talking about it will help me to deal with it." The alien sighed. "We were on the surface of the planet, studying the plants. Starmist always loved flowers. When we came upon this mass of purple flowers growing along the shores of one of the many ponds, Starmist shed her clothes and lay down among the flowers. There was something about these flowers. Suddenly, both of us were sexually turned on, and before we realized what was happening we were locked together like two animals in heat. Afterwards my mate walked into the water, headed for the huge purple plant that was floating in its middle. She climbed onto it. I heard her scream, and then she seemed to disappear into the plant."

"Disappear?"

"She was gone only for short time. Before I could jump into the water, she appeared again and waved. I lay back into the flowers. My mind was not clear, the fragrance of those purple flowers proved overpowering. It did something to my brain and body. Even though we just had sex, I was still immensely turned on. When Starmist straddled me, I closed my eyes and let it happen. We copulated for what seemed like hours." He paused, looked at Cunningham and smiled sadly. "It is not that unusual, because our females are easily aroused and can keep a male occupied for a long time. As for my own stamina? I thought it was just the fragrance of the flowers."

"So, what was wrong and when did you find out?" Cunningham asked, a little uneasy about the intimate details the alien was going into. After all, they were strangers. Cunningham was not used to talking about his sexual experiences with other people, especially not with a total stranger.

"Starmist tried to talk me out of going back to the station. When I told her it was out of the question, she reluctantly agreed to go back with me. I should have known something was amiss, when she refused to eat meat products. She told me swimming in the water changed her. I had no idea how true that was. She stopped eating altogether, and it wasn't long before she became ill. Her body deteriorated fast. She begged me to take her down to the surface again. I did, but it was too late. I stayed with her for a few days, and then she just died. Hers was the first body we performed an autopsy on."

"Exactly what did happen to your mate?"

"That plant devoured her and replicated her body. The woman who came back to the station with me was not Starmist, but a clone." The

166

agony the alien experienced talking about it was evident in his voice. "I copulated with a plant," he said.

A shiver ran down Cunningham's back. "If it makes you feel any better, so have I," he said, his voice a hoarse whisper.

Both men sat silent for a while.

"You know, we may have eliminated the threat here on the station," Cunningham said after a long pause of silence, "but how can we deal with it on Nu-Eden. I have one thousand colonists down there. Who knows how many of them are still human? I'm afraid to send down a team of scientists. How can we protect them? We can't destroy every plant on that planet. What are we going to do with the people who have been replaced?"

Starfinder nodded. "I see your dilemma. We don't even know which species of plant is suspect. Is it only one? Are there many different kinds? Should we worry about animals that may also be part of the threat?"

"You told me it was in the water," Cunningham said.

"Again, we're not sure." The alien man shrugged. "We believe the water is part of the cycle."

"I'll have the water in our tanks sterilized." Cunningham rose to his feet. "We have a small company of soldiers stationed near Alpha Colony, under the command of Sergeant Vicks. He and his men don't have much contact with the colonists, so there is a good chance none of them are affected. I must warn them." He heaved a deep sigh. "It seems they are of little use against an enemy you can't see."

"I advise caution," Starfinder said. "Take nothing for granted."

The elevator was empty when they stepped into it. Cunningham got off on the seventh floor and headed for his quarters. He didn't have to ask for Starfinder's destination. The alien was going to board a pod and float to the floor of the docking bay, then he would take an elevator down to the fifth level, where his people were living.

The aliens powered up the station, or at least part of it. Cunningham wasn't sure. He had not been given a tour. Most of the station was inaccessible to the humans. He knew that the Genaar didn't trust their uninvited guests, and Cunningham didn't blame them for it.

He didn't trust the Genaar either.

When Cunningham entered his quarters, he found a message on his computer from a Tom McClary. He was one of the bio-engineers living on Nu-Eden.

"Captain Cunningham," the message said, "please, send down a shuttle and pick up my wife and me. There are several important issues we need to discuss. We need the facilities of the Station to do some tests,

167

which can't be done here on Nu-Eden..."

Cunningham didn't listen to the whole message. McClary never said what exactly he wanted to discuss, except that it was urgent. The Captain decided to pick up the man and his wife. She was a doctor, and maybe she had information that could be important.

He put a call through to Commander Beringer. "I'd like to talk to you, Les. Come up to my quarters, please."

Chapter Thirty-one
Space Station

After leaving the Captain's office, Beringer decided he needed to talk to the alien man he knew as Starfinder. The vision of the beautiful woman in the park and the way he and his men killed her, wouldn't leave him. They had followed the Captain's orders.

Even though the Captain and Starfinder briefed him, Beringer kept on wondering. What exactly did they kill there? He still couldn't see how a plant and a mere woman could be a threat to the humans on this station. He saw the reaction of Starfinder when they destroyed the woman.

She called herself *The Xandra,* claimed to be a goddess.

Whoever she had been, she obviously had been delusional. You cannot kill a goddess.

Or can you?

When he arrived on the lowest level of the tower, he entered a room that had been hidden behind a door in the wall at the far end. It was one of the doors the humans had not been able to open. Since the Genaar started up their power grid, many of the doors were operational. Inside the room were a number of pods, which were used to cross the airless docking bay to get down to the next level.

Beringer stepped through the oval opening into the pod. It wasn't very large, just big enough to hold possibly five people. He put his hand on a small blue screen, the door closed and a light in the ceiling lit up the interior of the pod. A slight vibration told Beringer that the pod was starting to move. A few moments later the door slid open and Beringer found himself in another room. A door in one wall led him into another elevator, which took him down to the living quarters of the aliens.

One of the alien men greeted him with a friendly smile. Even though he never saw any weapons, somehow he couldn't believe that their newfound friends were unarmed. On the other hand, Beringer never brought a weapon. He felt safe in the presence of these gentle people. "I would like to speak with Starfinder," he told the alien, who nodded politely and said, "I will take you to him."

Beringer was amazed at the ease and speed that the Genaar learned the language of the humans. They were truly an advanced species.

Starfinder looked up from the metal desk he had been sitting at when Beringer entered. He smiled and got up to greet the Commander. Shaking Beringer's hand, he said, "What brings you here, Commander Beringer?"

"Concerns," Beringer replied and gave the alien a little smile.

Looking at their joined hands, he said, "You adapt well to human customs."

Starfinder pulled his hand away. "Association with many different species has taught us many things. Assuming the behavior of the people you're dealing with helps to build trust and friendship." He chuckled. "Besides, our two species are not that much different from each other. The custom of shaking hands is not unique to humans." He indicated a bench at one wall, "Take a seat."

Beringer looked around the room. "It seems you and I have much in common. My room is similar to yours. Some people may find it uncomfortable. But I'm a military man, used to little comfort." He looked at the alien. "Do you have a military background?"

Starfinder shook his head, went back to his desk, and seated himself. "I'm a scientist. I've always been. Most of my life I've spent in space, searching for other planets, studying different civilizations, their customs and their way of life. Once, I was a pilot, but that was only part of my training." He smiled. "Never a military man."

"But you do have soldiers?" Beringer asked.

"We do." Starfinder nodded. "However, we are pacifists. We do not condone violence."

"Never?"

"We are not strangers to it. A race as old as ours has not always been peaceful." His large purple eyes studied the Commander. "That is the reason we entered the relative safety of cryogenic sleep, instead of obliterating all life on a planet that attacked and killed hundreds of our people. Maybe it was the coward's way out." He shrugged. "Your Captain Cunningham does not agree with our decision. He wants to find out more about the threat you are facing. We are facing, because we are still involved. It seems a thousand years was not long enough to eliminate the enemy."

Beringer was silent for a moment. "I don't necessarily share my captain's decision," he said slowly. "That is the reason I am here. I just spoke to him. He informed me that he is sending a shuttle down to Nu-Eden to pick up a couple of colonists. I advised against it, but it is his decision, not mine."

"I was not aware of this," Starfinder said. "He didn't tell me when we spoke. Why are you telling me this?"

Beringer hesitated. "I've always had good instincts and I have learned to follow them. Somehow I feel uneasy, I have this queasy sensation in my stomach, this... this feeling of doom. If it were my decision, nobody on that planet would be allowed back on the station, not until we have identified the enemy. Something is wrong. I want to know if there is anything we can do?"

"Like what?"

Beringer stood up, approached the desk. "You and your advanced technology. You must have some way of identifying a person who has been infected by this, whatever it is we are facing." Beringer gave Starfinder a hopeful look.

"We have." The alien smiled ruefully. "But the person has to be dead before we can determine that."

"What other options do we have?"

"Not many. I advised your captain to be cautious. I suggest the same thing to you." Starfinder rose again. He stepped around his desk, faced Beringer. "Now, let's talk about something else. I saw that large vessel in our docking bay and I've seen you take it into space a couple of times. I assume it is a warship. Am I correct?"

"You are. My job here is to protect the colonists and the research scientists against any attacks from space or from hostile planets. Assuming we run into any hostiles. It seems we have, but what good is a warship if you don't even know you're under attack?"

"Not much, I agree." Starfinder nodded. "Can you land this vessel on the surface of a planet?"

"Unfortunately not. It is strictly meant for space. Why?"

"Cunningham told me about your people who are apparently lost on the fifth planet. He also told me that you can't use your shuttles for a search and rescue mission. I wondered why you couldn't use that big ship I had seen in the docking bay." Starfinder touched Beringer's arm. "I've spoken to your captain many times since we've come out of deep-freeze, but only a few days ago was the first time we met in private, without others around. He strikes me as a competent man. But I don't really know him as well as I do you, Beringer. I trust you."

Beringer chuckled. "I am honored. I hope I can live up to your trust."

Starfinder looked at him with a serious expression on his handsome face. "Whatever you do, don't send another shuttle to the fifth planet, until this threat has been identified and eliminated. Do not let anyone influence you, Commander. We don't want to spread the danger to another planet."

"I don't think we have to worry about that." Beringer smiled. "How about those spheres of yours in the shuttle-bay? Can you take those into a planet's atmosphere?"

"No." Starfinder shook his head. "They are maintenance pods."

Beringer searched the alien's face. "Do you have anyone on the fifth planet?"

Starfinder hesitated, then he nodded slowly. "Yes, we do. We've abandoned them also. We had no choice. There was no time to evacuate them."

A thought occurred to Beringer. "What happened to all your shuttles? How did you travel down to the planets?"

"All of them were on Nu-Eden. We destroyed them, except for one. I assume it is on the fifth planet now."

"I don't understand."

"Somebody had to operate the cryogenic chambers and close down the Station. Four volunteers stayed behind. When their job was finished they were supposed to take the shuttle down to the fifth planet, where they were to join the researchers who were living there."

"How many people did you have on that planet?" Beringer asked.

Starfinder lifted his shoulders and spread his hands. "I'm not sure of the exact number. Approximately 200 or so."

"They may still be around, then?" Beringer said.

The alien man chuckled. "We may be long-lived, but not that long."

Beringer grinned. "I'm talking about their descendants, of course."

"I know. I see you have a sense of humor. That is good. Another thing we have in common." Starfinder slapped Beringer on the shoulder. "Come, my human friend. You are just in time for supper." He laughed when Beringer gave him an astonished look. "You are surprised? Yes, we sit down for supper. We eat, just like you. I don't think our metabolism is so different that we can't eat each other's food."

"That's not what surprised me," Beringer said, "as far as I know you've never eaten our food."

"No, I have not," Starfinder agreed. "I knew that some of your food came from Nu-Eden. We take no chances."

As they walked toward the dining area, Beringer studied his surroundings. The new quarters of the Genaar were on the same level as the cryogenic chamber, but further down the corridor. Even though the power was back on, most of the station was still inaccessible. In the interest of good will, Cunningham pulled out all of the personnel who were stationed in the modified area of the corridor. No humans were present on this level.

The dining room was quite large, with low tables and benches. There were only a few of the Genaar sitting at the tables. Beringer counted five males and seven females. All of them smiled and nodded politely at

Starfinder and Beringer, then turned back to their meals and conversations.

None of them seemed to be surprised to see a human joining them for dinner. Of course, Beringer was not a stranger to them, he visited Starfinder quite a few times in the last couple of weeks. Not for the first time the haunting beauty of the Genaar females seemed to mesmerize him.

"Are all your women this beautiful?" he asked Starfinder in a low voice.

The alien man smiled. "On this station, yes. On our home world…" He shrugged. "How does anyone define beauty? It is true, we strive for physical perfection, but that is only on the outside. What's inside a person is just as important, don't you agree?"

"I agree, but it doesn't hurt to look at a beautiful body," Beringer said and smiled.

"No, it doesn't. I have to admit, the Genaar have always considered physical appearance as important, it enhances the attraction between a male and a female. Pursuing the pleasures of the flesh plays an important role in our society. Is it no so with you humans?"

"It is." Beringer chuckled. "There are some among us who would not admit it. They believe ignoring that fact makes it non-existent. What happens in the dark is evil, should not be enjoyed, even though they themselves partake in it. How else would a species continue to exist?"

"You only copulate in the dark?" Starfinder asked, surprise in his voice.

Beringer laughed. "I'm only speaking metaphorically. We can have sex any time of day or night. Of course, there are probably some who will only copulate in the dark." He shrugged, suddenly getting uncomfortable with the subject. He started thinking of Breanna McGuinness, remembering their sexual encounter. She had been the last woman. Before her, he didn't even remember. Looking at the beautiful alien women made him think again about sex and he was acutely aware of a gentle pounding in his loins.

Fortunately, Starfinder changed the subject, when he said, "Now, let me introduce you to some of our other pleasures, food."

Beringer watched Starfinder walk over to a wall-cabinet and remove a couple of small packages, which he put into another cabinet. After a few moments, he took them out again and brought them over to the table. He smiled when he handed one to Beringer. "Use your teeth to rip it open," he said.

Beringer took the offered package and followed Starfinder's suggestion. Watching the alien, he sucked the contents into his mouth, tried not to flinch when the bland flavor hit his taste buds.

"We're still living off ship's rations," Starfinder said, "I know our food is not what you are used to, but it is nourishing. Maybe soon we will have our kitchen operational again." He chuckled. "We do enjoy good food, just like you humans. This is not our regular fare."

Beringer swallowed, grinned. "I'm a soldier. Believe me, this is gourmet food compared to some of the gruel I had to eat already."

Chapter Thirty-two
Captain's Log
September 20, 2985

Much has happened since my last entry. We've sterilized the water and cleaned up the pond. With the giant plant gone, something seems to be missing. The pond looks empty. Jackson, the caretaker, asked for permission to put in some of the fish eggs we have in cryogenic suspension, but I denied his request. Who knows what still lurks in the water and what those fish could grow into. I've had a couple more meetings with the alien man Starfinder. Both, he and Commander Beringer, are against my decision to bring up people from Nu-Eden, but I'm willing to take the chance. The shuttle that is going to bring Tom McClary and his wife, Anina, will be arriving here tomorrow morning. I told the pilot to be careful and not to mix with the colonists while he is down there. Beringer is not the only one who expresses his concerns. All the personnel on the station have been briefed about what has happened in the park. There is a bit of paranoia spreading among the crew and the scientists, and many side with the Commander.

I hope I'm making the right decision. I can't abandon the colonists just like that. I have to think about the two thousand who are still sleeping peacefully on the 21st and 22nd floor, waiting to be awakened.

We don't have the technology the Genaar possess. They've been frozen a thousand years. We're lucky if we can keep anyone in that state for twenty years. After that, no guarantees. We still haven't heard from Exploration Team Delta. Brent McGuinness calls me almost every day and asks about news from the fifth planet. I have to tell him there isn't any. I wish I could tell him 'no news is good news', but I'm afraid it isn't true in this circumstance. We've been in contact with Professor Tennenboum. He and his research team are getting worried. A couple of his people want to come back to the station, but I told him I couldn't risk another shuttle. The atmosphere on that planet is just too rough and the weather too unpredictable at this time of year.

Maybe in the spring I will give it a try. I hope that by then Lieutenant Striker and his team will have made it to the research station. If they are still alive. If we can resolve the problem with Nu-Eden. If maybe the Genaar have a shuttle stashed away somewhere inside the bowels of this huge space station. A lot of ifs. We'll see.

Chapter Thirty-three
THE XANDRA

The Xandra watched through Anina's eyes. She'd have to be more careful from now on and adapt to new conditions.

Anina bent down, put her hand into the small pond. She let the tiny seed-pouch slide into the water. If everything went as planned the seed would grow into a plant that could thrive under water, clinging to rocks and other uneven surfaces, invisible to the casual observer.

"This is so beautiful," Anina said. "You've done a marvelous job, Captain."

Captain Cunningham smiled. "Thank you, Mrs. McClary, but I actually had nothing to do with it."

Anina laughed. "You are too modest, Captain." She put her hand on the Captain's elbow. "My husband will be busy for awhile with that biology-team of yours. This is a welcome vacation for me, with all that's happened on that planet. It is nice to be back in civilization for a while. How about showing me your quarters?"

Captain Cunningham raised his eyebrows a fraction.

She shook her lovely auburn hair and gave him an impish smile. "Are you afraid I might take advantage of you, Captain Cunningham?"

He laughed, slightly embarrassed by his failure to keep a neutral face. "I'm afraid it might be the other way around," he joked. "You are a seductive woman," and added, more soberly, "You are also married."

Her laughter was open and without embarrassment. "Keep talking, Jeremy, Captain. By the way, my husband and I have an understanding. Rules have changed since we've settled on Nu-Eden."

The Xandra detected the man's elevated pulse through Anina's hand, smelled the pheromones in his perspiration. The Captain would be the first; he tasted her once already; maybe she could persuade him to bring up Sister Angela and her Angels. All of them were of the Xandra now.

Conquest of the station would be easy.

Anina stepped closer. She was almost as tall as the Captain. Looking into his eyes, she put her hand behind his head and kissed him on the lips. Her tongue flicked against his teeth and he opened his mouth to let her probe the inside of his oral cavity. As if by accident, her hand touched his crotch for a brief moment. She laughed into his mouth when his body stiffened. Releasing him, she smiled and said, "Come, let's go up to your quarters."

He nodded, his breath coming a little faster. They didn't speak in the elevator. Once in the Captain's rooms they headed straight for the bedroom.

"Let me undress you, Jeremy," Anina said and began opening the buttons on his shirt. When she pulled down his pants and freed his manhood, he was already hard and solid. Slowly she sank down, took his penis into her mouth, and began flicking her tongue across the swollen head. He moaned loudly, grabbed her head between his hands, moved his hips back and forth.

Anina freed his member and laughed. "Easy, Jeremy, this is just a little teaser. Let's not waste your precious seed like that. Lie down on the bed and watch me as I undress for you. I understand man like that."

With agonizing slowness, she began taking off her clothes. Opening her shirt, she bared her full breasts. Then she pushed her slacks past her hips, let him look at the coppery triangle below her smooth belly. The Captain's eyes were glued to her exposed sexual organ. Between his legs, his penis stood straight and stiff.

She slid on top of him, rubbed her organ against his hard member. He groaned, put his hands on her round buttocks. She lifted up and let him enter her.

A loud sigh escaped his lips as he slid into her warm sheath. His fingers dug into the firm flesh of her buttocks and he began to push up with frantic movements.

She kissed him, dribbled some of her saliva into his mouth. Inside her, she could feel his penis swell and throb. Lifting her head, she said, "Take it easy, Jeremy, we have lots of time. Let us both enjoy this."

She sat up and let him look at her jiggling breasts as she rotated her hips in his lap. ""Come now," she said when it was evident he was fighting to keep from releasing his sperm, "it will be alright."

With a roar of pleasure, he came inside her then, but when he was finished, he was still hard. She sensed his surprise and laughed above him. "I told you it will be alright. Now, relax and let me take you to places you've never been before."

She churned above him for a long time, once in awhile she bent down, kissed him and fed him more of her sweet saliva. He came once more with great force. Then she lifted up, slipped off the bed and bent forward. She didn't have to tell him what to do. He stepped behind her, spread her white cheeks and pushed his stiff organ between them. Her lubricated sheath opened to let him back into her belly. Standing on the floor, he let his pelvis snap back and forth, his hands on her hips.

"I don't know how this is possible," he moaned behind her, pushing deep into her with forceful thrusts, "I feel like a young stud. I can't remember the last time I felt like this."

She just laughed, wiggled her bottom and squeezed her vagina walls tightly around his rampant penis. He shouted and pushed deep, filling her insides with his warm discharge. Then he pulled out. "I want to feel your breasts on my chest when I make love to you," he breathed hoarsely.

She turned and spread her legs wide. He let his fingers trail across her belly, put one of them into her pink slit, then he moved on top of her and with a deep moan he shoved his hard organ into her creamy sheath.

"Your husband is a lucky man and not very smart," he said between clenched teeth, trying to keep from coming.

"Why do you say that?" she asked and moved against him.

"I wouldn't let you out of my sight. No man but me would touch you."

She chuckled. "You are old fashioned, Jeremy. Lucky for you my husband doesn't think that way."

"Yeah, lucky," Cunningham almost shouted and let go. His hot fluid shot with great force into her, filling her womb. She sucked it into her, wishing she would have come prepared and brought a seed pouch to capture this precious seed.

When he relaxed in her arms, she stroked his head and said, "Why don't you come and visit us on Nu-Eden. We can make love in the grass, under the stars." She smiled. "There is nothing like it."

When he seemed to hesitate, she kissed him fiercely, let him drink from her nectar. She felt his penis grow again. She took him back into her, let her inner muscles caress his rigid rod. "Say yes," she whispered into his ear.

He bucked between her spread legs, shouted when he climaxed again.

"Yes!" he said with a voice gone hoarse. "I'll come down with you."

"Promise."

"Promise," he groaned and thrust into her.

Chapter Thirty-four
Exploration Team Delta

The temperature began to drop rapidly. The first snowfall brought over twenty centimeters of the white fluffy stuff. Most of it melted within a few days, when the weather became warmer again, but they received a taste of what was to come.

Their new home was sealed off against an environment that was beginning to become more hostile every day, but the cold winds from the north seemed to find every small crack in the ancient walls.

Windows were a problem, since they had no glass or any other transparent materials, so they installed removable shutters. Fortunately, lighting the dark interior was not difficult. Everybody carried a portable light with rechargeable solar-power-cells. Once fully charged they lasted for a long time.

There were several rooms, but only the common room held a fireplace.

One major issue no one thought about was warm clothing. Especially insulated boots. It was Adam who taught them how to tan the hides of a shaggy animal, the size of a small horse. It also provided them with meat. He called it *Ikkaraa,* but Rhea said it reminded her of a yak, without the horns.

* * * *

"I've seen a couple of those six-legged cats prowling around yesterday." Herm Woolf finished wrapping the short pieces of rope around his newly made boots. "Maybe Acram and I should go and see if we can bag them, before they surprise one of us."

"Might be a good idea." Kendrick rubbed his arm.

"How's the arm?" Woolf asked.

Kendrick flexed his hand. "It's healed well enough, thanks to the med-doc, but I haven't forgotten the attack. The next victim may not be as lucky."

"Take Remington with you," Striker said. "He's been itching to use that antic gun of his."

"I'll go, too," Kendrick said. "I'm good with a laser."

"All right, but be careful. We don't want any casualties."

Striker watched them go out into the frigid morning, four men wrapped in furs, like a band of prehistoric hunters; except their weapons were not spears and clubs, but modern lasers. They held the advantage, and yet, Striker felt apprehensive. These hunters were out of their element, their quarry was not.

He shivered, even though it wasn't cold in the room. The fire crackled in the old fireplace, not only throwing heat, but also roasting the peace of meat Striker speared onto a long stick. He looked at Sara and Concitta, who were sitting not far from him on a couple of furs, scraping the meat from a yak-skin, getting it ready for tanning. Both women wore vests made from animal-skins; they could have been females from a tribe of primitives on old prehistoric Earth.

Breanna, Monaca, Tamara, and Adam sat in one corner at a crude table. Striker shifted his attention toward them and was a little surprised when Adam said, "Tell more about people in sky, Breanna."

Adam made remarkable progress, and his vocabulary seemed to increase from day to day. Breanna saw Striker watching, padded Adam's hand and said, "Enough for now, maybe later I will tell you more." She got up, walked past Concitta and Sara, and sat down beside Striker. "What's the matter, Poul? You seem so quiet."

He smiled, pulled the charred piece of meat out of the fire, blew on it. "I don't think this is going to be very good." He looked at her. "You've been avoiding me lately."

"I know I have." She stared into the dancing flames. "I hate it here, Poul. This place. The way we live. We have no privacy. And it will only get worse." Turning her head, she stared at him. He could see the moisture in her green eyes.

"I want to go home," she whispered.

He put an arm around her. "So do I, Breanna. So do all of us."

From one of the other rooms came laughter. He could hear Gregorchuck's booming voice. Striker chuckled. "Maybe not all of us."

A series of shots outside brought the men running out of the room. Most of them ran out without bothering to put on heavier clothing. Striker grabbed his laser, followed them. "Stay inside!" he told Breanna who came behind him.

"I'm not a child," she flashed. "I can take care of myself." She brandished a small laser pistol.

Striker shrugged, not in the mood to argue with her. He turned at the sound of another volley of shots.

Girard, Kramer, and Chu were already running toward one of the towers at the edge of the city, where the shots came from.

"They must have found them," said Professor Findlay, who was standing beside Tamara.

"Has anyone seen Professor Banca?" Concitta asked.

180

"Is he not here?" Striker stared at the black woman.

"He left early this morning to check out something." Sara stepped into the open, a fur thrown around her shoulders.

"Damn it!" Striker cursed loudly. "We agreed nobody goes out by himself."

He began following the other men. He couldn't explain the sinking feeling in his stomach. Just because Banca wasn't here didn't mean something happened to him, or any of the others.

They were waiting for him by the tower. One dead cat lay between them, but none of the men seemed happy. They looked at him with grim faces.

"What happened?" he asked. "Did you get the other one?"

Remington nodded. "In there," he said, pointing at the ruins of the once tall tower. "He never had a chance."

At first Striker didn't even recognize the bloody, torn pieces of flesh, until he saw the head. It was miraculously untouched. He groaned and suppressed a curse. "What was he doing out here by himself?" he asked.

Remington shrugged. "You know the Professor. He was never one to take orders seriously."

The lifeless carcass of the beast lay beside the mangled body of Professor Banca. A number of large holes testified to the savage anger Remington must have felt when he found the killer.

"We'll bury him this afternoon," Striker said.

"What about the dead cats?"

Striker knew what he meant. "Keep the hides, but leave the meat to rot."

"It'll only attract vermin, or at worst more predators. It is meat, you know." Mian spoke quietly from behind them.

"You are right." Striker turned away, walked outside. The survival of the group was more essential than ever, now. Professor Banca had been an important member of this team. His death was a big blow. A reminder that they were living in a savage world.

Sara and Concitta broke down and began to weep loudly when the men brought the professor's torn body back to the house. He had been their mentor. Not just a colleague, but also a close friend. Everyone else was in shock, staring in disbelief at the remains of their former teammate.

"He was just so excited to be here," Sara sobbed. "He was probably the only one who didn't mind this horrible place."

"He was a good man," Professor Findlay said. "I think I would like to say a few words when we bury him."

Remington and Woolf went to dig a grave. They used their lasers to cut through the already frozen surface, and then dug a hole with shovels made from the shoulder blades of a yak.

Findlay kept his eulogy short. They buried the body wrapped in a fur, since they didn't have any means to build a wooden coffin. Adam watched the ceremony in silence and bewilderment. "Why you put friend in prison?" he whispered to Sara.

"It is our custom, Adam," she told him. "What do you mean by *in prison*?"

"He never…" he was searching for words, pointed north." No go…" He shrugged and smiled. "Not know say."

Everyone stood in silence, watching Remington and Woolf cover the body with dirt, when from the forest to the south they heard a strange hooting. Adam was the first one to react by running toward one of the old buildings and climbing to the top of the roof. He began to laugh and yelled something in his alien language.

"What is it, Adam?" Striker called to him.

"My people come!" Adam shouted and jumped down from his perch.

Mian scrambled up the same building and looked through his binoculars. Striker, Chu, and Kendrick joined him when Mian motioned for them to come up. Striker looked to the south, grunted and pulled out his own binoculars. The electronic screen inside displayed a surprising sight.

"Looks like people on giant birds," Kendrick said.

"And sleds pulled by huge rats." Striker put down his binoculars. "Let's get down. We don't know if they're friendly."

"I want everybody inside the house," Striker said to the anxious group. "Only Chu, Mian, Woolf, and Kendrick come with me to meet them. We'll take Adam with us, since he claims they're his people."

"Hold it, Striker," Remington protested. "I'm coming with you."

"I need you here, to protect the women, Remington. In case things go wrong." The truth was, Striker didn't trust Remington. He was too impulsive, and too eager to use his gun.

"We can defend ourselves," Melina said hotly. She took on a defiant stance and stared into his face. "I can handle a laser as well as any man."

Striker looked at her. They spent one night together, shortly after he slept with Sara. He knew her temper and he experienced her passion. "I know you can," he said, "but I'd feel better if Remington stays with you."

Adam had been listening in. "No need *Death,*" he said to Striker. "My people friends. Come." He began to walk toward the forest.

The five men followed him slowly, their weapons slung across their shoulders. "No hostile movements," Striker warned them. "This is a historical moment, we don't want to be the ones who screw it up."

Adam raced way ahead of them; they could see him running down the dusty, old road that lead out of the ancient city.

"Let's hope he doesn't forget the kindness we have shown him," Chu said beside Striker, echoing his thoughts.

There were at least a dozen of the giant birds; they looked almost like the ostriches Striker remembered seeing in zoos, with shorter necks and larger heads. Sitting astride them were men wrapped in furs, their arms bare, their heads covered by furry hats. It was not obvious if they carried weapons, but Striker wasn't fooled by their appearance.

A number of sleds, which were pulled by large rat-like creatures, with long legs and short tails, followed the riders.

The caravan stopped when Adam reached it. The boy pointed toward the group of humans, waved his arms up and down. One of the riders separated from the caravan. Adam climbed onto the big bird-like steed, positioning himself behind the rider. Together they came slowly to meet the five men.

"You stay here," Striker said to the others, removed his laser from his back and laid it on the ground. "I will go on alone. Like I said, don't do anything stupid, but be alert." He began walking toward the stranger on the giant bird.

They both stopped when they were about ten meters apart. Striker held up both hands, palms up, hoping it was a gesture the other one would understand. Adam jumped from the unusual steed, waited until the rider spoke in the same melodious language Striker heard from Adam.

"I greet you, Stranger." Adam translated the words.

Striker inclined his head. "And I greet you. May our meeting bring friendship."

Again, Adam translated. He seemed to have a little trouble with the second part of what Striker said, but apparently he translated it correctly, because the rider smiled and slid from his mount. He was almost as tall as Striker. His eyes were large and black, with a purple hue, his face handsome, without a trace of hair. Again, he said something. Striker waited for Adam to translate.

"My…"Adam hesitated, shrugged, "…says you come from sky… you live in Old City."

Striker nodded. "We do."

The alien smiled. "You save… Adam… life. He say you good."

Striker smiled at the boy and said, "Thank you, Adam. Tell your friend he is welcome to visit us where we live."

Adam spoke rapidly to the alien, who answered him in a lengthy speech. The boy turned back to Striker. "*Stasra* say thank you. No time. Time of cold come... you death here... come with *Stasra*... go my home, my people."

"He wants us to go with him, to live with your people?"

Adam nodded. "Yes, you come... no good here... death." He shook himself, like someone who is cold.

"We'll freeze to death, is that what you mean?"

"Yes, freeze. You come. Now." Adam pointed at the sky where dark clouds were beginning to gather. "*Palos* come... soon... from sky... much."

"I'll have to talk it over with my people," Striker said. "Tell him that."

Stasra nodded when Adam told him. He mounted his steed and rode back to where the others were waiting. Adam walked back with Striker, talking excitedly, but Striker didn't understand a word.

* * * *

It was Adam who convinced his human friends to accept the offer. He assured them that his people were peaceful and would welcome them with open arms. The *Sras* were the evil ones, the *Sras* murdered his family and they would murder the humans, too. Their safety lay with the *Jnaar,* Adam's people.

And so it was decided. The humans would go and live with the *Jnaar.*

At least until the winter was over.

Chapter Thirty-five
Alpha Colony

The huge globe of Nu-Eden began to fill the screen, and even though Captain Cunningham was looking at it, he didn't really see it. His thoughts were filled with the events of the last three nights. He had been in a state of constant arousal ever since Anina visited him in his quarters that first night. They copulated all night and part of the next morning. Only when Anina suggested they stop and have something to eat did his mind seem to clear a little. But only a little. She spent the next two nights in his bed. And now he was going down to the surface of Nu-Eden, against his better judgment and against Beringer's and Starfinder's advice.

Looking at the redheaded woman, he could feel the blood boiling in his veins. He never wanted a woman as badly as he wanted her, even though she was married. That was the reason he took her up on her invitation to accompany her down to Nu-Eden.

Her husband, Thomas McClary seemed to be oblivious to the fact that his wife spent three nights in another man's bed. Cunningham's brain was so befuddled that it never occurred to him that maybe McClary was aware of his wife's infidelity. She told him that she and her husband had an understanding, but he didn't even remember that.

"Captain, are you alright?"

Cunningham looked up at the man who spoke, his eyes slowly coming into focus. Wiping the perspiration from his forehead, he managed a smile and said, "I'm fine."

The man, one of the two marines Beringer insisted accompany him for protection, peered at the Captain. "You look tired, sir."

Cunningham waved a hand in dismissal. "Maybe I am. Don't worry about it. Once we get down to Nu-Eden, I'll be fine. Maybe I needed a few days away from the station."

"We're about to land," the voice of the pilot said, "please make sure your restraining fields are enabled."

A soft vibration shook the shuttle, then it was quiet. The door slid open and Cunningham stared at the lush vegetation outside.

"Welcome to Nu-Eden, Captain Cunningham," Anina said and laughed gaily. Her husband made a motion with his hand. "After you, Captain."

Cunningham rose from his seat and walked the short distance to the exit. He stood for a moment and took a few deep breaths. The air was humid and made him gasp.

"Exhilarating, isn't it?" Anina said behind him.

"I'm not used to this rich and humid air," Cunningham said. "Give me a moment to adjust." He breathed deeply. "The fragrance, it is familiar."

"It's the flowers," Anina explained.

"We had them in our park, before we…" he didn't finish the sentence. The memory of a beautiful woman who claimed to be a goddess was not easy to suppress.

He climbed down the ladder, stepped onto the alien soil. There were a number of small prefab homes not far away. Behind them a structure, that could only be a church. He remembered seeing churches like that back on Earth, a long time ago. He didn't remember the last time he had been inside one. Two more buildings, both larger, a short distance away looked like meeting places.

"That's our hospital," Anina said and pointed to one of them. "The other one is our mess-hall." She took his arm. "Come, let us give you a tour."

He walked beside her like a man in a dream.

"You show our guest around," Thomas McClary said to his wife, "I have a few things I'd like to check out."

Anina smiled at him. "Alright, dear. I'll take good care of the Captain." Looking back at the two marines who were following them a few steps behind, she said, "You can tell your bodyguards to relax and take some time off, Jeremy. There is no danger here. This is our home."

"You heard the lady," Cunningham told the two men.

"We have our orders, sir."

"What's your name, soldier?" Cunningham put an edge to his voice.

"Orman, sir."

"Listen, I am the captain of the station. Everybody, including Commander Beringer and you, Orman, takes orders from me. Is that understood?"

"Yes, sir, Captain!"

"Good. So, put away your weapons and mingle with the locals." Cunningham smiled to take away the sting from his harsh words. "Have some fun. That's an order!"

"If you don't mind, sir, we'll just stay close to the shuttle." Orman said slowly. His companion nodded, gripping his weapon tighter in his hands.

Cunningham shrugged. "If you so wish."

"You can't force anyone to have fun, Captain," she said and tugged on his arm. "Come, I'll introduce you to Sister Angela."

186

There was a garden behind the church. Gravel crunched underneath Cunningham's boots as they walked down a narrow path. He marveled at the mass of beautiful flowers in the large flowerbeds. A group of young girls was picking weeds behind a small grove of trees. Among them a tall blond woman. She turned her head when she heard them coming and got up to greet them.

"This is the famous Captain Jeremy Cunningham," Anina said.

"Welcome to Nu-Eden," Sister Angela said and smiled.

When Cunningham looked into her blue eyes, he felt himself drawn to her. She was even more beautiful than Anina. She wore a loose robe that hid the form of her body, but it didn't hide the slight bulge in her belly. She noticed his look and smiled. "You're right, I am pregnant."

"Forgive me for staring," Cunningham said, "I was under the impression you were a nun."

"Oh, I am." She laughed cheerfully. "This is Paradise, Captain. A place where we love each other. Anything can happen here." She turned and called to one of the girls, "Naomi, go get a pitcher juice for our guest. He must be thirsty."

Cunningham watched the pretty black girl walk toward them. She had her colorless robe rolled up to expose her slender legs. As she walked by, she gave him a big smile and said, "Hi, Captain."

"Let's sit down for awhile and enjoy the sunshine," Anina said, "you don't have sunshine on that dreary station."

"No, we don't." Cunningham sat down on a bench and squinted against the bright disk in the blue sky. It looked different from the surface of a planet; there was no artificial shield cutting down the glare. The rays were warm on his skin, possibly harmful. He felt himself perspire underneath his uniform. "I guess you get used to this heat," he said.

Naomi came back carrying a tall pitcher filled with a yellow liquid and three mugs. She filled one of them and handed it to Cunningham, who gratefully accepted it. "Thank you," he said and sniffed the mug.

"Don't smell it, drink it." Sister Angela laughed. "It's not poison." She filled a mug for herself.

He smiled, drank from the mug. The liquid tasted sweet, with a somewhat bitter aftertaste. It seemed to go right down to his genitals. "What is this?" he asked.

The women were watching him over the rim of their mugs. Anina lowered hers, smiled. "Secret recipe. Sister Angela and her angels are brewing it in the basement of the church." She laughed when she saw his expression. "Relax; it is *peach-juice,* freshly squeezed. This is harvest time on Nu-Eden." She looked at Sister Angela. "I'll be showing the Captain the pond tonight," she said.

Sister Angela smiled. "I understand."

Cunningham watched the girls moving around among the patches of flower. He realized suddenly that some of them were naked. They were all young and lovely.

Following his gaze, Sister Angela chuckled. "It is hot, Captain. And they are young. The trees shield them from prying eyes. If there are any. We have no secrets in our settlement."

He chuckled with embarrassment. "I guess I'm getting old," he said. "We are more rigid on the station. I shouldn't look at such young girls."

"This isn't the station, Jeremy," Anina said, "besides, their not that young. All of them are women. Not one of them is an innocent virgin."

"You called them *Angels*, I assumed they were nuns." He looked at Sister Angela. "Like you." His gaze wandered down to her belly. He shrugged, smiled. "A different kind of nun, I guess."

Sister Angela bent suddenly forward and pressed her lips against his. They felt warm and soft for a quick moment, then she moved away. She laughed and touched his cheek. "You have much to learn," she said softly. "If you'll excuse me, I have some more weeds to pull. I'm looking forward to seeing again."

Dumbfounded, Cunningham licked his lips. Shaking his head, he rose, followed Anina back to the road in front of the church. She stopped and hooked her arm into his. "Let's go, I'll show you the hospital where I work."

* * * *

He lay on his back, stared at the two satellites in the star covered sky. Strange, how things look so different when viewed through the atmosphere of a planet. Moaning, he let his eyes rest on Anina's beautiful breasts silhouetted against the bright light of one of the moons. She moved slowly above him. He heard her soft laughter as his penis began to grow even harder inside her.

Suddenly he realized they weren't alone. Someone else was bending over him; long hair fell into his face, and then he felt a pair of soft lips on his. Sweet honey-like nectar trickled down his throat. Anina released his still hard organ and stood up. The woman who was kissing him took her place. Straddling him, she gave him a big smile.

In the moonlight, he saw a beautiful face with oriental features. Her almond shaped eyes sparkled mischievously as she looked down at him. She took hold of his stiff mast, guided it into her. Staring at her pubic region, he saw that is was smooth, with no trace of hair.

She saw him stare and laughed. "Don't be fooled by that. I am older than I look. I just like it smooth."

She sank into his lap, she was tight, but soft, oh-so-soft. Her hips began to move, slowly at first, but became faster and faster. He came inside her with a roar, but she kept on going.

Surprised by his stamina, he studied her face. It was lovely, but so young looking. It didn't matter to him. She drove him crazy. After the third climax she slowed down and smiled. "I am Orona," she said.

"I am Jeremy, Captain Jeremy Cunningham," he said, trying to catch his breath.

Orona laughed. "I know who you are, Captain. We've been waiting for you. Welcome to Nu-Eden."

"I second that," said a familiar female voice beside them.

He looked at Sister Angela, watched dumbfounded as she switched places with Orona. His rigid penis disappeared inside her golden fluff and a soft gently vice gripped it tightly. She began to milk him expertly. Lifting her face to the sky, she laughed and said, "Welcome to Paradise, Captain Jeremy Cunningham."

After he climaxed inside Sister Angela, she let him suck on her beautiful breasts. He drank from the sweet nectar she offered and he felt a surge of power in every fiber of his body. He closed his eyes, thrusting deep into her.

Then there was a moment of emptiness, the weight of her body was gone, but another velvet glove slid over his aching shaft. Opening his eyes, he looked into Anina's smiling face. Laughing, she rotated her shapely body above him. He feasted his eyes on her beautiful breasts, watched the smooth muscles of her flat stomach ripple gently.

Later Orona took her place, again, and rode him with wild abandon.

How many times those three lovely women changed places he didn't remember, but what came next he remembered with great clarity.

They led him to the water. There was a giant water lily floating in the center of the pond. He climbed onto it. The women dove into the water and swam back to shore.

"Hello, Captain Cunningham," said a melodic husky voice behind him.

When he turned he saw the most beautiful and seductive woman he ever laid eyes on. Long jet-black hair curled around her smooth shoulders, cascaded down her back and front, partially covering a pair of perfectly shaped breasts. A thick black triangle hid her genitals below her flat belly.

When he looked into her face, he saw white even teeth behind her full half-open lips. She stared at him with shiny black eyes and opened her arms.

He moved forward, her eyes locked with his, he felt himself drawn into their depth. Smooth arms went around his neck. Soft lips touched his. Sinking slowly to the ground, she pulled him on top of her. Her breasts were soft and warm against his chest, her smooth thighs opened and her hand slid between them. Warm fingers curled around his rigid penis, guided it gently.

He entered her with a wild shout; his head swam as her hot liquid walls closed around his shaft. He became delirious. The universe stood still. Nothing else existed but his giant sex-organ and this incredibly animate vagina.

Chapter Thirty-six
Captain's Log
October 30, 2985

I don't feel any different. My body feels the same, my thoughts are my own, and sometimes I wonder if the Xandra is really truthful.

Most of what happened on Nu-Eden after I accompanied Anina and her husband down to the planet's surface is unclear, but my meeting with the Xandra is still fresh in my mind.

Nothing can compare with the pleasure I experienced in the arms of the Xandra. As my body joined with hers so did my mind. For a while I was a god. I saw and knew everything. I was alive like I have never been before. She absorbed my physical body and my whole identity became part of her great mind.

When I awoke, it was daylight.

The woman was gone, but the Xandra is still there, inside my head, inside every fiber of my body.

She told me to go back into space and secure the space station.

Anina, Orona, and Sister Angela were coming down the path as I climbed out of the pond. They hugged and kissed me. I felt close to them. They told me they loved me, the Xandra loved me, and everything would be all right.

The Xandra is gone. Or is she?

Am I still human? I don't know. She told me I am, in every detail. I don't know what to believe.

191

Chapter Thirty-seven
Space Station

There was nobody else in the small park as Commander Beringer stepped out of the elevator. He inhaled the warm, humid air and wondered what the air was like on Nu-Eden. The Captain asked him to join him on his now frequent trips down to the surface of that planet, but Beringer declined the invitation.

He walked slowly down the graveled path toward the pond. A new plant had grown into giant proportions. It was not quite as large as the one they destroyed, but at the rate is was growing, it soon would be.

The Captain seemed different. He told Beringer that they overreacted. The so-called Xandra was no threat to the humans on the station. She was gone now and the colonists did not report any more appearances.

Beringer didn't buy it. There was something about the Captain that seemed odd. When he talked to Starfinder about it, the alien seemed reluctant to make any comments, but he suggested Beringer watch for changes in the behavior of the people around him and take measures to protect himself.

A splashing in the pond made Beringer look up. He was taken by surprise when he saw the naked woman. She was facing away from him, but when she turned to look at him, he closed his eyes for a moment, thinking that his mind was playing tricks. But when he opened them again, she was still there.

Smiling, she climbed out of the water, came slowly walking toward him.

"Breanna," he said, his voice almost a croak.

"Les," she said softly. Rivulets of water ran down her naked body.

"When did you get back?" he asked.

"Today," she said, shaking the water out of her hair. "Did you miss me?"

He rose from the bench he was sitting on, took her into his arms. Lifting up on tiptoes, she kissed him gently at first, then with more passion.

When they broke the kiss, he held her away from him, studied her face. "We thought you lost and dead by now."

She laughed. "Well, you were wrong. I'm alive and well, as you can see."

"Why wasn't I told that you had been found?"

She shrugged. "I don't know, but what does it matter." She kissed him

192

again, then she whispered into his ear, "Come, make love to me."

He chuckled. "I will, as soon as we are in my quarters."

"I can't wait that long. Let's do it right now, right here." She pulled him down into the grass on top of her. Tugging on his pants, she pushed them down past his hips, freeing his already reacting penis.

Before he realized what was happening he slid into her warm, hot sheath. She took him deep into her, pushed up against him. It didn't take long before he climaxed inside her.

"I'm sorry," he said, apologizing. "But I lost control. It's been awhile."

She laughed softly. "Don't worry. We can remedy that." She pulled his head toward her breast. "Drink from my nectar," she whispered.

He fastened his lips on her long nipple, sucked on it. Sweet liquid flowed from her breast into his mouth. He swallowed it eagerly. He felt his penis swell again and with a shout of joy he thrust it back into her hot sheath.

They moved against each other for a long time. He climaxed several times, each climax more powerful than the last. She doused him with her warm liquid discharge, cried out when she experienced her own orgasm.

When they finally separated, he was exhausted, but happy. Rolling onto his back, he lay there, looking up at the ceiling above. Squinting his eyes against the glare of the micro sun, he could almost pretend he was lying on the surface of some planet, nobody else around, except he and the woman he just finished making love to.

"What are you thinking?" Breanna asked beside him.

He smiled. "I was thinking how nice it would be if it could always be like this. Just love and happiness."

"You could have that," she said. "But you won't find it spending your life in space."

"Are you telling me I should move down to Nu-Eden?" he asked and turned to look at her.

"Would that be so bad?"

"I'm a space-rat. I don't think I'd be happy living on a ball of dirt. The sky is too high, the climate uncontrolled, the air unpurified. No, thank you very much." He studied her face as she in turn studied him, marveled at the depth of her green eyes. Her skin was unblemished, except for the slight peppering of tiny freckles.

"You talk just like my brother," she said and moved closer to kiss him. Her lips tasted sweet, like freshly picked berries.

"I'd forgotten how beautiful you are," he said.

She laughed, sat up and rose to her feet. "Come into the water with me," she said. "I feel like swimming."

Chuckling, he let her pull him up. "I don't think that pond is deep enough to swim in," he said, slowly walking beside her toward the pond. He stared at the giant plant floating in the water. It was covered with purple flowers; they seemed to move as he looked at them. He stopped walking. "You never told me what exactly happened on the fifth planet," he said.

She waved a hand. "Nothing much. If you're really interested you can read it in the report."

"No, I'd like to hear it from you."

She gave him a sweet smile, pulled on his arm. "I don't want to bore you with it. Come, join me in the water."

"You go. I'll watch you."

Out of the corner of his eyes he saw a figure step into the open from behind a clump of bushes. A man. He was followed by two more. They were dressed in the uniforms of the crew.

"I think you should take the lady's advice," the first man said.

Beringer watched with narrowed eyes as the three men came closer. They carried what looked like pieces of conduit in their hands. "What is going on here?" he asked, glancing at Breanna. She shrugged and kept smiling at him. "Come with me," she said softly, "and everything will be alright. You'll see."

He stepped away from her. "Are they your friends?" He looked at the three men. "Have you been watching us?"

The first one grinned. "We've been here the whole time. What does it matter? Now, go into the water, climb onto that plant over there and I promise we won't harm you."

"If I don't?"

The man was still grinning. "Then we'll have to carry you in. No problem."

Beringer looked at his clothing, which he so carelessly discarded. He usually went unarmed on the station, but lately he began carrying his laser pistol. It lay hidden underneath his pants. Casually he began moving toward them.

"Aren't you going the wrong way?" one of the other two asked, trying to cut him off.

Beringer took another step, kicked the man in the stomach and raced in the direction of his bundle of clothing. He almost made it, but he did not count on the incredible speed the third man moved with. Before he reached his target, a shadow blocked him and he collided with a solid wall of muscle. The man went down with him, but he was on his feet a fraction of a second before Beringer could regain his balance. A hard object hit him on the side of his head. He went down, a black hand squeezing his brain. He didn't loose consciousness, but he felt dazed from the blow and his capacity for thinking clearly became diminished long enough for his opponent to pin him to the ground with a heavy foot.

"Don't fight it, Commander Beringer, or we might have to kill you after all."

The ringing in his ears subsided slowly. Beringer blinked a few times to clear his vision. The man above him gave him a warm smile, but the piece of metal in his raised hand spoke a different language.

"What do you want from me?" Beringer asked, lifting his head to look a Breanna, who was slowly walking toward him. Somehow she looked different. Her red hair was still the same, but her eyes seemed to have changed. Then he realized that they were not green, but purple. And definitely not human. He was looking into the eyes of a Genaar. "You are not Breanna," he said.

She smiled down at him. "You are correct, Commander, I am not Breanna. I am the Xandra." She bent down and squatted beside him. Reaching out, her hand touched his forehead. He felt a gentle tingling, like an electric shock. "You are a strong willed man, Les," she said softly, "so different from Thomas and Captain Cunningham. I want us to join."

He laughed cynically. "Haven't we done that already?"

Chuckling, she stroked his cheek. "I hope you enjoyed it as much as I did."

"I enjoyed it, because I thought you were Breanna," he said bitterly. "But how could you enjoy it! You are not even human."

"I am human in this body. And I have feelings, just like you." She rose. "But if you thought joining with me that way was pleasurable, wait until our minds and bodies join." She turned to walk back to the pond. Over her shoulder she said, "Bring him."

The moment the man above him removed his foot, Beringer kicked up, smashed his own foot into the man's crotch, then he rolled toward his bundle of clothing, grabbed his pistol and shot the big man in the chest. The other two men stood motionless, watching their companion collapse. One of them lifted his arm and threw his piece of conduit at Beringer, but the Commander rolled again. Still rolling he drilled a neat hole into the forehead of the conduit-thrower. Rising to his feet, he leveled his laser pistol at the third man. "Stay where you are!" he barked, "or you join your friends."

The man lifted his hands, smiled. "You can't escape, Commander," he said, "most of us are of the Xandra now. It is only a matter of time. Where will you go?"

Beringer looked at the woman. Except for her eyes, she still looked like Breanna and it was hard for him to do what he knew he had to. "Is he telling the truth?" he asked.

She nodded and came walking toward him. Opening her arms, she whispered, "He is right. You can't escape. Don't be afraid, I promise it won't hurt. You will experience pleasure beyond your imagination. You will be more alive than you have ever been. I promise you eternal life. Isn't that what every human wants? Eternal life, now you can have it. Without dying."

Setting his laser to wide beam, he shot her in the chest. He choked back a loud sob when she looked at him with Breanna's eyes. He burned away her beautiful face, sprayed the remnants of her body with his laser. Then he turned and shot the last man, reduced his charred carcass to ashes.

He dressed without looking at the burned remnants of what once had been some sort of life form, he didn't know what. His laser still in his hand, he stepped into the elevator. There was a coldness in his chest and his mind seemed numb. His suspicions about the Captain were now confirmed and the next steps he needed to take were quite clear. The Xandra had been wrong, there was a way out, but he wasn't sure if it was the right way.

He left the elevator on the fifth floor, headed for his quarters. Then he called Lieutenant Wang and Sergeant Stasnowski.

They met him in his quarters only moments later.

"I want all the men in battle gear and spacesuits. I'll see you in twenty minutes on the fourth floor. Have the men ready to move out. Now, go!"

Both men had been briefed days before about his suspicions. He ordered them to keep the marines confined to their quarters until further notice. There was no need to ask any questions.

After Wang and Stasnowski left, Beringer put a call through to Starfinder. The alien gave him a communications device, for his own private use, in case he needed to contact the Genaar. That moment had arrived.

"I've been expecting your call," Starfinder said. "We are ready to proceed."

Twenty minutes later the Commander stood in front of his assembled men. They were all dressed in spacesuits, with only their faceplates open.

He didn't make a speech, just told them that this was an emergency and it was time to take evasive action.

They took the elevator platform to travel down to the floor of the docking bay. While going down, Beringer looked at the big battle cruiser. As menacing as it appeared, it was useless against what they were facing. They climbed the stairs down to the fifth level of the station, where Starfinder and two of his people met them.

"Tell your men to follow the technicians," the alien said to Beringer. "The chambers have been prepared for them."

"Have you found a way to…?" he didn't finish the sentence.

Starfinder nodded. "Yes, we have."

"What will you do if one of them is affected?" Beringer asked.

"We'll deal with it." Starfinder smiled grimly. "All of them will have to be scanned, including you, my friend."

Chapter Thirty-eight
Captain's Log
January 12, 2986

Things have changed. The station has shut down again. We are only in control of the tower that we first occupied. The Genaar have taken refuge in the bowels of the station. They've created an energy barrier that locks us out. We can't force our way in.

Lucky for us, we had some shuttles on Nu-Eden, because they also closed the docking bay. Our only access to the tower is through the pressure chamber on the 21st floor. Commander Beringer and his marines have joined the Genaar. Too bad.

All the humans in the tower have been changed. The giant water lily, which is home to the Xandra on the station, covers most of the pond in the small park. One hundred ninety-seven human bodies can supply a lot of building material.

The thousand settlers who are still in suspension will soon be revived and shipped down to Nu-Eden. They will be split into two groups and will settle in different parts of the continent. They will not be processed. The Xandra has decided to let them live as real humans. It is an experiment. If they become a problem, then they can always be absorbed and changed at a later date.

The Xandra has made me a gift. She gave me back my wife. She created her from my own sub-conscious memories. I know it is not really her, but it has been so long since I've seen her last, I will probably never know the difference. She had always been a beautiful woman, but now she is gorgeous. Her breasts are large and full, without the slightest bit of sag; her buttocks are firm and round, her skin as soft as velvet. When we make love the universe moves, and she is totally devoted to me. What more can a man ask for?

I am happy.

We are the children of the Xandra.

WE ARE THE XANDRA.

* * * *

(Look for Book 2 of The Xandra Series, now available.)

198